KU-504-657

Praise for

OBLIVION

'A Dantean descent... In a steely translation by
Antonina W. Bouis, *Oblivion* is as cold and stark as a glacial
crevasse, but as beautiful as one, too, with a clear poetic
sensibility built to stand against the forces of erasure.'

Wall Street Journal

'Astonishing... Ingeniously structured around the prog-
ressive uncovering of memories of a difficult personal and national
past... with a visceral, at times almost unbearable, force.'

Times Literary Supplement

'Opening in stately fashion and unfolding ever
faster with fierce, intensive elegance, this first novel
discloses the weight of Soviet history and its consequences... Highly recommended for anyone serious
about literature or history.'

Library Journal

'Packs a wicked emotional punch through
fierce poetic imagery... Lebedev takes his place beside
Solzhenitsyn and other great writers who have refused to
abide by silence... Courageous and devastating.'

Kirkus Reviews

About the Author

SERGEI LEBEDEV was born in Moscow
in 1981 and worked for seven years on geological
expeditions in northern Russia and Central Asia.
Lebedev is a poet, essayist and journalist. His novels have
been translated into many languages and received great
acclaim in the English-speaking world. The *New York
Review of Books* has hailed Lebedev as 'the best
of Russia's younger generation of writers.'

About the Translator

ANTONINA W. BOUIS is one of the leading
translators of Russian literature working today.
She has translated over 80 works from authors such
as Evgeny Yevtushenko, Mikhail Bulgakov, Andrei
Sakharov, Sergei Dovlatov and Arkady and Boris
Strugatsky. Bouis, previously executive director
of the Soros Foundation in the former USSR,
lives in New York City.

OBLIVION

SERGEI LEBEDEV

TRANSLATED BY ANTONINA W. BOUIS

An Apollo Book

First published in Russian as **Предел Забвенья** by Eksmo in 2011

First published in the US in 2016 by New Vessel Press
This paperback edition first published in the UK in 2022 by Head of Zeus Ltd,
part of Bloomsbury Publishing Plc

Copyright © Sergei Lebedev, 2011
Translation Copyright © Antonina W. Bouis, 2016

The moral right of Sergei Lebedev and Antonina W. Bouis to be
identified as the author and translator of this work
has been asserted in accordance with the Copyright,
Designs and Patents Act of 1988.

All rights reserved. No part of this publication may be
reproduced, stored in a retrieval system, or transmitted in any form
or by any means, electronic, mechanical, photocopying, recording,
or otherwise, without the prior permission of both the copyright
owner and the above publisher of this book.

This is a work of fiction. All characters, organizations,
and events portrayed in this novel are either products of
the author's imagination or are used fictitiously.

9 7 5 3 1 2 4 6 8

A catalogue record for this book is available from the British Library.

ISBN (PB): 9781800249219
ISBN (E): 9781800249196

Printed and bound in Great Britain by
CPI Group (UK) Ltd, Croydon CR0 4YY

Head of Zeus Ltd
5–8 Hardwick Street
London EC1R 4RG
WWW.HEADOFZEUS.COM

No resident of this town,
no dead man,
but something in between.

—Joseph Brodsky

PART 1

South Dublin Libraries
www.southdublinlibraries.ie

I stand at the boundary of Europe. Here, every cliff above the ocean reveals the yellow bone of stone and the ocher-red soil, looking like flesh; the bone crumbles under the blows of the waves, the flesh of the soil devours the tide. The ocean is so vast that eyes cannot encompass it. Here, Europe ends; the shore recedes, as if the continent was drawing into itself.

You came here out of the taiga and tundra in order to see the Columns of Hercules, to discover the world that gave birth to the Atlantes holding up the grim sky of your homeland, to breathe from the mouth of Gibraltar the life-giving air of the lungs of the Mediterranean—for those born in Russia this remains the limit of the inhabited world, as the ancient Greeks had thought.

This boundary has challenges: a new, different life lies only beyond the faceless ocean waters, similar to death; dry land is unfolding constancy, while the ocean interrupts this, demanding spiritual effort, a great goal for which you can renounce the familiar solidity of land and step onto an unstable ship deck.

My soul and heart are filled with the memory of spaces yearning for the polar circle, filled with their muteness craving a word, filled with the eye-bleaching whiteness of the snows, the blackness of the night, the blackness of the mine where the air is impoverished by breathing and does not know the dawn.

That is why for me, having come to the edge of the world, the goal lies not ahead but behind: I have to return. My trip is over and the return trip must begin in words.

I sense—this sensation is sudden even though it ripened

long ago—that I am a European to a greater degree than the inhabitants of the country that looks out onto the Atlantic as a balcony looks onto the street.

I was at the other edge of Europe, which breaks off with rocky ledges into the swamps of Western Siberia; I saw the dark back alleys of the European continent, its Finno-Ugric sheds, its backside, its foundation; I stood beyond the polar circle in the Ural Mountains, where Europe and Asia meet: on the European slope, only the polar birch grows, low and twisted by the winds, while on the Asian side there are cedars, tall, powerful, their roots breaking stone, and in the sky overhead storm fronts collide from the two great plains.

It was there, where Europe's life force weakens, where it is only enough for reindeer moss and lichen while the thick Asian forest and grass threaten to overflow the crest, that I first felt I was European.

There, in the middle of the range, thinking or speaking, trying to write something down, you suddenly realize: you have reached the *edge of language*. On the Asian side you have to make some effort to name objects; they seem to slide away from being named. Or to put it a different way—between name and thing arises a thin and tight film similar to the caul that surrounds a baby in his mother's belly; things here have not yet been born for the language you speak. Fir and pine will be fir and pine for you, but the names will be alien to their essence, which requires different sounds and responds harmoniously only to them.

The edge of language, the outskirts of the European world; beyond there is only the flatness of Siberia's swamps. Here you will learn what muteness really is: you can speak, but the world does not respond to speech. You realize that your homeland is your language; its strengths, its defects are your integral strengths and your defects; outside language you do not exist.

I recall being in a village in early, frosty spring: huts

squashed by the long-standing gray snow, hardened prints of felt boots and sled runners on the road; the reluctant awakening after winter—the shaggy winter dreams reeking of lime and felt are dissolved in the air inside the house.

They had recently closed the village school, there weren't enough pupils. The building, an old manor house, was boarded up. The school stood on a conspicuous hill, and for several months the village lived with a view of the former house of landowners, abandoned as if in retreat.

A monument to a cosmonaut was stuck in the schoolyard, as if he had landed there and being unneeded was placed on a pedestal and painted a silvery color to match his space suit. The school, despite the cold that froze out odors, smelled of damp wallpaper and mice. By the stove in the corridor the watchman sat on a stool, a man composed of felt boots, quilted trousers, quilted vest, and hat with earflaps; the floorboards creaked and it sounded like chalk on the freshly erased blackboard; through the keyhole I could make out desks and chairs, clumsy and heavy to match the children's backpacks; a ruler lay on one of the desks, as if the teacher had forgotten it and would be back.

The watchman sat by the stove; piles of worn, scribbled-over textbooks that had been through many hands lay by the wall—Our Mother Tongue, fourth grade. The watchman took one book at a time, tearing off the cover and crumpling the pages so that they would catch faster into flames, and tossed them into the stove. "They shut the school," he said. "They don't issue firewood. So we use this for heat, you can't defrost them anyway. It's a big library, it'll last until April."

They fed the stove in the shut school with the Russian language textbooks. How you hated those books as a child, those "Questions on the text," the paragraphs marked "Test yourself," that enlarged, easy font, rounded like the corners of the desk, so that children didn't hurt themselves! You were ready to weep, because now none of it meant anything.

There in that Volga village, in the midst of fields covered with birch shoots, I learned what a person's mother tongue meant, mother tongue without quotation marks, without a school's edifying insistence.

Birches, snow, firewood, sky, road, fire, smoke, frost— I repeated the words that I remembered for only a slightly shorter time than I remembered myself. Birches, snow, firewood, sky, road, fire, smoke, frost—the words grew, as if they were material, had material energy; the words sounded symphonically, one through another, without blending, the frost was frosty, the fire fiery, the smoke smoky; the words became translucent, melting slightly, like pure flame, their phonetic casings lost their hardened precision, and the eye perceived the pure essence of meaning—like a bubble of air in a precious stone, refracting the light differently.

A bubble of air that is fractionally older than the stone— the air was there before the mineral appeared. This tiny gulp of older air, the integral soul of the word—it was what made the word real, belonging to life and death—that is what I saw and felt then in the snowbound village, where the white roof of the school was covered with splotches of book ash—the textbooks burned smoky and dirty, and the ash metallic and greasy from the thick typographic ink.

I learned that the Russian language was my homeland, my fatherland; those who populate the Russian language are my fellow citizens, my comrades. What I am writing now I write not by the right of memory but the right of language. I see and remember; these lines are as necessary to me as the pianist's need to touch the keys, to test the resilience of the silence before playing; beyond them I hear the sound of letters coming out of the dark.

Here, on the boundary of Europe, I see people on the beach, as beautiful as the Nereids or dryads of Greek mythology, hybridizing man with animals or plants to produce an immortal creature. Human beauty has a vulnerability, a presentiment of dying, which defines its individuality.

I see people playing golf, endlessly repeating a lesson in Cartesian geometry, the lesson of articulating space, capturing it in a grid of coordinates. I picture them in the middle of the tundra with ball and clubs—and I think that they would freeze in amazement: there can be so much space that you cannot master it even in your imagination; they would leave their game and go off in various directions to make sure that what they saw was not a stage set.

I see a café by the ocean where every evening the stiffening breeze mixes up snatches of conversation in ten languages, plays with them, like a simultaneous interpreter at a conference switching now to French, now German, now Polish—and I remember the cemetery of exiles where there is the same mixture of languages and dialects spoken by the man who became a watchman there of his own volition. There were no crosses, no peripheries, no graves, only barely visible ditches, covered by damp spring soil, over which he pronounced names from memory. The consonances, foreign to this area, fell into the soil like seeds, and it seemed that this was a prayer composed by an only survivor who had almost lost memory and reason in order to make room for those who had no other refuge in the world.

I see the smooth asphalt of the highway—and I recall the northern road that led to the gold mines. Along it drove long-haul Ural and Kamaz trucks, all-terrain vehicles, bulldozers, the road's shoulders infused with diesel fumes, dried to an oily crust that crunched under your boot. The powerful machines traveled alone and in caravans; from the high cab you could see how the engine noise made tundra hares scatter, partridges fly up into the air, and fish flee upstream, barreling through the water; it seemed that this low-lying area, giving birth only to tubercular trees, froze at the sight of the ribbed wheels and shiny bulldozer blades, ready to trample mosses and berry patches, to rip open the thin soil.

Suddenly, after a steep downhill, the Tsar Puddle is revealed: all the drivers call it that. Some say that this spot is cursed by shamans in revenge for the mining tunnels hacked into the sacred mountain, others say that this was the site of a mass reindeer pestilence, still others that an entire transport of prisoners froze to death in a blizzard here, hundreds of men herded to the gold mines in the forties. In general drivers were a tough crowd, not superstitious, not believing in God or devil, but the human mind truly could not cope with the sight of the Tsar Puddle.

It was impossible to go around the Tsar Puddle: the long stretch of swampy land saturated with the water of melting permafrost extended for a hundred kilometers between two rows of hills. When the vehicles braked before reaching the edge of it, the drama of the place was revealed: all around the land seemed to be bouncing, everything was covered by rotting rusty water, jutting out from which were logs and boards smashed and turned into kindling by caterpillar treads, rocks scraped by metal, and squashed barrels of sapper pontoons that people had tried to use to pave the Puddle, vanishing islets of gravel and sand—traces of attempts to fill the gaping pit. In the distance the skeleton of a tractor cab, losing the last of its paint, rose out of the swamp, bent crane dangling. A bizarre forest grew along the shores of the Puddle: dozens of iron pipes and concrete reinforcements hammered into the ground, some torn and twisted out—drivers lassoed them with the winch loops of stuck trucks. Frayed, torn ropes, each with dozens of knots, unable to withstand the deadly clutches of the Puddle, were scattered about. If you come closer, stepping carefully so that your boots don't land in the drying sticky ooze, you can see the remains of minor dramas, desperate attempts to restock when work stopped at the mines; they needed fuel, explosives, and food, but the weather conditions kept the helicopters on the runway at the airport, and the bosses sent two or three trucks out, promising the drivers whatever they wanted as long as the cargo made it through.

Thus was born a caste of drivers who knew the Puddle, northern augurs who told fortunes by the water level, by animal tracks on the Puddle surface—it was believed that elk and roe deer chose the driest path; some drove to the side to risk a new spot, and then tractors worked a long time to haul them to shore; the majority tried to get across along the old track. Remains of these restocking trips were visible from the edge of the Puddle: spilled cans, the metal siding of the vans, benches, heaters—everything was thrown into the ruts to let the truck drive over it, and everything was inexorably consumed by the Puddle. Sometimes the Puddle became bloated, and corpses of things, decayed and digested by the juices of the earth, appeared on the surface; as if choking, the Puddle disgorged tarps, slate, drill pipes, all stuck together, fused into gigantic likenesses of rooted-out stumps, spat out the garbage dumped into it, bottles, packages, hacked out with a clot of dirt a skeleton of a fox tempted by leftovers, and then once again, in the course of a day or two, swallowed everything it had purged.

I see a German shepherd on a leash following a man on the embankment; the dog is hot, it steps gingerly on the hot stone pavers, panting wildly, sticking out its tongue, pink with purple veins; the dog is pathetic, overfed and old, used to a collar, indifferent to the bloated pigeons searching for crumbs in the cracks, but I do not feel sorry for it: I remember other shepherds, I remember the thick, viscous saliva dripping from their upper fangs, the roseate upper palate, ribbed like butchered meat on a counter, in their jaws, I remember the bark, which had nothing canine about it.

Usually the sound of barking, however furious it may be,

reminds you of a city square or a village street—the distant echoes of a dogfight heard on a night in the boggy woods, you realize that somewhere nearby there are houses, people, a place to spend the night. But the bark of a convoy shepherd is not the bark of a fight, skirmish, flight, or hunt. You don't need to chase a prisoner, he is entirely at the dog's mercy, however in the bulging eyes, the clumps of sounds torn out of its throat, the degree of hatred reaches human levels; human—by nature of the feeling—hatred, grafted on to the dog, becomes bigger and stronger than the creature, and it must unload it upon the prisoners. That is why the barking of convoy dogs immediately makes you think of fangs, yellowed as if by tobacco, of the hatred that separates man and animal more profoundly than it does man and man, because the animal follows it to the end, to destruction, to the crunch of tendons and vertebrae; about the hatred spilled out with the barking into the air of a thousand places, living in the canine and human descendants, absorbed with meager milk and the marrow of chewed bones.

I see fishermen, the tips of their long rods glowing in the twilight, as if they were catching flying fish with that greenish light; after fishing, the men go to the café on the shore, drink beer or wine while the fish is cleaned in the kitchen; a local white wine in bluish bottles goes very well with the fish, clean and light, slightly bitter; this wine does not intoxicate, agitate, or weigh you down, it seems to rinse the feelings.

You take a sip of that wine and the woman you met and fell in love with here, the soft bonds of bed sheets, doubly salty sweat, from the seawater, the reddish pollen of the shameless palm flowers on her skin—all this recedes, and desire itself suddenly turns into an almost sexless tenderness, the sense that she is merely the vessel of her life, inaccessible to you. You look not at her anymore but at how her life lives inside her, perhaps unfamiliar to her as well; how the blood ebbs and flows, the blush grows, the hair curls. This quotidian nature of her body becomes precious and necessary; you want to take her hand to feel her pulse: the beating of the heart that was conceived in her mother's body, appearing out of nothing, out of a few cells.

You know that no one was ever closer to you than she is; but even she is not close. They bring the fish, dorade for her, swordfish for you, because swordfish does not resemble the flesh of fish; it has large fibers, it looks like bleached beef, and that is why you can eat it. You could tell her why you turn away from her plate, drink wine, and stare at the ocean, and she—sensitive and understanding—would empathize, but it would be only a story; there is the final definitiveness of experience that cannot be shared.

So you watch the fishermen on the beach, watch their rods tremble and bend when they drag the fish to shore. Farther along the transparency moves into darkness and then into color: there is a whirlpool, and the water spins slowly, thickly, and light circles float on the surface, like traces of drops fallen into hardening molten glass—the grayling snatching insects.

The summer is coming to an end, the early darkness thickens, the mornings grow cooler, and the winds toss the light-winged dragonflies onto the water, as if sweeping out rubbish—skins, wings—from the space between window frames; the grayling is the fish of death, the river hunter—it swallows up flies, mosquitoes, dragonflies, so that soon it can go downstream and huddle in the holes in the riverbed, to lie dormant until spring; the rainbow wings splash, and the rainbow bodies of the fish flash through the water.

A pause. A pot steams on a rod, fish soup cooking; grayling is tender, it should not be overcooked. As a treat, we have raw fish, rubbed with salt and pepper and marinated under a press to release its juices. But then you follow the route along the river, the path leaps from bank to bank, and in one of the fords someone steps on a human skull trapped among the stones, covered with slimy green weeds.

A skull. A skull in the water. Higher upstream, we see a crumbling cliff and a black peaty carcass. In the peat there are more skulls, bones, flesh half-decayed, flabby like berries that spent the winter under snow; a camp cemetery that was being washed away when the river changed its course and began a new tributary. And you vomit the fish, that flesh is the grayling meat, and now you are a cannibal, all of you are cannibals because you ate that fish, drank that water, in which the dead are dissolved. You threw up, but the uncleanliness remains, it is in your body, in your blood forever.

And now you curse the rod, the line, and the bait: a barbed hook is stuck in your lip, you swallowed the fly that is tearing up your intestines. Fish skeletons tossed into the river and human bones—you suddenly realize that you had always been a link in the food chain, your memory had been a weapon of destruction.

And then you understand that the deathly communion was not accidental. Through it, as through newly granted vision, you see your body, your memory, your fate as predestination: the inheritance of blood, the inheritance of memories, the inheritance of other lives—everything wants to speak, seeks to complete itself, to happen to the end, to be recognized and mourned.

You see and remember; this text is a memorial, a wailing wall, for the dead and the mourners have no other place to meet except by the wall of words—the wall that unites the living and the dead.

PART 2

Summer days, long, expansive, like an enfilade of bright rooms; days when nothing is missing in nature and wakening comes with the dawn—summer days, the summer of life!

Autumn memory absorbs nature's decline, the transition from volumes of foliage to the emptiness of bare forests, and this disembodiment continues, as if its strength were undermined by disease.

The darkness of winter days multiplies the lacunae of memory, confined to the circle of light from the desk lamp; you travel from one memory to the next as if from village to village in the snow, sinking, losing the road, barely hearing the guiding thread—the hum of the power lines.

The memory of spring is timid, unsure, resembling the dreams of a recovering patient, as fragile as the ice of morning frosts, unsupported by the body's strength.

Only the memory of summer says: remember, all this has happened to you and will not be repeated, but there will be room for everything in your reminiscences; remember—here's a blue spike of delphinium, bowing under the density of color, here are the smoky blue juniper berries smelling of tar, clean arboreal sweat, here is a butterfly flying without will, like a bit of white cloth carried by the wind; remember and it will be you: delphinium, juniper, and butterfly, they will become the rigging of your feelings and thoughts, they will help you when feeling will seek words and thought—images.

August is the month of your appearance in the world; you were born in the summer, and the world appeared summery to you. It was hot, the thermometer kept climbing; body temperature coincided with air temperature, and you must have felt the world accepting you.

August—in August you fell, climbing up on the handle of the stroller, and crashed with it onto stone; blood spurted from your smashed lips, your mouth turned into a wound, your milk teeth crumbled; you sensed pain that years later returned with the metal wires of braces retaining the metallic taste of blood; pain that deformed and paralyzed speech, as if every word was pushed through the bars of its cage.

The unspoken words when you wanted to say them accumulated in you; other children collected cars and the older ones, stamps, but you started collecting words. Just as the rectangle of a stamp held out for some the promise of another life, other countries, where fame and glory were so great and triumphant that the hero's face radiating his portrait into space was captured on stamps, the smallest part of the world's mosaic—so for you every word reflected the bigger life that had produced it.

Hidden beneath my childish appearance was a real and profound age of silence and life among words and conversation with words that allowed all the insights that shaped my early development.

A man whom I will call Grandfather II insisted on my birth—I called him that to myself as a child; naturally, he had a name, patronymic, and surname, but they are inessential; my receptivity accurately sensed this man's extreme alienation, hidden by politeness. It wasn't that he kept himself aloof, taciturn, it wasn't about his behavior or character; he was alienated from life almost in the legal sense of the word and only as a consequence of that was he alienated from people as well. Everything that happened in the present did not involve him directly but only brushed against him—not because he was unreceptive but because he seemed to have already lived his life, his existence outlasting his destiny, and no event could touch him now; he was omitted from the blueprints of daily life as if he was being punished—left out—denied.

Grandfather II was blind. It is difficult to give a physical description of a blind man; sightless eyes not only deprive a person of one of the usual features, they create the sensation that the defect is greater than an external one, in the organs of sensation, that the blind man is lacking something more than the inability to orient himself in space.

The eyes are something unusual for the human body, smooth, solid, as impenetrable as a wall; they seem to be clots of energy of a different sort than the energies found in blood and muscle. There you find blood corpuscles and formulas for breakdown and conversion; the eyes contain something of an order more mysterious for all their obvious openness. Time is light, the physicists say, light enters a person through the eye; perhaps they are the organ of time.

The blind seem lost in time, they are not entirely present in every moment; being lost blurred his features, as if he had moved while being photographed.

That is why Grandfather II did not persist in the viewer's retina, he seeped through it, remaining a vague silhouette; you remember his profile better than his face, he somehow was always turned sideways, behind something, as if in a crowd, among others, even when he was alone; you remembered his clothing, perhaps the set of his shoulders, something of his walk, but that did not create a whole portrait.

Now trying to picture his face, I see some moment of recollection in which everything should be there, I see it with photographic precision, but there is no face; it could be overexposed. I can list external features—medium height, thin, gray-haired, but the key to description is not there; rather it lies in the layer of perception where the impression is no longer directly tied to what we see.

Grandfather II—that was the only way; when you spoke his

real name, you felt that you were throwing a letter across the fallow no-man's land by a border, and the letter never made it, falling halfway; you call the man by his name, but the sound of that name does not create a link between you, no closeness; the anonymous numeral—Grandfather II—corresponded to your actual feeling.

Grandfather II was not a relative; he was a neighbor at the dacha, an old blind gardener. Apparently having spent his past life encased by the harsh contours of an army or some other uniform, he now wore only soft linen that followed the lines of the body; he had lost his vision long ago, decades before my birth; he had gone beyond his blindness, beyond the habits that trap the blind in their blindness, and he was free in his inability to see; he reduced his life to a few routes, the main one being the route from his apartment in the city to the dacha and back. He relied on a cleaning woman for the housekeeping—and over the years by ear and touch created an image in his mind of the limited space he allowed himself for habitation.

In essence, he lived on a few islands with the solid ground of familiar sounds, smells, and touch; you might say he lived in the midst of this ground, perceiving it with his entire body, leaning on it, and in that sense his situation was more stable than that of the sighted. The only danger for him was something new. A new bridge across the ravine, a new front door, a changed bus stop destroyed the dummy Grandfather II had created out of sounds and physical impressions; for the sighted this destruction is not visible as destruction, they see only a change, while the blind are closer to the true understanding of things; new means death, innovation is murder; and therefore, although not only because of this, Grandfather II treated the past more seriously than others.

What Grandfather II had been earlier, no one knew; there were almost no old-timers left at the dacha settlement to ask.

Dacha life predisposes people to friendliness, to collecting biographies and the names of local celebrities—and this is where so-and-so lives!—but Grandfather II was always beyond such inquiries.

He was alluringly uninteresting; next to him everyone seemed a bit more significant than they actually were; Grandfather II blended into the background, the epitome of obscurity—not modesty, not discretion, but obscurity; modesty and discretion are distinctive traits, and he had none of those. Grandfather II sought to pass through life by never drawing attention to himself and achieved this with almost monastic perfection.

As the senior bookkeeper of a concern, remnants of the managerial habit appeared in him, but very weakly, when he sat down in a specially important way, weighing the pen in his fingers before signing a receipt; it seemed that the eyes behind his smoky eyeglasses had been eaten by the ciphers. Yet some of the old villagers—the dachas were built on the site of a mushroom woodland beyond the village—said that Grandfather II was no bookkeeper at all. The village gives you a different vantage point on people, a different sensitivity to destiny, than the city, its inhabitants have a different sense of a person's belonging to the state, whether he had been only a mailman or a forest ranger—and the old men thought that there was a stench about Grandfather II; he had "the stench of official boots." Of course, the villagers did not go far in their thinking—a police accountant or administrator; official boots, in their opinion, did not have a powerful odor.

The dacha residents did not judge by city standards, but by those of dacha life. Owning a dacha in those days and among those people was considered a kind of amnesty, an absolution of the past, whatever it had been; not of imagined or actual sins, but of the past per se.

One's past life became a treat that could be served up

as something light and tasty with tea, for an evening chat; people moved to the dacha in order to reexamine their memory, reorganize it through a retrospective gaze, to be assured thoroughly and meticulously of its fine quality. The dacha residents sensed a vague similarity of fates, an affinity in attitude toward life; finding themselves in proximity, they discovered that they were a community; and dacha life in that sense was perceived as a different life—following upon the one already lived and separate from it.

It is unlikely that morally inexcusable acts were among the things they wanted to remember. Rather, the very position in the middle rungs of authority, which presumed a slightly greater moral conformity than what a person could exhibit without having to inwardly justify himself, forced them to assume a dignified air. They were the abstract "elderly" who were supposed to be given seats on the train and bus, according to the proper rules.

Naturally, the question of what Grandfather II used to be simply could not be uttered in this circle—the sound would be lost in the air; everyone there was a decent person, and this combination of words—*decent* person, not "worthy," not "good," but *decent*—was the highest praise at the dachas. In essence, this is what united all the residents: they managed to come out of difficult times as decent men—that is, people about whom for a variety of reasons you couldn't say anything bad.

At first glance, the dachas were an oasis, an island of conciliation, tranquility, amiability. But the children— the children sensed that it was all a sham, a show: we were brought up too strictly and fervently, shown no forgiveness or mercy in moral issues. The adults had a clearly marked area of eclipse in their heads, and if that eclipse came on—if you stole, lied, didn't keep your promise—the punishment was so incommensurate—not in cruelty, but in readiness to deny your son or daughter, to become strangers instantly—that it seemed you weren't a child but an enemy who had sneaked into the family, a changeling from the maternity hospital.

The family played out an entire scene: Is this our son? Is this our daughter? I remember how my friend, eight years old, unable to stand these questions—they were investigating the theft of plums—suddenly came up to his parents and repeated loudly: I'm your son! I'm your son! I'm your son!—and they stepped back, they didn't know what to do with the little boy who was shaking, missing an unbuckled sandal, and shouting without anger, without stubbornness but with the sudden firmness of the weak: I'm your son! I'm your son! I'm your son! They, the adults, were at the moment afraid of an eight-year-old child, they stood there, mother, father, and the person whose garden the plums had come from, until the boy quieted down, climbed into a ditch, and started to cry.

Children were seemingly being prepared for a life in which any misdeed was not in and of itself bad but bad because it cast a shadow on the family, made people take a closer look at them—Who brought up a child like this?—and the family did not want to be looked at closely; the result was forced morality, and reciprocal hypocrisy permeated everything: the order not to lie, accompanied by fear, only multiplies the lie and forces to you operate within it.

Childhood in those dachas—they are long gone, they have become the suburbs, the houses have changed, been renovated, there are solid fences—childhood was a school of hypocrisy; I cannot say that in full measure about my own family or the families of some of my friends—but the general field of relations was like that. Every one of us dacha kids led a double life to some degree; I'm not talking about secret mischief, rule breaking, omissions, or enforced furtiveness. We—each in his own way—were betrayed by our families, who saw all too clearly other children we were supposed to become.

However, I am thankful for my childhood; if not for the enforced study of split personality almost to the point of schizophrenia, I would not have become who I am; and certainly I would not have been able to see and figure out Grandfather II's real nature.

One day—I am getting ahead of myself—I understood, naively, childishly, that seeing is a mirror; we see not people but how people are reflected in us; I thought I had discovered a secret and all I needed was to figure out how to get beyond my own gaze to see what you're not supposed to be able to see.

I began playing with my shadow: I tried to stand so that you could not tell who my shadow belonged to; I stood next to the stump of an apple tree, a barrel, a scarecrow, held my head down, hid my hands, and tried to make my shadow look like theirs; I played for several days, choosing the evening when the shadows were clear, thick, and long, I played madly, forgetting the time. And suddenly, weary and just fooling around, I turned and froze; my shadow was *not mine*. I had missed the moment of the switch and stood there, afraid to move: what if moving didn't help, what if that alien shadow followed, but remained alien? But I had frozen in a very uncomfortable position, I moved my feet as soon as I shut my eyes, and when I opened them, I saw that it was my shadow.

The game now had a dangerous meaning: I consciously sought the state of excited oblivion when I was playing so hard, so inside the movements and the last rays of the sun, that I lost consciousness for a second and became a stranger to myself; I acquired another's shadow.

Of course, I never experienced that state again; then I started studying the grown-ups' shadows—this wasn't an amusement, not a game, but a path to knowledge. I thought that their shadows differed in more than outline: my father's shadow was much bigger than he was, and when he put the light out in my room after wishing me good night, I imagined that it remained, dissolved in the dark, growing and threatening, watching if I was really asleep. Mother's shadow was fluid, musical in outline, I thought if you touched it, it would respond in a singing tone like a cello; grandmother's was flickering, like a spindle, like knitting needles—a kind shadow.

I couldn't get a feel for Grandfather II's shadow; it did not respond to my imagination, no matter how hard I tried to find something in it; I couldn't say that it was ordinary, average, without a hook for my fantasy; it seemed that Grandfather II knew what his shadow was like, that he directed it and watched that it did not tell anything more about him, that he was constantly pulling it closer, like the skirts of a long raincoat.

However, this is a subject for later; I merely needed to clarify the circumstances of my childhood and the starting point of the story—the story of Grandfather II's gradual entry into our family, my birth, and my separate and special relationship with him.

Our dacha plot was next to Grandfather II's; there was no fence between them, the water pipe served us both, and somehow it turned out that the sellers of our dacha also passed along the voluntary obligation to take care of Grandfather II. All the separation of the dacha lots, the delineations between neighbors depended on visual clues—fences and pipes, in our case. What can you expect from someone who can't see? So the border did not work, and relations with Grandfather II crossed the line of neighborliness.

As far as I can judge Grandfather II had no obvious interest in being close to us; he was not looking for listeners and he didn't need comrades; it happened on its own, Grandfather II even subtly pretended that he was acceding to neighborly socializing under pressure. Now I think that this nearness was a test: he had lived privately for decades, outliving the past,

31

and now he was trying to be close with strangers so that he could use their eyes and their feelings to check just how well hidden were the things that needed to be hidden.

However, that's too simple an explanation; there were other reasons. Grandfather II's health was excellent; nature, having taken his vision, seemed to have exhausted the bodily harm due him, and the woes of aging passed him by; only his bones ached when bad weather was coming—he must have suffered freezing temperatures long ago and now his body warned him of cold. Grandfather II sought—and found in my family—people among whom he could die; what he sought most was not reliability, not help "if something happens," but fastidiousness toward other people's secrets.

He was building a relationship—not for life, but for his postponed death; this vantage point, this turn of events was hard to see from inside the relationship, and I can judge it only in memory. Grandfather II didn't join the family, he didn't try to become a dependent—on the contrary, he tried not to be a burden, not to beg for intimacy, and did it all without stress or artificiality, without engendering pity. Yet there was something of a well-rehearsed dramatic role about it, when the actor never makes the slightest deviation from his chosen method.

Of course, this could be the behavior of a man of impeccably noble objectives; however, such a man would have been natural in his nobility, while Grandfather II's actions always seemed slightly off, dissociated from himself.

However, this remark is from subsequent times—back then no one thought this way; on the contrary, as far as I can tell, the family considered Grandfather II a sincere man, albeit rather reticent.

Grandfather II knew how to be useful—with considered advice or needed information; his presence elicited the sense of the steadfastness of life arising when you know that next to you is a man who has been through a lot and learned to live amid adversity. Both my real grandfathers had died in the war, and Grandfather II gradually took the place of the oldest man in the family, even though he did not openly count himself a family member; he did not seek to replace them, did not try to block the memory of the real grandfathers, on the contrary he treated them respectfully. Slowly, over years, he worked his way in: gave up some land for a garden, taught us how to graft trees, selecting the most viable cutting, grafting it to the trunk, covering it with tar, and tending it the first few years—and he gradually grafted himself to us, joining us, as if he knew the long power of time, which does not tolerate haste but allows only the small daily effort—the way texts are written, the way impossibilities and contradictions in relations are solved—a small effort creating and increasing the field; the field that first grows quantitatively and at some point takes on its own qualities, creating new connections, new events, incidents, thoughts, and actions, previously impossible.

At the end of summer, we made jam at the dacha— Grandfather II helped, washing the copper tubs; foods were canned—he brought over jars sterilized by boiling. Gooseberries, currants, apples—the fruity summer moisture, the summery juice was boiled, thickened, the summery fruitful time was canned for winter, cold and dark; the summery aromatic herbs were put into jars with cucumbers, tomatoes, and squash, they were used to separate layers of mushrooms in pails, which emitted burbling, drooling juices.

A family is made up of various people with a shared attitude toward time, and Grandfather II was gradually accepted into that circle, first as not a stranger and then as one of us. Novels, magazines, and newspapers were read aloud to him—his housekeeper read woodenly, without intonation, the book did not let her inside—and he talked about the past, very abruptly, as if constantly bumping into the borders of an area he had promised himself not to discuss, and my family formed the opinion that somewhere in his past there was a drama, an injustice, perhaps an arrest, an exile, a prison term. Grandfather II liked table games, lotto, cards, but someone had to sit with him and with a touch tell him what move to make, and the dacha evening under the cloth lamp shade became quite proper thanks to him—the way evenings at the dacha should be when people of different generations got together, when no gaps existed in the generations, and everyone was kindheartedly connected because there was a person whose need was appropriate, not burdensome and who could be easily helped; the tubby lotto barrels tumbled along the table, the cards were placed on the tablecloth, it grew late, and it was probably even too agreeable to sense that evening was closer for some and farther for others; the evening of life.

Thus, bit by bit, Grandfather II entered our family. Of course, he never interfered in affairs that were profoundly personal; if something important was discussed in his presence, he settled himself in the chair in a way that showed that he considered himself properly present but without a say; with each year in these situations he sat ever more confidently in the chair, millimeter by millimeter approaching the stance of a family member and not just a friend; he became something like a notary, and he was invited when there was a serious conversation to be had.

And then once, when my mother was pregnant with me, the doctors said that giving birth was very risky and recommended an abortion; naturally, this was not discussed at the table, but the whole family knew and worried. Unborn, I was already present, grandmother was already searching the trunks for old diapers and wool to knit a cap and socks; but everything vacillated, grew, and the family—belatedly—tried to be more careful in their speech and controlled their gazes; a life was being decided and no one wanted to place the wrong calibration on the scales.

Everyone expected the decision to ripen and occur on its own; life in the household changed, swollen like a pregnant belly, filled with the murky waters of expectation. Mother was determined to give birth, but too many unspoken concerns, unfinished questions had accumulated in the house. The closer the day approached when an abortion would no longer be possible, the more some members of the family, who felt she should not carry the baby, watched with frightened and squeamish astonishment—as if looking at jars in a medical museum—as the new life, still totally belonging to physiology and therefore comparable to a disease, a tumor, prepared to appear at the cost of the possible death of the person bearing it.

All the old grievances between the two branches of the family, mother's and father's, manifested themselves; two bloods, two heritages met, and the fact that I—still nothing, still only a fetus in the womb—was preparing to be born this way, through mortal danger, exposed old contradictions; pitting blood against blood, family against family.

Father bore the receding, weakening blood of an ancient noble dynasty; my three great uncles on my father's side died missing in action during the war—having set down roots in the eighteenth and nineteenth centuries, the line was dying out, finding itself in an alien time and conditions.

Mother had the blood of a southern family in which every generation bore at least ten children, and each child was much more someone's brother or sister than himself or herself; where, if the whole family gathered, they set tables in the garden; where they were strong bodied, and when they died, they were not lost or unknown, as if the family ties—direct, second cousin, third cousin—left no one unsupervised, did not permit them to vanish without a trace; as if the blood of this family in some sense ignored the individual person, and new shoots came up, as it did after grass was mown—three times as thick.

Two bloods, two family fates were mixed in me; two past tenses sought the future verbs in me. Two forces, related to me but not to each other, my mother's family and my father's, came together implacably in me: Which was I to be, whom would I take after? Each side was prepared to fight to the death to keep the other from winning. People were merely weapons of those forces, blood donors.

I know that this incompatibility, just as objective as the incompatibility of proteins, this irreconcilability of two sources, not opposite but different in some other way and therefore unable to become one whole, forms the contradictions of my life today. Two loves, two hatreds, two fears—from my mother, from my father. The feeling of disunity in myself, desire bifurcated—two different desires for the same thing, arguing and competing; and fear multiplied by two. Twice as much strength to quell, stifle, sate; half as much confidence, validity, firmness; two bloods—tenacity and vulnerability, lust for life and openness to mortality—two bloods, two mutually exclusive legacies. Even when my mother was pregnant with me, they grappled with each other, tying the knot of the delayed event—the threat of death in childbirth.

It was then that Grandfather II came to our house. Unable to see the tension of the hidden conflict manifested in every look, gesture, and pose, he nevertheless learned of the argument or disagreement. In the timbres of voices, in the changed sounds at home—What do we know of what a blind person learns from the sharp and fractured sound of a fork on porcelain, the strained creak of door hinges, water pouring more voluminously and loudly than usual from the kitchen tap?—Grandfather II sensed the score of discord in the changed sounds (the way animals sense an earthquake, hear the noise of the future, for every catastrophe is also a catastrophe of time, violating its smooth flow). Silence and quiet for a blind man are material phenomena, objects grow still for him, and the edge of a chair or table is the acute angle of silence; Grandfather II recognized changes in the silence of the furniture, the drapes, chandeliers, doors, and parquet; he recognized it and like an engineer, a composer in steel and concrete who sensed that the construction did not sound right, he tried to find the region of altered sound, the region of the cavern, the split, the crack. He sought it in questions—he must have heard not only the words but also how they bumped into one another, head-on or obliquely, in passing, swallowed by the atmosphere or on the contrary, forcing it to resonate; words for him were those invisible particles whose existence physicists can determine only by the sum of the effects they produce, and these effects, of intonation, of meaning, Grandfather II literally absorbed; he straightened up, as if listening with his whole body, turning it into a resonator or radar, and he received hidden currents of events with the surface of his body.

Quite quickly—they had been at table about an hour—Grandfather II must have comprehended the situation; one remark about mothers not eating spicy food, and the tone in which it was said, was enough for him to see that pregnancy was dangerous for her. And here—everyone knew that Grandfather II was childless—he unexpectedly, after a long pause for thought, delivered a speech, revealing everything that was hidden, bringing himself into the family with full and permanent rights.

Grandfather II spoke hesitatingly, jumping from one subject to another, which in itself was amazing. His judgments, for all their reason and experience, were always somehow memorized, rote; he never supposed, never considered possibilities and probabilities, as if his blindness had taught him to trust only hard—in every sense of the word—facts. He valued the hardness as a quality even more perhaps than the content of the fact, which gave the impression that he was an encyclopedia reader, a lover of dates, metrical information, and legal definitions; but here he stepped onto the unfamiliar ground of conversation about life per se, and this gave his speech an additional sense of sincerity.

He spoke the way one might conjure away a toothache—repeating intentionally, leading away from the present with its constant reminders of the pain; lulling, calming the unborn child, as if giving the mother a relaxing massage. He began for some reason with the thirties in the village where he had lived; the former landowner there had a huge apple orchard. In the olden days, he let in the villagers, giving them a third of the harvest, and even though he always offered people allotments, no one took them—it was more familiar and easier to gather apples in someone else's orchard in the fall. After the revolution the orchard belonged to the public, and every village family decided to have an apple tree in their yard; the old orchard trees were dug out and brought by cart to the village. It was fall, harvest time for trees, and the yellow-leaved crowns of the apple trees floated across the fields as if the orchard had decided to leave the area; not a single tree took—they were the wrong age, even though the villagers had dug big holes and lined them with hay and manure; the apple trees froze the first winter.

Grandfather II spoke with a sense of having been injured by the apple trees, by the laws of nature, according to which an old tree cannot take root in a new place; then he spoke of the North, of the fish spawn coming from the ocean, where the whole world becomes a fishing net, and it tries to break through the nets, seines, swim upstream through rapids, overcome the force of the flow, and its movements are so powerful that it breaks through—but it breaks through into death, it dies creating its descendants, as if there are obstacles that cannot be overcome without accepting first that you will die if you do.

But note that from Grandfather II's speech it was impossible to tell whether he sympathized with the apple trees and the fish that died in the nets; they were echoes of his thoughts about himself. He had something planned and was now trying to prepare my family to accept his idea without naming it. He could barely keep up with his own speech, he had spent too much time, perhaps decades, deciding something and now the energy of those unspoken deliberations, liberated, unleashed, poured out of him, and he could only manage to place dams along the way, to separate it into flows, cover them with masks and euphemisms, so that whatever he had said to himself clearly and directly should not be heard in that directness.

Of course, it was listened to and heard differently; the people gathered around the family table sensed that Grandfather II was searching for an approach to what could resolve the general tension of many days, and they interpreted his speech as he was speaking not about himself but exclusively about the situation in which he found himself. The no longer fruitful apple trees, the dying fish spawning—there was something vague in this and it was not clear onto which side of the scales his words were to go. But suddenly, coming to his senses, he sharply changed course: to everyone's surprise, he began to speak as if he had discovered all the unspoken trepidations—and tossed them aside. He said that she should definitely have the baby, medicine was advanced now, and the doctors were being overly cautious—he listed births in trolley cars, the lamp room of a mine shaft, a cornfield, on a Central Asian steppe near the space center, in a bakery, a dentist's chair, a bomb shelter. A more attentive listener would have realized that Grandfather II was inventing these incidents, choosing the locations from the life he knew or from newspapers, but he filled and overpopulated the room with these unexpectedly born infants, the endless contractions of birth, until the listeners' focus dissolved. Grandfather II was already promising to get Mother into the best hospital, an exclusive clinic for the elite, promising that everything would go well, as if he were a midwife himself; he spoke of himself, his childlessness—I end with myself and there is no continuation of me—and asked and begged her so persistently to have the baby, pleaded with her to fear nothing, that no one ever thought he was asking for himself.

This conversation settled it: she should have the baby; and this is how Grandfather II appeared among the people who stood at the source of my life. The contractions lasted a long time, I exhausted my mother; with every hour she grew weaker, we needed to be separated, she needed to be freed of me, but they couldn't; she hemorrhaged, the bleeding would not stop, and the doctors later said that at one point they didn't know whom to save, mother or child. I was born in part on the word of another, I was born a hair's length away from death, mine and my mother's; it was luck, but in hindsight it strengthened faith in Grandfather II's successful presentiments.

And so Grandfather II entered our family; it was unspoken, but I was established as his grandson; through me came the connection, through me this relationship was created and subsequently retained. With his words, his vital force, embodied as certainty, Grandfather II redeemed me from nonexistence, made me real, opened doors for me; the connection of savior and saved, creator and created. In some sense I was relinquished to Grandfather II; many disagreements among those bringing up a child are over who has the final right of ownership of the child, and Grandfather II held this right of mental property, creating a slavery more subtle than treating a human being like a thing.

However, he did not rush to use it in my early years; as far as I understand, he removed himself, as if taking a break after the main deed was done. Additionally, he did not care for infants, he avoided being in the same room with them, as if they were disgusting to him, babbling, suckling, crying, screaming, unable to speak; unintelligible creatures to the ear.

He must have been waiting for the infant to grow up quickly, acquiring reason and speech—then he could talk to him, treat him like a small adult—that is, behave as Grandfather II behaved with everyone else. Infancy requires a different attitude: you don't have to adore, flirt, make kissy noises, you can be aloof but have an inner conviction about the scale of the event; this person had not existed and now here he is, called upon to live. In fact, infants are a gauge of the ability to have serious and altruistic feelings between people: he is yet no one and at the same time already someone completely autonomous, a concentrated "ego" that will only be dissolved by the years. And if an adult can truly comprehend the revelation of a new life that belongs only to itself, if he has the inner hearing and vision, he would never encroach on a relationship with another; the other for him is a goal, not a means. So when an adult absolutely must do something with a small child and he has no idea how—then you can presume that this person is a seeker of use and profit in relationships; none of his usual methods of secretly manipulating others works with infants, and he is lost, in an uncomfortable situation fraught with exposure.

Thus, the fact that Grandfather II disappeared after my birth, which he had so wanted, could have been food for thought; could have, but was not.

I've already said that Grandfather II lived like a man without a past; one external flaw—blindness—hid another: that absence of a past. A displacement occurred—it was impolite, uncomfortable asking a blind man what he had seen, how he had lived, what he used to do. The idea was that such questions would remind him of his handicap, his infirmity, and Grandfather II hid behind blindness so naturally that no one noticed the maneuver. He did not pretend to be powerless, he did not parade his lack of vision, demanding special attention—he merely did not see, did not see with all humility and realization of his inability; he did not grumble or complain and I was probably the only one who understood that Grandfather II had made himself an appendage to his own unseeing eyes; it is unlikely he could have restored his vision, the diagnosis was final, but his acceptance was feigned.

He had the kind of pride that is unknown to ordinary people who cannot imagine that a person can be the sculptural shell of his pride; a pride so strong that its bearer would be humiliated to reveal it; pride and scorn.

Later I managed to see all this only because Grandfather II's habits, his scrupulous self-control, which was tripled or quadrupled by the need to keep in mind the accidental gaze that he could not notice, were all calculated for adults; they do not play hide-and-seek, do not sit silently, breathing through the nose, under the table when someone enters the room.

Grandfather II seemed to have forgotten there was another pair of eyes in the house. He had never seen me from my very birth, and probably at the beginning I was something like a speaking breeze of air for him. He could follow my growth only in his mind, and not knowing how I looked, not being able to picture me made me—in his perception—a plant capable of reason or a domestic pet. Grandfather II concentrated too much on always appearing the way he wanted to adults, keeping a mental picture in his head built on sounds—who came and went, where they were going, where they were now, who might be looking at him—that I "fell out" of the picture, or rather, did not appear in it for some time. Grandfather II did not expect astuteness from me, did not target me as a possible danger; he could judge me only by the conversations adults had with me, and those conversations—for this is the common attitude in conversations with children, if you listen objectively—could create only the image of a dawdler and bumbler.

Had Grandfather II been internally closer to his own childhood, had his memory not been so crammed with events that blocked one another, he might have understood that one should beware of a child most of all; that the absent-mindedness for which I was always scolded was in fact a sign of a different sort of attention: not narrowed but expanded, embracing and absorbing the margins, the things that did not fit into a focused crystal. But Grandfather II—I guessed this only later—had lived the kind of life that separates a man from himself; he was unlikely to remember anything about his own perceptions in childhood.

When I turned seven, Grandfather II at last laid claim to me. In the final dacha days—the family was already seeking suitable gladioli for a bouquet to bring to school—they found I had lice. There were only a few days left before class started, it would be impossible to get rid of them in that short time; the adults met to hold a council and I waited in the next room; I thought they would decide to cut my hair short, and I was already suffering: not only was my hair perhaps my only freedom, but I did not regard the whole haircutting business as something ordinary and safe.

My inner anxiety was always disproportionately high before a haircut. The mended sheet that my mother used to cover me seemed like an ancient shroud, its whiteness no longer the familiar white of bed linens and it took on—probably because it was an old, much-washed sheet—the shade of invisible twilight that you catch on white death shrouds: they themselves are not touched by decay, but the shadow of decay lies upon them, as if sunlight from the cloth is absorbed into the air, leaving behind particles of the purplish blue that appears on the sharpened cheekbones of the dead.

The loneliness—looking in the mirror—of the human

head separated by the sheet, the nearness of scissor blades, hair falling on the floor which had just been part of you, and was already being swept up; a haircut seemed like a little death to me. I invented a hierarchy, and a haircut was on the same level as the death of a cat or dog; the animal dies, while a person is not killed by a death like that, a human needs a larger death—but I wasn't very big, and so I froze on the chair, and to this day I have to walk anxiously past the barbershop several times before stepping inside. The scent of soap, powder, foam whipped up by the hot currents of the blowdryer, sweetness and stickiness all refer me to something else, two biblical stories merge into one: Delilah cutting Samson's hair and Salomé carrying John the Baptist's head upon a plate; cut off hair and the separation of head from body—something about life and death is understood in those images which is revealed in anxiety even to a child; I learned later how such feelings are euphemistically transformed in the Book.

And then, when something had to be done with my head, Grandfather II proposed: shave it and smear it with kerosene.

Shave. Completely.

I was not worried that I would be teased for being bald; rather, a complete shave was equal and equivalent to death, not the little death, as in a haircut, but the full-sized real death. They were going to "nullify" me, turn me into an infant, that is, to deprive me of the little I had lived and which was expressed visually in the length of my hair.

I got even more scared when I realized that the adults would not argue with Grandfather II; they were happy that he proposed what they were thinking but, out of pity, had not said. It was fitting for Grandfather II to propose it; lice, kerosene, shaving the head—it all smelled of ancient times, homeless children, severe measures; if anyone else had suggested it, the adults might have argued, but here we had the charm of severity; stop whining, shave the head, imagine you're in the army, no one's asking you, you've got to put up with things, learn to man up. This was all said as if he had right of age and experience, with the intonation of superficial and therefore cheerful people who like the phrase "don't turn this into a tragedy." People like that become sergeants, trainers, gym teachers, they don't like sloppy and careless bums; they think that even feelings should be energetic and brief—three minutes for a farewell; nothing bothers them, nothing gets through to them, everything heals quickly. Grandfather II spoke that way, and the adults probably thought he was playacting, that this was the right tone to take to cheer me up, but I had the growing awareness that this wasn't just about the haircut; Grandfather II had decided—and no one understood!—to take me in his power.

There was a backstory to this feeling; I had noticed long ago that Grandfather II resented and even hated long hair.

Blind, he could still guess whether the unknown woman who came into the room had her hair loose and not up in a knot. A woman, for instance, our new neighbor, would visit for the first time, and Grandfather II could sense the invisible agitation coming from the unbound, curly, long hair—and run his hand over his gray crew cut; that meant that Grandfather II was angry. In the liberated locks, in the lightness of tresses sweeping her shoulders, he probably sensed vague danger: a symbol and source of sensual freedom—that is why he really loved, forgetting his relatively masculine nature, all kinds of hairpins and slides, all the metal ammunition used to tame and restrain women's hair. The housekeeper spent her life wearing kerchiefs, he bought them for her with almost every pension deposit; she used them to cover the television, laid them on shelves like little tablecloths, she secretly gave them away, for Grandfather II could not count them; much later I learned that Grandfather II burned her hair, allegedly by accident, with a curling iron. When Grandfather II hugged me and patted my head, his fingers grabbed my hair at the root and moved as if the middle and index fingers were scissors. In our dacha house, the scissors hung on a nail near the cupboard, and Grandfather II sometimes went over to check if they were in place. The fact that they hung on a nail and were not put into a drawer created a special sensation; they were old, made in an ironmonger's workshop in the twenties—you could make out the mark—blackened, as if over the decades the metal had absorbed candle soot, stove smoke, and coal dust; the scissors hung on the wall like a sign and reminder, a sign of power. The only object equal in power was the pencil—once a year, on the eve of my birthday, Grandfather II stood me in the doorway, put a book on my head, then I stepped aside, and he made a pencil mark along the book—to mark how I had grown, and then he notched the line. How I feared that pencil, ribbed and sharpened: I thought that one day I would not meet the measure Grandfather II had already intended for me, and my failure—I could not grow, the bread of our house was wasted on me—would be so great that no one would even say a word to me: they would turn away, and that would be all.

Scissors and pencil: if a coat of arms depicting Grandfather II's power over me were needed, I would pick those two objects. Scissors and pencil, and maybe also a protractor: when I first saw the drafting tools in his room, when I saw the ascetic precision of the tools, the gaunt extension of the legs, I didn't even understand at first that these items were meant for drawing on paper; I assumed that they were intended for drawing on a person, anthropometry, and decided that Grandfather II had called me in to compare me with those instruments to some diagram: Was I suitable to be a person, was there some discrepancy?

So, I sensed that the haircut would have a second, additional meaning; in getting rid of the lice, Grandfather II actually wanted to get me in his power, and I saw my shaved head as the hairless head of an infant. I might not have felt this so acutely and morbidly were it not for yet another recollection.

Besides hair, the second mysterious and special part of the body were nails; they were cut with small curved scissors, and for me it was a ritual of leave-taking, a ritual of growth and loss; sometimes there were white spots, like stars or clouds, on my nails, and I tried to tell my fortune by them, thinking they held signs of the future. I knew that nails continued to grow after death, and therefore thought they belonged in both worlds simultaneously, and that we without knowing were always standing before the veil of death and penetrating it with our fingertips. Those white dots and stars come from over there, from death, from the unity of time.

I brought my hand very close to my eyes and looked at the nail as if it were a screen, the sky in the planetarium where messages were projected from the other, dead side, shadows of approaching events; that is why you can't simply cut nails, you have to catch the mood and moment, do everything not to scare off the shadows; my nails seemed to be the most sensitive—if we mean premonitions and other sensations that combine feeling and time into one—and the almost forbidden part of my body that did not belong to me.

So on a spring day when frogs were laying eggs and their gassy clouds, full of black dots that would turn into tadpoles, glowed in puddles, I ran into Grandfather II's house; the house was illuminated, white woven curtains in the doorways rustled in the draft, and Grandfather II did not hear me. He was in the middle of the room on an oak stool, cutting his toenails; nails as yellow as last year's fatback *salo*, ingrown, like bird claws. Grandfather II was soaking his feet in a tub of warm water and clicking his clippers; with the same indifference to yourself you could chip at a sugarloaf or slice a sausage. I was astonished: not only did he not see the signs I saw, he could not even imagine that these signs occur; he was snipping off particles of himself dispassionately, meaninglessly; he was a thing to himself.

As I sat awaiting the haircut—the adults were consulting on where to get kerosene, there wasn't enough left in the lantern—I recalled those moments; I was sure that Grandfather II wanted to make me just like him; a thing, a thing, a thing ran through my brain; I suddenly saw the room as a conspiracy of things; my steps had made a narrow bright path in their dark life, and I realized I was trapped; Grandfather II knew whom to leave me with, to whom to entrust me.

He was the only adult who truly mastered things; the relationship between him and things was mastery, not possession or ownership.

The difference is that possession and ownership deaden the object, root it in the ossified nature of matter; a person repeatedly enslaves things that are already there to serve him—out of fear that he will lose them, that they will refuse to serve him, that someone else will take them; he enslaves them without actually having real power over them.

I watched Grandfather II pick up an axe, rusty, with a splintered handle, and it was suddenly clear that it was *his* axe, the way it was his arm which lifted the axe; the category of belonging did not apply here—Grandfather II and the axe became a single organism of flesh, wood, and metal, and the tool quickly regained the forgotten meaning of its form; I realized that Grandfather II could chop until the axe handle broke, but even then the axe—if things could speak—would bless the hands of Grandfather II, who had provisionally restored meaning to its existence.

This happened with things other than tools: Grandfather II could pick up someone's pen, a spoon in someone's house—and I would have the feeling that he left those items happy, left them recruited by an idea, the conviction of agents, and the sugar bowl from which he took a cube of sugar was ready to drag its glass belly on its stubby nickel-plated feet to the telephone, to inform Grandfather II what people at the table said about him after he left. It seemed that things sought his patronage: they fell at his feet, rolled across the floor to him; he was blind but he constantly found things and never lost anything; and every rare loss turned out to be someone else's oversight or error.

I was alone in the room; I was not alone; things—Grandfather II's eavesdroppers and servants surrounded me. I was caught; I was too scared to even think about running. I imagined that the couch upholstery and the old curtains were like the carnivorous sundew plant, electrified, sending out tiny threadlike whiskers that listened to my inner vacillations; a trap—I was trapped—I knew that Grandfather II had set it, and I even wondered if he had not given me head lice. He had told me how homeless children used to stop people on the street with a box of lice and threaten: We'll shake them on you if you don't give us money. I started looking for a hole I could escape through and got stuck even deeper in the feeling of being caught, identifying myself with mice, the house was riddled with their holes, mice, whose inconspicuousness I envied.

Grandfather II killed the mice; some adults considered this hunt a manifestation of his preference for order: the mice in this case were something irregular, petty, and nasty; others—who thought they saw more deeply and accurately—assumed that the mice were too much a reminder of the days that Grandfather II never talked about; that in the image of mice creeping up on grains of sugar and wheat, Grandfather II saw the deprivations of his past.

But I saw that he found a special eerie pleasure in how the mice died in the traps he, a blind man, set out; he did not need to see their holes, or seek the right place to put the mousetrap, or select the right bait—it was enough to set down the mousetrap and the mouse would find it, as if it was not the bait but the trap that attracted it by its very existence. Grandfather II was not killing mice, he probably did not care about them at all—he was seeking over and over confirmation of the law he discovered by intuition: the trap is important, not the quarry, it is important to insert the spring, raise the toothed arch, and the victim will appear—only because the trap was there.

Now in the room—there was silence behind the door, they had made a decision about the kerosene and they would call me in at any moment—I sensed that I was right; Grandfather II had a trap for every person. I realized that if I allowed them to cut my hair, if I sat in the chair, snuggled into the sheet, the scissors snipping metallically by my ear, my hair falling to the floor like rubbish, the blue blade, which made a ringing sound if you snapped it with a fingernail and which was honed on the suede reverse of a belt strap—if the dangerous razor touched my scalp, I would lose the future. The future tense—in premonition—was taken away, petrified, lost its visual perspective; it was taken away in language, too, verbs became a third lighter in weight. I sensed that if the scissors divided time into "before" and "after," the "after" would be alien to me, but I would not know that it was not mine, I would not remember how I had been afraid and wanted to run and thought about the trap. Acting on my own, not giving in did not mean exercising my own will; it was not will—it was life versus not-life, in which I could be taken like a thing, shaved and acquired.

Suddenly *the presence of spirit*, previously unknown, appeared, as if in that moment my entire future was being decided, and the person I was and would be in every moment of my life stepped into the compressed moment of the present, in the room that was a trap—and the trap cracked and fell apart. It did not require courage or boldness—just the presence of spirit; I saw that I was more extended than any particular moment of the present; and this extended "ego" in three tenses banished fear and opened up the conspiracy of things.

Hair—growth—time; razor and strap; a minute ago I had considered slashing my throat with the razor, hanging myself with the strap; but now I simply left the room. The adults told me to sit at the table, but I promised to be back in five minutes; they stayed in the house, and I unlatched the gate and went into the woods.

This wasn't running away; I had run away many times, hiding, but this time I simply needed to walk through the woods to the field. Something had happened inside me that needed space so it could complete itself and start living and breathing, and so I walked to the field; rye grew there every year, it was the end of summer, but it had not yet been harvested, and I soon crossed the twisted, cracked earthen lips of the fire ditch.

The grains slept in the dry grass spikes; the road cut into the field like a long tongue, disappearing beyond the edge; beyond the woods the commuter train moved, picking up speed; and I felt that I was alone; this was probably the first time I felt the sentiment—Where are the adults?—without fear, without an instinctive wary look.

They looked for me; they told me later that Grandfather II blamed himself, said it was all his fault; he was so frightened it seemed that some time in the past he had previously suggested shaving some other boy's head and smearing it with kerosene and then some accident befell the boy, not related to the shave, but the two events were so close together that they were somehow combined; Grandfather II roused everyone, sent them out searching, but he wasn't concerned by the insult I suffered; my hurt did not worry him—he just needed to know I was alive.

After my flight, Grandfather II stopped noticing me for a while; I think he realized that I had figured out his ulterior motive, and now we were united by that knowledge; my family fussed about my oversensitivity, my unacceptable childishness, but Grandfather II kept quiet; he probably understood that I would be thinking about him, that I would risk trying to find an explanation; he was sure I would not talk about it with the other adults—it was one thing to be scared of a haircut, another to even hint that you suspect Grandfather II of something.

He started behaving so that we were alone more often. I remember the dacha room that had pieces of carpet runner, probably bought from a hotel that had remainders—wine red with a dark green border; all the rooms of our house had them, we were used to them and did not notice that along with them unheard steps had crept in, and long corridors with nowhere to sit. The runners—which Grandfather II had obtained through his connections—were reminiscent not of a hotel but of Party headquarters, ministries, even the agency that people preferred not to mention; you could say that Grandfather II let them in along those paths—what a gift, what a service!— but I thought he had them laid because they were more familiar to the soles of his feet than painted floorboards.

I remember the room where I was alone—I had to work on my English, which I was taught in summer, and Grandfather II came in and stopped at the window. He did not pretend to have been passing, did not hide behind some errand— he simply stood there and allowed me to regard him; I was supposed to see something in him, be enticed in the neutral examination, gradually shortening the distance between us, coming closer and closer—in my gaze; like a big fish with its jaws wide open stopping in the water so that the small fry can swim in on its own.

And so it went: Grandfather II no longer tried to influence

me directly; he appeared on the periphery of my vision in the house, in the garden, as if trying to soap up my eyes— or, despite his own unobtrusiveness, enter my retina piece by piece. I soon discovered that he appeared in many separate moments of my day, like photographs. He did not try to make his presence known—he seemed to be counting on peripheral vision, knowing that it was a crack through which he could sneak into my awareness, just by visual repetition.

Grandfather II had figured it out correctly, but he underestimated my fright over shaving my head; of course, the fear receded over time, but the caution remained, and now trying to behave differently, but still with some sleight of hand, he merely heightened my wariness and essentially set in motion my formation in feeling and thought.

When we speak of a child's liveliness of perception, we think that liveliness is practically a synonym for friskiness; that it is alive in the sense of being changeable, distractible, unstable. But perhaps a child's perception is really alive, that is, endowed not with the gift of subtle differentiation but the gift of sensing—the game of "hot or cold" is not accidental here—what is alive and what is not in the ordinary sense; to see through the substitute image, to feel not nuances but the very nature of human relations.

This ability to understand the nature of relations, recognizing the live and the not-live is what bound me to Grandfather II with ties that could not be broken then.

I sensed that he was dead inside, unconnected to the world of the living; not a ghost, not a specter—but a solid, physical, long-lived (what could happen to him?) corpse; yet he had a strange concern for me and in his own way a liking. He— perhaps unconsciously—tried to bring me up in order to untie some knot in the past, to solve a drama that made him what he was. But in the present there were no explanations for his actions, from insisting on my birth to the haircut and kerosene for lice. My family got used to accepting current events as a given without seeking reasons, but if you looked at things from a different angle, the whole story between Grandfather II and me seemed superfluous, like a goiter or an appendix; he could have lived perfectly well without me and no circumstances forced him to have a relationship with me.

I felt that there was no life, nothing living in Grandfather II's attitude toward me; there was something else, unnamed; and I understood it only twenty years later.

A woman loved me; she confessed her feelings to me and not finding reciprocity tried to receive it with extreme persistence for a while; she called at night, wrote letters allegedly from my girlfriend, and then stopped, and I thought that her passion was spent or she had found someone else.

A few years later she died in an accident but was not immediately identified, and we, her coworkers, began searching for her while she was still missing; we got the police to open the door to her apartment, in case something had happened to her at home.

When I saw what was inside, I asked my friends and the policeman to wait outside.

My scarf hung in the coatrack; it had disappeared from our coatroom at work, worn and inexpensive, and I wondered who could have wanted it. The table and windowsills held pages with my handwritten notes, drafts of scholarly works. Everything that could be borrowed or taken unobserved she had gathered in her apartment; my pens, lighter, a pack of cigarettes; CDs, key chain, driver's manual, pocket calendar, the five hundred ruble note with a torn corner which she'd borrowed for a taxi.

She created a phantom of my presence out of those trifles. She lived her real life here with me, and in her ordinary life she was just a shadow. I suddenly realized how great was the constant tension with which she created—out of insignificant things!—this life of a double.

Her inner existence was revealed to me: desire, passion, jealousy twisted into a tight whip. Inside, there was another life in which I was a slave of this woman, the more obedient the farther apart we were in fact. That was the locus of the forces that were unleashed by her death; they had vision that did not see other people or were totally blind, blinded at the birth of her irrational choice rejecting other men. The eyeless hunting dogs followed the scent, hurried to fulfill their destiny, to pass unto me the passion that had created them—and at the same time to attach themselves to something in this world, the world of the living.

She had killed herself while alive, destroyed herself in order to live through me alone, and therefore her love was the love of a corpse; an almost otherworldly equivalent of emotions, which however were capable of participating in the entwining of fate.

Grandfather II's attitude toward me was of this nature. Back then, as a child, I felt only this nameless, unknown force; I couldn't have imagined that there was another life in which I was the star unwinding in Grandfather II's mind, and that he no longer correlated it with reality, like that woman who loved me many years later. In his head—blindness in this case played into his hands—I was already the person he wanted me to be; and the way he behaved in real life—which I took as the only behavior—was merely an edited, partial reflection of his plan.

Grandfather II carefully brought me closer; he asked that I accompany him when possible on his walks and errands, and my parents consented. I became more than his guide, I perforce walked his paths, moved in his orbits. Some would have thought that I was leading him, a blind man, but in fact he led me; we could go mushroom hunting, I looked for porcini or orange caps, Grandfather II carried the basket, and the mushroomers we met were touched, praising me for my kindness and care; but I knew that I was the blind one and Grandfather II saw what he was doing, saw his own intentions, invisible to me. In the woods on a hot day a spiderweb stuck to my face, and I thought that the web was the materialization of Grandfather II's plans, and I removed it, washing with black musty water from ground puddles, just to keep from feeling those threads; in the early twilight—we could go out for long periods—the forest turned into a layering of shadows, inky springs of darkness appeared between tree trunks, and I would relax—I didn't have to watch out for a trick anymore, I no longer felt that the sunny day was just a cover-up, that the two of us were moving in a different space that only seemed light. I wandered after the figure showing white in the twilight and I knew that this is how everything really looked—dark, formless, with the invisible touch of grass and branches.

My age gave Grandfather II power; whatever happened, he would be believed, not I. And Grandfather II, moving beyond making me his guide, began playing a game with me. It began by the well; we had gone for water, Grandfather II turned the handle and I filled the buckets. "Do you want to get in the bucket and I'll send you down?" Grandfather II said. "You can see the stars from the well even in daytime."

I looked into the well. It was hot, flies were swarming—the cows had been herded nearby recently; everything was burning, sparkling, heating up; the world itched like a scratched bite, blistering, stinging with nettles, dusting, shimmering, but under the well roof, pulling back the lid, you were suddenly, without transition, on the underside of that overheated world.

I was always a bit afraid of well water—I thought you shouldn't drink it until it had been in the light for a while, had gotten used to air and space. The buckets were covered, and I secretly removed the lid so that the water would not keep what it had absorbed underground; my parents told me once about groundwater, how it collects, dripping along layers of rock, forming underground rivers and lakes; a second landscape was revealed to me, a second world which contained the mysteries of the circle of matter, everything that was washed away, carried, dissolved, everything that the water had seen with its transparent tight eyeball-drops; it contained decomposed fallen leaves, spring-melted snow, the rain from two days ago; there, beneath the present was the past, flowing its own way, and the well water in a bucket seemed different than water from the tap—thicker, like a trembling ingot, as if the attraction of molecules was stronger in it. And now Grandfather II offered to lower me down there, into the round hold of the well, into the cold of yesterday's water.

I was afraid of being near the water that had not yet been brought to the surface, still underground and dark. Grandfather II said: if you don't want to go down there, just have some water—it's hot. I wasn't allowed to drink water from the well for fear of catching cold, and Grandfather II's suggestion seemed such an understanding gesture: go ahead and drink, I know you do when no one's watching, go on; but I knew that I had never in fact had a drink of water like that.

A tin cup was attached to the well by a chain, Grandfather II scooped it full and handed it to me.

There were many cups on chains later—by wells, by the hot water urns in rickety trains, by cisterns in Kazakhstan mines; the water in them either had a musty smell, or had been boiled a dozen times, or had a rusty aftertaste; a prison camp, shackled kind of mug, dented, scratched, wrapped in dirty adhesive tape, with an uneven bottom and edge shiny from many lips; but this was the first, most memorable mug.

I didn't dare refuse and took a tiny sip; the icy water burned my lips the way metal does in winter, and Grandfather II started telling me how in the North water can be so cold even in summer that it can stop a man's heart; it wasn't water anymore but the embodiment of cold. I drank from the cup and Grandfather II waited; then he scooped up more and drank himself.

After his mention of the icy water of the North, our relationship was firmly established, strange, full of unspoken words, pauses, and tensions. Grandfather II had selected me to be a junior comrade, a confidant, knowing that I would understand very little of what would be revealed to me in hints, circumlocutions, and riddles; it was my inability to understand that must have tempted him to begin a conversation extended over time.

Sometimes he gave me "a sip from the mug"—as if he was giving me communion, permitting me a sip of the past, which I could neither picture accurately nor fit into a bigger picture. Grandfather II told me about polar nights, when people went mad and could be saved only by showing them a picture of a new, different face cut from a magazine; about mountains that were always hidden by thick clouds, where German planes had crashed during the war; about gnats and midges that could get past any mosquito net, crawling over your face and neck, seeking dead meat. It was all carefully selected to suit my age—distant parts, extraordinary events—but the more Grandfather II told me, the more I felt that all these stories were just the edge of the envelope; Grandfather II set out the hunting flags consistently and irreversibly, turning my perception in the right direction; he sketched the contours of an unknown continent, Atlantis, which would float up on his command, gradually preparing me to step on its soil.

Occasionally he said nothing, stopped maintaining the image that he was presenting, and those were moments of stupefaction. His features did not change, but he stopped radiating familiarity and he appeared as a stranger.

That happens when you're exhausted and look at someone you've known a long time, but you are completely drained and the comprehension of the gaze ceases; someone new and unknown appears before you. But in this case my vision did not lose its clarity and strength, did not fail me—it was Grandfather II's inner tension, which twisted him like a cramp, letting him loose, and you could see another old man who sat inside Grandfather II.

This could happen anywhere, on the platform between train cars, in line at the doctor's office, in the woods, at the pond. Grandfather II, knowing that I could see, would suddenly start touching his face, fingering the lapels of his jacket, bending over to fix his shoelace, run his hand along the row of buttons, as if checking that everything was buttoned and covered. If strangers saw him, they would think it the necessary habit of a blind man, but I knew that in just a minute Grandfather II would turn, stand so that I could not see him whole, he would be in a space between bodies, trees, or furniture, as if in a random photo, fleetingly, for a second, and I would not recognize him, neither his clothes nor the location would help. He would be a stranger from a different era, he would be years behind, and then, covered by a chance passerby, he would return to my field of vision as his former self, as if he had changed outer shells, time-traveled, behind the screen of someone's body.

From the outside our connection looked like the friendship of an old man and a boy; everyone thought so, explaining Grandfather II's good feeling for me by his reserved complaints about being childless. This explanation obligated me even more: it was assumed that Grandfather II—soon, not soon—was close to the grave, and therefore I was not supposed to "upset," "anger," "let him down," or "make him worry." I knew that Grandfather II was completely healthy, and my family knew it, too, but still they made him out to be a helpless old man who could be killed by any strong emotion—that was more convenient, it was a wonderful way of bringing my life into a subordinate state.

As a result, Grandfather II strengthened his power over me; every action, every word was evaluated by what effect it would have on Grandfather II. Interestingly, despite all this, no one particularly loved him; even I at some moments, when he seemed a completely harmless person, wondered why I couldn't like him—it would save me from the constant feeling that he was trying to dominate me, and maybe I would be able to accept his power gladly. I even—quite childishly—tried to love him; I tried to clarify the map of my inner workings, find the area on it where the physiological background of love is located—warmth, a sense of openness, as if shutters were flung back; I tried, but failed—it was impossible to love Grandfather II.

I think no one actually had any feelings for Grandfather II, the attitude came from the mind rather than the heart; probably everyone was ashamed of this, thinking it was his own fault and not Grandfather II's, and tried to express false emotions—you don't want to hurt the old man, who didn't deserve it. Maybe if members of my family had once talked to one another frankly and discovered that no one liked the old man, even though there was no reason, they would have stopped to think; but there was no conversation, and each one added his or her lines to the illusion of universal liking of the old man, never imagining that the rest were also pretending.

I thought a lot about why it was impossible to like Grandfather II; I realized that love could not arise in his vicinity. If you take cowardice to be the highest degree of egotism, Grandfather II was a coward; he could exhibit many different qualities, including self-sacrifice and concern, but they all served his cowardice: to preserve himself as he was. No one could love him: he loved himself so much, not in the sense of emotion but in the sense of self-preservation, that there didn't seem to be any love that could be added, it was excessive as it was; and almost all his actions had a thin layer of fear for himself, the apprehension that events could interfere with his plans and destroy his plots.

I understood this when I was still a child; I had often asked Grandfather II if he had fought in the war and he replied that they didn't take him in the army. But I knew from his cleaning woman that he kept his medals in an old candy box; I decided that Grandfather II had done something horrible in the war, never spoken, never reckoned with, which was behind all the films, paintings, and stories; I thought that those heroes killed the enemy with a first death—the one that happens on paper, canvas, on film; but there had to have been someone outside the pages of the book, the frame of the shot, who killed Germans with a real, fatal death, and I thought that Grandfather II could have been one of them, one of a few.

One day we kids were playing with Uncle Vanya the Iron Neck, who came from the village; right by his carotid artery he had a piece of shrapnel which doctors would not risk removing, and our favorite game was putting magnets on his neck, for they stuck right on living flesh. Uncle Vanya was an old man who had been burned in a tank; they tried to keep him away from children because his face and head were disfigured by drop-like growths that resembled the flesh of a rooster comb, missing a layer of skin and covered by blood vessels; it looked as if his face was melting and the flesh had frozen in those drops, trembling, hanging on thick threads, repulsive because they revealed—on his face!—the reverse, animal side of the body, like the rooster comb.

But children were not afraid or repulsed; Uncle Vanya the Iron Neck seemed to us to be the only person we knew who had something significant happen; we knew—and we could see— that he had been in the war. Of course, children avoid the pathetic and the sick, unconsciously protecting trust in life and in the future; but Uncle Vanya was so ugly that it was almost a caricature of ugliness; the destruction of his face was so horrible that it didn't seem striking.

And then—he didn't need pity or sympathy; Uncle Vanya carried a postponed death of 1944 in his body, a death that had killed four of his comrades; it had needed just a few more millimeters to get through his flesh, but the shrapnel was moving slowly through his body, like a drifting continent, heading toward the artery, and essentially, that explosion that hit the tank still existed for Uncle Vanya—he had carried away the trajectory of the shrapnel's flight and lived in that trajectory.

Another person who survived death and was then disfigured by disease would probably have formulated a supporting philosophy, with the disease interpreted as the cost of his survival; commander of a tank that burned German dugouts, pillboxes, and trenches along with the soldiers, who crossed the battlefield in flames, flames that punished Germans, and who before the war had been fire chief of the district, Uncle Vanya didn't even remove the mirror in his village house. Probably those flames destroyed all concepts of proportion, of beauty and ugliness; only one thing remained—man was not meat, even though he saw more burned men than live ones; the spirit of life breathed in him freely and easily.

We played with Uncle Vanya; he taught us to make stilts, nailing planks for our feet on long poles; we walked around him on our wooden legs, passed a ball, and he kept bending his neck so that the magnet stuck to the shard under his skin but did not fall. Grandfather II came over to us; he was looking for me, and Uncle Vanya said hello. By the way Grandfather II replied to the greeting and the way he asked when I would be back, I suddenly realized that Grandfather II was afraid; afraid that I would get too attached to Uncle Vanya, that I would not return, would slip away, taking advantage of his blindness. So blatant was that childish, offended fear in an adult next to the benevolent friendliness of Uncle Vanya, that I—from that single feeling—sensed that Grandfather II truly had not fought in the war, that he was of a different human breed than Uncle Vanya.

I was struck by the realization that Uncle Vanya was sick, that his life was ruined by his ugliness, while Grandfather II was marked by a tidy, unnoticeable blindness; I suddenly saw—again by intuition—that Uncle Vanya's face, a face in meaty drops, should belong to Grandfather II, and the clean, untouched face of Grandfather II should be Uncle Vanya's.

I decided then and there to learn Grandfather II's past. I thought that every adult in our house was privately glad that Grandfather II was secretive and that any potential knowledge of his past remained unexposed.

The adults tried if not to forget the time about which Grandfather II could have spoken, then to at least make it palatable for their own private memory. They broke it up into small impressions, personal stories—what an ice hill there was by the ravine, now covered up; what nuts, all with rotten, wrinkled kernels, they once bought at the market to make jam; what pale, water-diluted ink they used to pour into the inkwells at school, and then the teacher complained that she couldn't read anything in their notebooks. That kind of past was like keys, wallet, and papers that you can stuff into your pockets when you go out; it was small, domesticated— everyone diligently reinforced the little sport of personal memory, and no one remembered for the collective.

Looking around mentally, I realized I could not combine the stories of the past into something general; people remembered their families, remembered their youth, but it was all narrow, cramped, like the rooms in the new neighborhoods built in the sixties and seventies in the outskirts on empty lots where it was so hard to get rid of dusty soil, burdock, and weeds; new houses came up, and in them, new life, separated by thin walls, and everyone learned to live quietly—how else when the neighbors could hear you cough—quietly and separately; live the way survivors do, stunned by having survived and forever maintaining the apartness of survivors.

I wanted to learn about Grandfather II's past, but all I could manage I already knew; I was his guide, I walked the same roads, I put his few letters in the mailbox; there was only one area where he would not let me in: his passion for fishing. He went to the pond alone and returned alone; it was wholly his time. Once I crept after him, but halfway there he heard me and ordered me to return home. I had only wanted to see how a blind man could fish, but Grandfather II clearly sensed in my attempt the desire to spy out something else that he knew and I did not. I came up with a circular approach so that I would not be following his footsteps. Alders and sedges grew along the banks, and every fisherman had his spot, hidden from view and reached by squeezing through branches.

A blind fisherman, yet Grandfather II did not look silly— you couldn't find a feature or detail that made him vulnerable to being a laughingstock. For all the potential ridiculousness of the image—canvas trousers, patched jacket, straw hat—he did not look ridiculous; even the bamboo rods, which always seem unserious and boyish in a grown man, were somehow separate from him, did not add another brushstroke to his look, even though he carried them in his hand.

He was not part of the brethren of fishermen, he had his place at the pond which no one else used, and the other fishermen did not come to him for bait or a cigarette or even to chat; he had set himself apart from the first day.

I started sneaking up to the pond and sitting at a distance from him. If you got too close, no matter how carefully you crept, Grandfather II would turn and fix his sightless eyes on you; at the moment you felt like a water rat that crawled out of its hole right in front of a hunting dog. I was amazed by the sensitivity in that self-contained and passionless man, whose movements were so measured you thought he was turning a windup handle, like on an old gramophone, inside himself that moved the various parts of his aged but still solid body. I even thought that he was expecting someone; someone who was supposed to come and ask him about something; waiting so as not to be caught unawares.

The more I sat at the pond watching Grandfather II catch fish, the more clearly—slowly, day by day—I understood that there was no mystery in Grandfather II's character; there was only a strong ban, a securely locked door, the metal bolt, the heavy curve of the padlock's shackle. There, behind the door, was something that had no place in the present; Grandfather II carried all his past with him, like a refugee at a short halt who does not unpack all the stuff from his city life.

Once I caught a glimpse of Grandfather II writing a letter; he must have written so much that blindness did not hinder him, the memory in his fingers connected the letters correctly. At the end of one sentence he placed a special question mark, drawn with additional meaning.

Grandfather II used a fountain pen, and the evaporating violet ink made the letter seem prematurely aged, and the sharp nib, divided like a snake's tongue, gave the drawn letters a persistent intonation. The question mark, which I had written in school exercises so many times, appearing like the contour of a hot air balloon from the basket's point of view or an ear with a drop earring—the sign suddenly appeared in a new meaning which I could not explain to myself then.

It was only later, at the pond, watching Grandfather II tie the hook to the float that I recognized the question mark from the letter—I recognized it in the snagged hook that sticks in the fish's belly and does not let the creature escape.

Grandfather II had a strange way of fishing; I could see but I couldn't tell from the movement of the float that the fish was biting, that its lips had touched the bait, I thought that the float was bobbing from wind puffs, but Grandfather II was already changing his grip on the pole the better to make the pull. He seemed to have a special sense of when the carp touched the bait; he could feel the live beating of the fish, he could feel it with the seeing fingers of a blind man, it reverberated moistly and sweetly in a hidden, clearly constructed corner of his soul.

A voluptuary of death, Grandfather II could feel—in general could feel—only through the mechanism of the fishing pole, in which the pain and fear of a living creature was transmitted by the tension of the line, the bend of the bamboo; he felt those surges, the thrashing weight of the fish as a caught life; without a fishing pole, touching live flesh, he apparently felt nothing.

I remember his fingers—I crept close and watched him put a worm on the hook. There is a peasant skill for killing chickens, breaking necks of geese, sticking pigs; the rough, domestic, accustomed dealing with death, without an admixture of martyrdom, of dependent animals and birds. This was something entirely different—Grandfather II's fingers moved as if he was threading a needle, and not for work but out of curiosity—will the thread pass the eye or will he need a needle two numbers larger?

Worms have red blood, and the worm sullied his fingers. When you're fishing your fingers are constantly covered with dirt or fish slime, and wiping them on grass or your clothes is automatic, repeated dozens of times. But Grandfather II took out his handkerchief and wiped his fingers thoroughly. There wasn't an iota of squeamishness or excessive fastidiousness in this, it was an inappropriate and marked thoroughness, which he did not notice; thoroughness, which was only an edge, an unexpected protuberance—the way a sharp angle of a sculpture sticks out from a cloth tossed over it—of his real nature. Behind the thoroughness was his knowledge of himself, so habitual for him, albeit hidden, that being blind and not seeing himself from outside, he did not catch it motivating the gesture: to clean his fingers.

Did he feel blood on his fingers, did he sense something wet, or did he understand, with his mind, that it was blood? I don't know: maybe the feeling of wetness on his hands fit some picture from his visual memory in his mind.

Deprived of light, most of his visions from the past must have fallen apart into dust; he was healthy for the present moment, but in the measure of the past he was sick, his visual memory, if I can put it this way, was going crazy: a live amputation, a stump, left alone with itself. The gap in time remained—and grew!—in his mind: his past, wrapped up in darkness, could not meet the present. And when it tried, the blind memory took what reached it through smell, touch, and hearing, and fit it into and rhymed it with a few remaining pictures where it fit; but the meeting of times could not take place this way: only the blind past via hidden fear directed the blind present.

Now I think that the blood of the worm he set on the hook seemed like human blood to him; externally he remained the same, unflappable, inspiring caution more than respect, as if he would open his eyes and say "I saw everything!" and that "everything" would be X-ray knowledge of what you hide in deep inner shame, which should never be revealed, because that which you experience so painfully may in fact be the reason you have a conscience, and revealing it would be moral murder; externally Grandfather II remained the same but I think inside, condemned to darkness, he was sentenced to being torn apart by the manifestations of his memory.

Now I understand why some of his memories seemed more stable through time than all the rest. These were memories leading beyond the border of life; killing and destruction contradict the work of memory—to preserve whole, which is why the memory of a death in which you are involved is a tragic oxymoron; if you clear away the component of external action from this memory, its foundation will not be the bas relief of presence, the existence of something, but a gutter of absence, unfillable but never-ending like the water in the Danaides' vessels. Such a memory is not quite a memory; it is fed by an unrealizable desire, used to punish sinners; it does not strengthen, it weakens existence in a person.

But Grandfather II—it seems to me—did not regret anything; you couldn't approach him from the moral side. However, the categories of being and nonbeing are more primary than moral ones, and vengeance got him through a fear of death; the worm's blood did not remind him of the blood of his victims or of their suffering—the less he could feel the horror of his deeds, the more palpably did death, as a naked, dispassionate fact arise before him, elicited by that blood; what had previously served as a defense—perceiving it that way—turned against him and became the only weapon that could hurt him.

This explains the death of Grandfather II and our posthumous blood tie.

It all took place at the dacha, in early August, the day before my birthday. It was so hot that the chocolate candies in the hutch were melting, sticking to their wrappers; the bread kvass in the crawl space fermented, popping their corks, and the sour intoxication spread through the floorboards into the house, dozens of flies were dying on the sticky paper, so many that the paper ribbons moved as if in a breeze; but the air was heavy, unmoving, stale, like the water in a glass for dentures; grass flopped heavily, breaking at the geniculum, the pond grew shallow and fish rotted in the dark green, dried slime, bubbling on the surface; crows gathered at the pond, perching on the low trees on the shore, digging in the slime, untangling fish innards with their beaks; sated, the crows flew to the high-voltage lines and it seemed that the lines were drooping under the weight of the heavy bird mass and not the heat; the crows sat in silence, burping occasionally; Grandfather II walked along the bank of the stinking pond, feeling the presence of the birds above, and he threatened them with his cane, copper-clad, knotty, darkened by the tar the wood had absorbed, resembling a mummy's sinew-wrapped bone.

In the dachas, where behind the white swoon of lace curtains old people breathed heavily, the thermometer's red thread trembled and crawled upward; all the thermometers looked like glass tubes for collecting blood, and all the thermometers measured life and death. Blood pushed at calcified arteries, flushing faces, pumping into weak, flabby hearts; blood seemed to be dispersed in the air, and the dogs, hiding in jasmine bushes, in pipes and ditches, swollen tongues lolling, clawed at the dry earth. The heat cracked the tender skin of cherries, unpicked for several weeks—and dark ichor dropped from the cherries, making spots on the eggshells tossed beneath the trees; the sweltering heat accumulated in the sky, and feeble, age-spotted hands touched the body, which had become alien and distant—farther than the tubular metal pillbox, farther than the voice which could no longer call for help.

Dust storms swirled on the adjoining fields, convulsions of space; something was brewing, gathering amid the whispering oats; there was always a line at the dacha guard booth for the only phone, people turned the dial that clicked when it sprang back into place, and through the fading foliage we could see the red and white of the ambulance, and only Grandfather II was sprightly and brisk, as if on good terms with death, like a doctor, and the heat merely dried his body to make it lighter, allowing him to stride faster.

That day I went out to the alley of garden plots; our children's gatherings had ceased a long time ago, as if the element that brings children together had evaporated, gone with the play of breezes, rustles, whispers, and trembling branches that form the melody and milieu of children's games; the air was sickeningly thick, sticky like the skin that forms when making jam, and had an acrid taste.

Why I went out I can't remember now; there are actions you perform without knowing what prompted them and in that sense are unintentional, but not done out of momentum or habit. Probably I just needed to get outside the fence, to free myself of the sense of being surrounded on all four sides by pickets; the fence in a dacha lot very clearly defines the place where a child is both protected and hemmed in at the same time, while right outside the fence the street begins, where things impossible inside the fence can happen.

A fence is the border that separates life built on repetition, like a school lesson—have breakfast, weed the garden, read a few pages of a book—from life where you are on your own; the gate, which could be locked if you are being punished and not allowed out, the lock and shackle are guards protecting you from imaginary and real harms: the year before a boy had jumped from the shore and cracked his head, at the beginning of summer another boy went into the woods and got lost, a third boy tried crossing the tracks beneath a standing train, but the train started and caught his shirt, a fourth boy went for a walk in the sand quarry and fell into a hole ... These supposed corpses were "registered" in the dacha topography, like pagan spirits of lakes and forests, they even included a pilot shot down in the winter of 1941 and buried near the pond under a small pyramid with a red tin star; they deprived the area of safety but also announced its realness: the forest wasn't a forest but the forest-where, the pond was the pond-where; thanks to them, this locality took on an additional dimension, stopped being a dacha suburb and turned into a village district that incorporated life and death in such proximity, like the village and its cemetery.

Under the dark forest canopy, in the impenetrable, intoxicating denseness of the raspberries at noon, in the cattails and sedges on the pond shore that blended into a thick green haze over the black water, in the moist moss of the swamp, in the hidden source of the forest stream, buried under tree roots, everywhere there was something that called to you, touched you questioningly and invitingly, as if testing to see how conscious you were, whether you could be enticed, lured, abducted. The boys from the stories told by grown-ups, to whom something "bad" happened—you understood that was a lie, but a lie caused by not knowing, a guess, which therefore unexpectedly revealed the area of truth.

Therefore the fence was not simply a guardrail: all the scrapes, wounds, and hurts, everything that made you bleed and left scars happened outside it. If you cut yourself at home, it was from a carelessness that was instantly nursed with iodine and a bandage. But out there, beyond the fence, the concept of careful and careless did not exist: sunny fields and dark woods worked together so uniformly, blood flowed so easily and almost merrily from a cut that you did not see it or any wound as an attempt by death on life; you didn't see it and in that sense you were protected.

Coming out to the alley, I stepped on the sand that marked the border between it and the garden plots—and saw a chunk of concrete the size of a fist; it was studded with smooth pebbles the color of frozen meat and sharp shards of flint speckled with conch shells. The piece of concrete must have fallen from a truck carrying construction materials from some lot; it had fallen recently and was not yet pushed into the sand, catching my eye.

Before I understood or remembered anything, my mouth filled with the taste of blood—without any blood; pain shot through my lower jaw like surgical thread in an unhealed wound. The world around me turned blurry, like the corrugated glass in hospitals, like the walls of a vortex; I looked at the piece of concrete but it seemed to be at the bottom of the vortex; the only clear thing in a blurry world, but extremely far away, discovered at the bottom of memory. I was slowly drowning in myself. Numbness entered my muscles, and I understood that in parts of my body an incessant telegraphic conversation had been under way, and now the components were falling apart, it went silent and was becoming empty, like the line where I stood, empty, like a book without letters, and my breathing stopped.

I saved myself—the way a diver finds a pocket of air underwater and takes a breath. My memory found a previous moment with a rock just like this one, and at that point, the opening which connects time like a nerve canal was revealed, and a fragmentary and flickering recollection came to the surface.

That other concrete block was just like this one, bristling with flint and pebbles. I had leaned too hard on the handle of my stroller and tipped it over, falling face-first onto the concrete. I was about a year old; my memory of that time was like amniotic fluid, better at conveying sound than image, and I sensed only my own long-ago scream. I did not understand then that I could die, the scream was older than my age, as if it was not a year-old child screaming but someone who was conscious of the horror of death and cried to stave it off. The sound was so piercing that it thickened and slowed time and the moment of the fall, and pain lengthened in it, lengthened in memory.

As soon as I recognized the rock the vortex vanished and the world stopped spinning like a top; however the sensation of alienness coming from the rock did not go away. I knew that my father had put the block in a wheelbarrow, smashed it with a sledgehammer, and thrown it away in the distant forest;

when he told me that—those were his words, "in the distant forest,"—it frightened me that somewhere a chunk of concrete splattered with my blood and that had almost killed me, was still lying around, smashed but not destroyed. I wanted to find it so I could bury it, or better, take it out in a rowboat to the middle of the pond and submerge it beneath the water and the silt. Father just laughed and said he had forgotten where he threw it; as if to say it was all nonsense and if not for Grandfather II he would have used the concrete as planned— for the foundation of the shed; he and my mother were to blame for not keeping a closer eye on me, but the concrete was just concrete. Father admitted that Grandfather II had insisted that he take the concrete to the woods; "nothing good will come from such a foundation," Grandfather II said and Father obeyed.

Now a chunk of concrete just like it lay before me. Or was it part of the block I fell on? There are moments when you sense that you must live carefully: it's as if the protective layers have been removed, habitual as clothing, you are left naked, exposed, vulnerable, and the event that has been stalking you, following you outside your field of vision, is close, but you don't know where it's coming from.

Reliving death exhausted me—I did not feel weak but I sensed that I was defenseless, and defenseless in a different way than even an animal in a hunter's sight; the deer and wolf have the ground beneath their feet, they are certain at least of that, confident in their ability to rapidly flee.

Sand. Sand was under my feet. A drop of sweat fell from my face and was absorbed, leaving a fat, convex blotch. In the sand I could see shiny grains of quartz, flakes of mica like particles of dragonfly wings, and pieces of feldspar as pale gray as ground grain; my body seemed too soft, pliant, sadly doomed; this is the way you look at places you are leaving, you become relaxed and compliant because in your mind they are already abandoned. I felt as if I had discovered a crack in myself and the fear that the break would increase fought with my desire to look inside, to follow that break, as if it had opened a path into depths previously inaccessible, or perhaps not even existing before.

At the very end of the desolate alley, by the far gate that opened to the place we called Concrete—there used to be a railway to the airfield there, abandoned, with crookedly diverging rails, where once they pushed concrete blocks like stelae from the loading docks onto smashed tanks, the lids of pillboxes, the wild wind of the outskirts whistled over broken glass and cardboard shelters for tramps—at the far gate a black dot appeared, growing like an abscess, a wormhole in the jellylike, greasy flesh of the day.

It was a dog, a black dog that could have come only from the Concrete side: it was running toward me, unsteadily, trotting from ditch to ditch, jaws open, scattering thick cottony saliva in the dust. There was no one around: just me and the dog, we were connected by the straight line of the alley, the geometry of fate; the dog was rushing disjointedly and kept itself together by running—if it were to stop, it would fall apart—and I stood, nailed to the ground by its attack, and the flesh in my calf could already feel the touch of its fangs.

The black dog—there were no black dogs in our neighborhood—black, frenzied by the heat, came close and prepared to jump, but its muscles could not lift its body into the air, and it just attacked, knocked me over and bit into my left leg as if my blood could cure it. Then the dog got on top of me, held me down with its paws, and started crawling toward my throat—and suddenly it howled, moaned pathetically, bent as if death were taking its measure which it could not fit while still alive. Grandfather II stood above us with his cane; he broke the dog's back, striking the protruding vertebrae with the copper; the dog was dying, and Grandfather

II moved his boiled egg-white eyes, not seeing but sensing how the fur fell out, the legs straightened, and the dog's life ran out; blood gurgled out of my torn leg, and Grandfather II listened attentively to that sound.

How had he appeared there? I remember that Grandfather II was not nearby when I went out into the alley. Apparently he must have been hiding behind the brambles at the gate—he liked to play with them, bring his fingers close to the prickly branches, following their curves with the palm of his hand, bringing his hand so close that the thorns seemed to trace the lines of his fingerprints like a needle on a record; he seemed to be testing, calibrating, adjusting some sense that replaced vision, and he hated being caught at this; then he would intentionally—and I was the only one who guessed it was intentional—prick himself and pretend that he had wanted to pick a flower or a berry.

It must have been that other sense that told Grandfather II that something important or dangerous was happening to me; once when my parents assumed I was riding bikes with my friends, we were actually planning to climb the power line tower to retrieve someone's kite stuck in the lines; the kite fluttered, I was trying on the rubber boots and gloves I had taken from the shed, and my friends were egging me on—and Grandfather II appeared on the road. He was probably going off on some business of his own, but the anticipation of my triumph was blown away; his appearance seemed to say: What do you think you're doing! Don't you dare!

So it's unlikely to have been a coincidence: Grandfather II was behind the bramble rose and heard my screams ... He was guarding me, nursing me; not me, but my future. Then the ambulance came flying through the fields, siren wailing, driving consciousness deeper, down into my heels, it smelled of tobacco and gasoline, and the belfry swayed and swayed over the hospital courtyard, I had seen the belfry many times when

I fished on the dammed lake; the belfry was like a needle on some apparatus, leaning first left then right, it bent toward me like a question mark, shot upward, blocking the sky, shrank, waving in the far corner of my vision and then blocked the view again. In the room, plaster was peeling off the walls, there was a black spider in a web in the corner; I watched it with strangely changed vision, which omitted the objects nearby; the spider moved right in front of my face, while my torn leg—this was probably the drugs—seemed to be back in the courtyard, my body was being dragged through the hallway, and only my head had been brought into the room.

The spider was going to weave its web over my face, get in my mouth, hang up its sticky threads and wait for the flies that were buzzing in the hospital room; I wanted to wave my arms, shout for them to take away the spider.

But as soon as I tried to speak the dog appeared, its eyes rheumy, bulging, as if the touch of the dry lids caused them pain, and I realized that it was not the hound looking at me. I had crossed an invisible line, marked perhaps only by faded buttercups or scattered gravel; the way you can catch swamp fever, I caught death, seeing a mole pecked to death, a dead hedgehog covered with black horned beetles; I wandered out on Concrete in the evening hour when nature trembles at someone's presence, when you feel it, too, and every shrub watches, it seems that they're looking at you, but they're really looking at the one standing behind you. At that hour you can't play hide-and-seek far from home, beyond its allure, where voices and smells don't reach—you will get lost, climbing into a dark space that turns out to be the crack between day and night; it is the hour of interstitial, indeterminate time, the hour the birds try to wait out in the air. I let in the pestilence somehow, brought it home without noticing the way you don't notice illness, thinking the slight temperature is due to running around, and that your throat is dry from thirst;

I let it in and it grew in me, settled in like a worm in the intestine, and that is why the black dog ran straight for me—I was careless and learned too soon what is hidden from a child by the indissolubility of body and mind, the indivisibility of the individual and the universe.

It was all decided there at the hospital; I had lost so much blood I needed a transfusion, they didn't have the right type, and then Grandfather II, who had forced his way into the ambulance—my parents were in the city, leaving me in his care—offered his blood. He wasn't supposed to do that because of his age, but he insisted—I don't remember it, but I can imagine how he spoke to the doctors in a voice that crushed his interlocutor the way his stick broke the dog's back—they took his blood, they took a lot, and I lived and he died, as if the part of his blood that was transfused in me contained his life and the part that remained in his veins was empty, used up blood, the blood of a dead man.

Now I think that he did not plan to die, counting on his good health; if he had lived, having saved my life, I would have belonged to him totally, by right of the blood in my veins; he took a risk and he would have won, but something happened that he could not have imagined, he was sure he would be transferred to Moscow, where they would nurse him back, replenish his blood loss: the break in our lives, the dangerous threadbare patch, coincided with a tectonic shift in history; an epoch—the epoch of Grandfather II, in which he could function, his milieu—was over; he did not survive the first moments of general confusion, the moments that did away with the old but did not yet usher in the new.

A few hours after the operation, tanks and armored cars from the neighboring base moved along the concrete road outside the hospital; I watched them through the third floor windows, and I don't remember anything except the turning tank rollers and wheels of the vehicles. A whole hour while the column moved, stopping, compressing and stretching, driving into the invisible funnel of the highway leading into town and the tank treads and wheels spinning before my eyes.

I had seen tanks before on parade, but there you had the triumph of form, coordinated movement, no room for details, the parade was perceived as a whole, as if a text was marching, carrying the structure of letters. But here, on the concrete road outside the hospital, the tanks moved one behind the other, stalling, jerking in place, the caterpillar tracks grinding and coming loose—probably not all the vehicles were ready when the alarm was sounded—and therefore, my perception, affected by pain and the medication, involved two mutually exclusive images.

It seemed that the column of tanks, constantly braking and falling into two or three tank groups, the soldiers waving their flags furiously, the cursing officers speaking on the helmet phones, the very metal of the tanks that suddenly lost the connection that brought them into motion, the evaporated fuel that lacked the power to push the tons of steel—all this was the disintegrating speech of that time, the speech of a paralytic whose lips had forgotten the shape of sound. Some words tried to be spoken, but too late: the lips were already rimmed by the deadening frost, like anesthesia. I later learned that Grandfather II started dying just as the first tanks moved past the hospital; the nurse thought the noise and rumbling were killing him, and she shut and curtained the windows tightly, but Grandfather II still thrashed in the bed as if the tanks were driving over his legs, accidentally in the way.

There was a second image my mind would let in, pushing out the image of disintegrating speech, and then let go; the rollers that propelled the caterpillars and the wheels turned into the gears of a clock that needed winding, that couldn't start turning; the clock had been stopped for many years, the mechanism had disconnected, and now all the gears from biggest to smallest turned on their own, the cogs catching and then not, and the hands on the clock jumped forward and then stopped again. The tanks got bogged down, angrily backfiring, their engines roared, but the tension of men and motors seemed incommensurate to the slow, disjointed movement, as if there was something ahead on the highway blocking the column, as if it—the vehicles and people—basically did not know whether there was any point or necessity in the expedition; as if time were trying to start and could not.

August days last a long time; in the distant fields beyond the hospital windows, they were harvesting the rye, and two different types of vehicles, as different as predators and herbivores, tanks and combines, seemed to look at each other in amazement, discovering that there were others types of mechanical creatures. Young soldiers waiting for the tank in front to restart its ignition amused themselves by turning their turrets toward the field, aiming at combines and trucks, which kept moving away, until work stopped completely. The combines ended up wedged at the very edge of the fields, the necks of their chutes raised; cars were parked along the sides of the road, one had a sofa on the roof and it looked as if the stuffed, plush creature had climbed up to save itself from the tank treads. An agricultural plane circled in the air senselessly, like a bumblebee on a string.

The rumble of the tanks and their number—there must have been a hundred vehicles—first overfilled the day and then, when the column had passed, emptied it the way a house stands after it's been slated for demolition, when the people move out, finally and irretrievably. It feels like that when you are on the edge of sleep, dozing, and the pause between heartbeats seems unbearably long, you fall into it, cease existing, until a pulse of blood comes from deep inside your body; you feel like a shoreline: the heart is located outside, the blood wanes and waxes like a wave, and consciousness grasps at the tide, in the emptiness of the interval. That day, after the passage of the tanks, became such an interval: the past had finished but the new had not yet started. Even noises seemed not to know how to sound, as if the hospital's glass vessels had forgotten how to clink and the floorboards how to creak.

The hospital was old, wooden, full of cracks; and mice began emerging out of the cracks. The wood of the walls and floors was so brittle that it was pointless to fill mouse holes with ground glass, and the mice ran sidling along walls and occasionally darted diagonally across the floor. But now, feeling something that people didn't, the mice grew cold and came outside. They sniffed and ran around, they were chased with mops and rags, they brought in a cat, but the mice did not leave, and the cat got under the wardrobe and sat there, not afraid but as if he knew something, too. The mice climbed up the curtains, the legs of the beds, there were hundreds of them and it was suddenly clear that there were many more mice than people, this was their abode, and the hospital had rotted down to the last board; I imagined that mice were climbing out in all the other houses in the district, mice that had seen only old newspapers that lined the walls beneath the wallpaper and were now seeing the world.

Of course, the mice had been upset by the tanks, the noise chased them out of cracks and nests, but their exodus was an accurate reflection of people's reaction: the nurses stopped struggling against the mice and tried to find something monotonous to do, but nothing worked: the mop end came off the mop, the water splashed, dishes fell from their hands. There was no anxiety or excessive concern in this: every action is a link in a chain extending from yesterday into tomorrow, and every action is given meaning by the proximity of other actions, proximity repeated and fixed in time; wash the floor, iron clothes, water flowers, take a temperature, give a shot— each action on an ordinary day exists in a series of others, in the outline of time moving in order, a series that imperceptibly supports you, does not let you feel that time is in the least benign, that midnight is breathing down the neck of noon, and that at every moment an internal light is extinguished.

That day time stopped for everyone; each was left with what was in his hand—a scalpel or a mop; no action became meaningless but it did become unclear in which greater time these actions were taking place—the past and present no longer gave a clear image of the near future.

The hospital was housed in a former estate; space opened up too generously from its windows, the view was meant for a park that had already been cut down, and now it seemed bizarre that the architect had decided to reveal all that emptiness lying in front of the grain fields, the emptiness now crowded with self-allotted garden plots: their fences were hammered together out of crooked planks, wrapped in wire used for fruit crates and scraps of barbed wire, reinforced with uneven sheets of rusted iron hanging so crookedly that they could have been thrown against the fence by a gust of wind; beyond the garden beds—and always in a corner—were windowless tool sheds just as sloppily constructed.

The egg-yellow hospital building with its two wings, four columns at the entrance, and tall windows—if all were opened, the house would splash out the foam of the curtains and become airy, swaying like a sailboat—shrank at the sight of the tanks beyond the gardens; it seemed as though the ceiling moved closer to my face.

The tanks left, and the garden allotments filled with people; someone started a bonfire, the smoke of rotting matter rose up, and in that smoke—it was a weekday, the gardens should have been deserted—men and women bustled around with shovels, not quite sure what to do: it was too early to dig up potatoes and the cucumbers had been harvested. Some were digging things out, others digging holes for compost, and it felt as if the tanks had awakened memories that they were too young to have; a little more and one of them would realize that he was digging a trench or a foxhole; the soft soil, worked for many years, seemed to be calling, offering shelter inside its womb. At first the shovel bayonets dug up dusty chunks, but then the moist interior was revealed, untouched by drought, embedded with thin, white, grass roots, and riddled with the pathways of worms and beetles.

There is something indecent in soil unearthed by a shovel, in its friability, as if it were black farmer's cheese, black buttermilk from a black cow; in its formlessness, readiness to fall apart—and in the cold wet grasp of its chunks clinging to a boot. I once saw flooded tank trenches in the woods, filled with impenetrable water, oily as overbrewed tea, which had absorbed rotting aspen leaves, year after year, until they dissolved; the water was a deadly infusion as deep as a coma, and in the midst of the clear leafy forest full of sunny glancing light, each trench was like a death cup filled with the earth's juices.

People were striving to reach that dissolving blackness, its shelter; the village was emptying, the garden plots filling up, as if the residents had smelled the diesel fuel of the tanks, the smell of war and disaster, and were leaving their houses and everything that meant their ordinary lives—to temporary shelter by the garden plots.

The ambulatory patients understood that the medical strictures were suspended for the moment and also headed out to the gardens; they walked cautiously, attuned to their diseases, trying to catch the secret signals, hear the flaw in their heartbeat, the additional twist in the rhythm caused by the illness; the illness hid itself, and the patients tried to find it, to see how far it had spread, which territories it occupied; the patients stretched their necks, straightened up and stood on one leg, in an unstable position, so that fundamental support would not hinder the perception of what can be perceived only in nonequilibrium, in turning yourself into the fine needle of a recorder that registers the quakes of the earth's core unfelt by humans.

However, an observer would not need to search for the illness, so clearly evident was it in their faces and figures. What I saw was beyond the limits of ugly and repulsive; freed of aesthetic significance, it was a sculpture, a plastic picture of what life can do to people if they don't have inner changes that give them the strength to withstand it and not give in.

Bulging bellies, sunken cheeks, drooping breasts, paralyzed arms—the injuries were so varied that they read as monotony. The hospital, a sorrowful house, gathered all possible traumas; but the missing fingers chopped off by an ax, or a leg severed by a train were just the visible extremes among them; the general human figure suggested that people lived in a concentration of constant pressure in different directions, which broke, bent, sprained, and twisted them; people were crushed, pushed, stretched, they expended labor and exhausted themselves in effort, and now when they couldn't hammer in a nail without clutching their hearts or falling into a coughing fit, it turned out that the labor had not strengthened them internally. People were used to the form created by the pressure; and when the pressure vanished and a long pause ensued, a rarefication of time—then people walked as if they had forgotten how to walk unaided.

Sick and healthy—everyone gathered at the garden plots, trestle beds were quickly covered in newspapers and the vodka appeared; someone had brought a battery-powered radio and a television and people clustered around them, no one tried to leave, or follow the tanks, or take part in anything—they all watched the TV or stared at the woods, beyond which the plane engines at the military air base warmed up, and there was the sense that the television and the radio were the latest secret mechanisms that decided destiny, pronouncing a verdict calculated by tubes and micro schematics: what would be, what would not.

In was during this pause, this general stupefaction that Grandfather II's life ended; it wasn't that no one risked driving him to Moscow—for a brief period all human duty was suspended and people even tried not to pick up the phone, for who knew what the call might bring; the ambulance carrying medicine for him got stuck on the side of the road, letting the tanks go by, and he died—the new era might have accepted him, but it was the interval, the disconnect, that killed him.

Thus my existence coincided with his existence, and I was never just myself again—Grandfather II's blood, which saved me, circulated in me; the blood of a scrawny, blind, old man flowed in the body of a little boy, and that separated me forever from my peers; I grew under the sign of the inestimable sacrifice made by Grandfather II; I grew like a graft on old wood.

I was in the hospital during his funeral, and later it was an effort to go to the cemetery: I thought that Grandfather II had not died completely, that he had passed into me, and that when I stood by his grave the two separated parts of Grandfather II's soul encountered one another, one unsatisfied and the other I carried under my heart like a fetus; they met and experienced voluptuous pleasure because they had managed to deceive death, cling to life, while all around lay decomposed bodies, and the stage props of gravestones, photographs, and dates meant nothing.

I looked at other people wondering if there were those among them who like me carried a dead man inside them; maybe someone else is brought to the cemetery by a corpse, looks out from inside at the handyman sweeping the paths, piling up fallen leaves, and feels like a sneaky and nasty child who has hidden where no one will ever find him.

It was almost unbearable being in the apartment where Grandfather II used to live; I thought that his things, reverently preserved in their place, knew who I was and that the apartment had turned into a mausoleum, a crypt, where memory tactfully rested in peace, and it knew who I was. His ivory cigarette holder seemed a part of him; the housekeeper had filled the shelves with dozens of his pairs of glasses, of growing thickness as his eyesight dwindled; probably she wanted to create the impression in every corner that he had not died but just stepped out, leaving his glasses on the table, and would be right back, but for me the murky lenses meant Grandfather II's gaze, he was inside me and at the same time looking at me from outside, from every spot in the room, wherever I might hide, under the bed, behind the drapes; the only place I could hide was the full-length mirror, but I had to be careful not to look in it—on the opposite wall there hung a photograph of Grandfather II and in a way that made him appear over my right shoulder when I looked in the mirror. His Sig Sauer, the double-barreled shotgun the Germans used during the war, which hung on the wall, also looked at me, but crookedly, with the dark holes of the barrels, two zeroes, assessing whether the previous owner would have the strength to pick it up with *my* hands, and deep in the attic there were boxes of shells, filled with still potent gunpowder.

Now remembering Grandfather II, I sometimes think that he summoned the death he wanted, even though he expected to survive giving me blood.

He was afraid to die the usual way; he thirsted to live through me, in me, and he was so fiercely afraid of death that he must have known whom he would meet in the other world; Grandfather II sought salvation for his soul, salvation as he understood it; his unconscious idea came out better than if he had lived; his death obligated me wholly and irretrievably, indebted me independent of any possible knowledge of him;

whatever else may be, he saved me, sacrificing his own life—and tightened the knot by the fact that the sacrifice was accidental and the goodness a calculated risk.

I often wondered why Grandfather II had chosen such a housekeeper—a widow with a fifth-grade education, from an orphanage, who had never had a family, had gone through the Volga famine and retained the hunger forever—it lived in the depths of her large female body, and all her cooking was either too rich or too fatty; I remember the amber drops of fat in her cabbage soup and the pinkish gentle dew of fat on the *salo* striped with meat. Unaware of it, she fed not herself but the old hunger that was never sated; a sucking, irritating hunger like a foreboding that is actually the voice of remembrance pretending to be a premonition because we do not want to see it as a memory. Now I understand that Grandfather II picked her as if preparing a justification for himself—he helped a woman who did not expect anyone's help, and she repaid him with loyalty.

The housekeeper executed the terms of Grandfather II's will: she burned all his papers in the park, she threw away his clothes and shoes; they say that in those days—the August days—she was not the only one acting this way; while crowds stood outside government buildings, people of the former era, the most careful ones, hid their wealth or destroyed evidence, sometimes, along with themselves; if you added up the trophy guns that were used for the first and last time, it would reach the highest number in decades. My parents were taking care of me then, so no one could go to the funeral; the housekeeper later told us that he had left her a number to call in the case of his death, and when she called, people came, apparently military; they took care of everything, quickly, with military precision, and took away his medals with an inventory list, there turned out to be almost a dozen—she couldn't remember what kind; they buried him as if they were afraid of the still-unclear new times, as if they didn't know whether there should be honors or whether everything should be done quietly, and so they hurried; when we later visited the grave, there was nothing but a funeral wreath without a name.

Grandfather II passed away anonymously, as he had lived; as if there was a special service dedicated to his total obliteration; one of my relatives called the number the housekeeper had used, but he couldn't even find out where he was calling: and when they learned that he was not a relative of Grandfather II, they refused to give him any information. Probably if he had died in a different time, we would have managed to learn a few things, to find friends, colleagues, to understand which agency had sent the funeral team; but the country was falling apart, all the agencies had stopped working, no one knew anything about previous positions, officers' shoulder boards and insignia, forms and signs were meaningless; in this chaos, Grandfather II sank without a trace, as if he had planned this exit. Everyone preferred not to know, not to talk, not to inform, but to forget; and extensive research into who Grandfather II was led to nothing. Once he had hinted that he had headed a major construction project; now that lie was revealed, but there was nothing to replace it; therefore—probably for my sake—Grandfather II remained simply Grandfather II, the man who had saved my life.

His will left the apartment to his housekeeper and then to me upon her death; a large sum was left in my name, which I could receive when I came of age; Grandfather II left the dacha also to the housekeeper and then to me.

Thus I became an heir; the money soon became worthless, the thousands turned to nothing, and in fact the only thing I inherited was the secret of Grandfather II's life; money, once a weighty thing, had turned into paper, which, as I later learned, was trucked away to be buried—you can't burn money because the dyes are too toxic; later, in a northern region, I visited a mine into which they had dumped money in plastic bags in the early 1990s.

Somewhere among the violet 25-ruble notes with the profile of Lenin brought from branches of Sberbank was the money left to me by Grandfather II. I took a banknote as a memento—not of my lost wealth but as evidence of how quickly and irreversibly the materially embodied powers and possibilities of an era can vanish; evidence of the instant onset of historical illness; and I saw that along with time, the thing that had comprised Grandfather II's posthumous power over me had also vanished; time, I realized, had loosened those bonds.

But this very pile of bills reminded me how I had gone to tidy up Grandfather II's grave as a teenager; I thought I could go to the cemetery safely now, no longer fearing the revulsion of having the old man preserved inside me. I must have wanted to come to terms with Grandfather II, let go of those old memories and replace them with new ones, and I chose a time on the eve of my birthday: I thought that I would clean up the grave and step into the new year of my life on different terms with the past.

It was spacious and cool at the old cemetery; the mosaic on an ancient crypt depicted Charon bearing the dead across the River Styx, and in rhythm with the oarlocks came the creaks of the cemetery caretaker's cart; dirt protruded onto the paths from beneath the gravestones, as if the dead needed more space.

I swept around the grave and watered the ferns and peonies; I smoked, looking at the neighboring plot, where a husband and wife were buried, Ivan Pavlovich and Sofia Vasilyevna Bessmertny; the black slab produced an iridescent play of blue shimmers, like the eyes on a butterfly wing; crows squabbled high in the branches.

It was empty and fresh, as if on the edge of a meadow;

I thought that the past had finally gone and Grandfather II had left me in peace; I even thought that I could come to the cemetery more often—I had gotten over his hold on me, it was past its sell-by date determined by some unknown but active laws, and in the new times I would distance myself even more from those old feelings, cover them with another attitude toward Grandfather II; an attitude which essentially did not presume an attitude but only an elastic habit of memory, which actually makes you forget more deeply; you don't remember what had been but only a memory of a memory, and the past moves away and diminishes, like an object reflected in opposing mirrors.

I walked down the path, not looking around, bearing this new mood in me; there was only a slight sorrow that everything happened too easily and imperceptibly. The cemetery fences, crosses, trees—everything was freed of the heavy feeling created by memories and appeared with a new ease; I walked slowly, I wanted to stay longer, to remember it all anew. The cemetery had changed even in its color scheme, there were light green and straw tones I had never noticed before.

Suddenly I saw an old crumbling stump and on it a floury and plicated tree mushroom, looking like a fat ear.

An ear—the underground world was listening, it was here, I just hadn't noticed it in the sunny omens of the day. It all came back: fear, loathing, chills; the mushroom looked like the flesh of a corpse and it lived a vegetative existence; Grandfather II had not let go of me.

Part 3

My craving to escape my parents' home as a young man was multiplied by the desire to be where nothing reminded me of Grandfather II; I could never be myself on the streets of our hometown—I was always a little bit him, as well: here I had taken Grandfather II to the shoemaker, here we'd walked from the train station, here we'd bought him a suit.

In this city I had lost the ability to be anonymous; for true anonymity is not in being unrecognized but in the fact that the environment does not mirror, does not return you to yourself with the help of memories.

There are places that become obsolete: many things are tied to them, but they are tied to a former you; there you are mostly a person from days past rather than now. The whole city and all its streets had become like that for me; when I was in the last grades of high school, I even tried to find new ways of getting there, instead of the usual routes, overlaying a new map on the old one; but decades of life without moving made that maneuver impossible: every road had been traveled, every sight seen. So I chose geology as a profession; I needed to get as far away as possible, to be in new areas, freed of a binding legacy.

I saw the world; but the important thing is that I traveled the country from edge to edge. It turned out that there is the gravity of destiny; there is a field that is always wider than how we see it; my departure, my work in distant places was just a path for returning to what I had hoped to escape. But I returned a different man, ready to accept and assume my inheritance, even though I did not know about this readiness until life summoned me.

In an old city, and especially in a capital, passing eras leave behind the significance and passion of architecture; the legacy of various years creates a contradictory urban ensemble, splendid and magniloquent; the buildings emit a glow, and it illuminates them. Therefore the past is not visible there; only magnificent façades remain. What lies behind the façade cannot be understood without archives and witnesses.

But in nature, everything a man does remains exposed; you cannot hide anything behind architecture, behind high-rises, bridges, or monuments; there is also little that can be hidden in a city whose cultural patrimony comprises only one era and which emanates the general aesthetic of that era.

Therefore, the first time I flew in a helicopter over the taiga, approaching a northern town, and I saw the star-like pattern of logging radiating through the heavy forests, dozens of kilometers of logged forests and the low camp barracks, some still active, some abandoned, I learned more from my impression than I could have read in books; I saw the effect created by the camps, the catastrophic vision of an environment organized in such a way that you could not recognize the evil of it.

Many people were deprived of life, of fate, of freedom; in the context of that enormous, all-encompassing evil any lesser evil became invisible; it became possible to live where everything—from the look of the housing to speech—dehumanized instead of humanized; the camp and the housing for former inmates expanded, settled in, and began reproducing itself without the state's involvement. My passage through these parts, changed by the camps, became my path of return: to Grandfather II and his life and works.

I can't set down everything I encountered and saw in my wanderings, to bring it all together in a text; so now I am holding the 25 rubles from the mine where they buried money; I feel there are passages through time that can briefly connect what should have been learned and understood; for me such a passage, a keyhole, is Lenin's profile—if you don't look at it but through it.

The first look—through the portrait—is into the time before my travels, in my last year of school.

Behind our school stood the burned-out remains of a two-story house: the broken walls guarded piles of charred beams and crumpled iron sheets; the house gave off the sense of a dead catastrophe, and it summoned you inside, to study its core, see the ugly frozen agony of things—to come close without risk to the hardened face of death which could no longer look back.

I climbed into the house; the destruction inside was not as bad as it looked from outside. But as I opened a door in the hallway I almost stepped into a void: the door opened right below the ceiling of a large space, a former sculptor's studio. The stairs leading down had collapsed; the studio was filled with rubbish that fell when the house was burning, and you couldn't tell it was there from the façade; a hidden room, the secret of the burned building.

Dozens of Lenins stood on the floor: just busts. Plaster, granite, metal, plasticine, the size of a child's head and waist-high on an adult. The Lenins looked at one another, the beam of my flashlight was weak, and in the far corners the sculptures easily blended with the dark, like ghosts incarnate of former times, the shadows of monuments.

The air smelled of ash, stone, dust; dust covered their heads, the floor, the scattered sculptor's tools; this was not wispy household dust, practically weightless—this was solid dust that could have been the remains of a plaster sculpture; too heavy to be moved by a powerful draft.

If one of the busts had been unfinished or, say, marred by an obvious flaw, the moment would have had a different feeling. But all the Lenins repeated one another without variation, they weren't even copies, but copies of copies; they had reproduced here, in the cell of oblivion, six steps from the Garden Ring Road, splitting off like amoebas; they had no relation to the real Lenin, each was but a monument of a monument, a bust of a bust.

I realized that the dust everywhere was the dry residue of time; it withered and fell here, fruitless, unable to overcome itself. It seemed that the big Lenins had come first, before the smaller ones: a chain reaction of degeneration was taking place in a hidden crevice, dying time tried to reproduce itself, save itself—and it could not create anything new, not even anything equal to the past.

The real mausoleum was here and not in Red Square; here I understood what the death agony really is—a person doesn't die right away, but through the extended death of all his "I"s.

The monuments also tried to die, but nonexistence would not accept the multiplied sculptural image which had never been alive as an image, which had appeared stillborn, and it simply grew smaller, and smaller, and smaller. Probably if one were to go down and look, somewhere under the table, under the workbench, under the pile of newspapers, under the rags there would be a rat-sized Lenin, a mouse-sized Lenin, and so on down to the dust particles, which must consist, like chalk, of calcified algae, of micro-Lenins, limestone sculptures visible only under a microscope.

Death-within-death; a dead time—for me that was the multitude of busts on a dusty floor in an abandoned studio; the house was torn down, but the decay was infinite and still continues somewhere.

The second look—through the portrait of Lenin—came in the years when I worked in the North, in the mountains where our expedition was studying old deposits started by the work of prisoners and then abandoned.

The mountains were foggy then; objects lose their material component in the fog and become more image than thing; fog transforms the external world into something similar to the inner world, inhabited by ethereal substances in a spectral environment; whatever you see—a hut, a tripod for land surveying—everything first appears as a symbol floating out of the swirls of foggy murk; the fog seems to present that which is usually hidden—the substantially defined form, the soul of a thing as if it manifested consciousness. And the mind then perceives the object differently: not literally, scanning all its potential imagery and meanings.

It was through a break in the fog that I saw the barracks in a mountain pass. Barely visible through the white mist, they somehow did not seem to belong to a concrete place. Cut out of the landscape, blurred, vanishing at the edge of vision, the barracks came closer without becoming clearer; but the details were not important. From the fog came contours and outlines unburdened by volume—the important part was in the lines.

You can draw a house in which you would not want to live; and you can slightly break the lines of the drawing so that even though it will still be a drawing of a house, there will be something in the lines that Filonov or Kandinsky could understand: the lines will be grief, misfortune, death; it is not the composition that will mean something in total, but each line will express what seems inexpressible in the graphic arts with such clarity it could be a visible sound instead of a line. This will be Munch's *The Scream*, but presented not through subject and color, but the agonized scream of geometric figures before their death, hacked apart, squashed in torture vices, stretched on the rack.

The outlines of the barracks appeared to push the barracks themselves into the background; you couldn't say you were seeing buildings, human dwellings. The barracks stood like plywood cargo crates in which people were stacked, unnaturally long—this correlation of length and width appears only in coffins.

These outlines felt like a long scream, the scream of a form that was suddenly horrified by itself.

In that camp I learned the features of many other places that were present and unrevealed but here displayed themselves with the explicitness of the absolute. They were not literal, physical features, rather they were the features of the emotional sensation that a place makes on us; the features of its sensual and mental portrait.

In the barns of kolkhoz farms, in the Khrushchev-era slums on the outskirts of cities, in railroad station warehouses, in the one-story village houses and the houses of worker settlements, in sheds, in provincial hotels, in timber offices, in army dormitories, in district hospitals, and in many other buildings scattered across the country, I intuitively recognized those camp barracks. They were hidden inside the buildings, clad in pathetic architectural dress—and yet they were revealed in general outlines, corners, and most important in the sense of deadly (and I don't mean that figuratively) dreariness.

Once I visited a miner's home; the apartment windows had a view of the refuse heaps of the coal mines—huge cones of tailings, the waste that remained after the minerals are removed. The heaps gave off dust and smoke, and froze: the man lived with a view of the futility of his labor—here is the residue, the wind carries it far, even the monument of a miner in the middle of town had a black dusting on its face; he lived here but this view ate at him, like acid, even if he didn't think about it. Hence the dreariness, the deadly dreariness—the angst of a man who was only the material or tool of a great construction project.

I experienced the same feeling—multiplied many times—in the mountains; not only multiplied but on a qualitatively different level; the camp barracks, the heaps from adits, the horizontal tunnels on the mountain slopes—it expressed a great concept, it was part of a gigantic plan, but when applied to an individual fate it served as a way of making it meaningless.

Slave labor, the lifeblood of the place, was anachronistic in the twentieth century; an anachronism only perpetuates itself, it always falls out of its time and does not participate in it, no matter how active the imitation of participation may be.

But besides the time gap there was also a spatial gap. I understood why they exiled people to the taiga, the tundra: they were crossed out of the general existence of humans, exiled from history, and their death took place in geography, not in history.

Everything there was made so that the place where people lived and died would not absorb anything from their lives, so that the place would have no attraction, not even a weak one. There was nothing there to elicit compassion, nothing for feeling to cling to—and that was the irreparable harm.

Just wood and stone all around; gray slate, lichen-covered and soggy in the rain, and gray planks and logs. The gray color of the wood, with the shimmer of the nap on an expensive coat, was a sign for me; the wood was drying out, like an old man's muscles, its fibers were beginning to show, and that patina of gray covered it: the muted shine of death. I had seen planks like that in abandoned villages and now here, in the mountains of the North. They resembled—there is no sacrilege here—wooden relics: even if it turned freezing, I would not use them for a fire.

I walked from barrack to barrack: they were built hastily and cheaply, using wooden wedges instead of nails; wood and stone, no iron, no ocher shades of rust. The place was dying with unnatural thoroughness, trying to vanish into nature. I found only one nail, forged and four-sided, its head deformed by many blows. The nail gave me hope that the place would not vanish completely, a trace, a memory would remain; the nail showed that these barracks were not a mirage, a spectral settlement of wind and fog, that there had been people here.

I recalled all the nails I had ever hammered: how you put the sharp tip to the board, strike with a fifth of your strength so that it bites into the wood, and then when the nail is going in precisely, you hammer, enjoying the precision—and with the last blow you drive the head even with the board, like making a period, connecting what should be held together, should be connected.

The nail; it came out easily from the rotting wood and lay in my hand. Its form—the form of a period with a deep root that cannot be pulled out of where it is placed by the meaning of what was said—was asking something of me. Looking at the nail, the logs, the boards, I suddenly understood what I had not understood before: how there can be a connection between true faith and a form of superstition which demanded material proof: the devout preservation of a nail from the Cross of the Savior, or a sliver of its wood. I saw that it was not about proof or a literal, museum preservation of the object—the objects we consider inanimate that were the weapon or merely witnesses of suffering take on a threatening cast; they receive a second existence, a resemblance to a voice breaking through its own stammer—the soul of the event, the quintessence of its providential meaning settle into objects and speaks to us.

Standing with the nail in my hand, I felt that the place was weakly affecting me. Small islands of soil appeared amid the rock, so thin that even moss could not take root in it. And then it was as if I had taken a step away from myself and saw the place with different eyes—I saw that these handfuls of soil that plants avoided were human remains; or, what the remains had turned into; once they were remains and now had become soil.

I saw that what had happened here had happened

conclusively; death is not instantaneous, it lives on after itself: a person dies; then those in whose memory he had lived on also die; the traces of his existence are washed away, like particles of ore in stone. This waiting work of death, which knows more about the time allotted to men and things, rarely finishes in visible time: people may not remember anything, but death is more demanding of the purity and completeness of oblivion.

In this place it had completed its work and had been aired out.

Speaking mentally or emotionally to the dead is only possible when there could be an echo from something in response; when there is a mold of presence, symbolically depicted in a death mask. But if death has shattered the death mask as well, then no one and nothing will respond.

That was the feeling I had there among the rocks; the sense of loss that cannot be overcome by feeling or thought. The earth was too clean and in the thinness of its layer too open to being seen, making it impossible to draw a connection between it and the people who had died here. Just the nail, as if it were the only thing left of an entire house, the nail was in my hand; retaining the meaning of its form, but representing the singularity of an object, and therefore it was simultaneously meaningful and useless.

The fog was lifting; the wind was chasing it away. I went up to the adits along the path among the rocks, following the way the prisoners took to the top. This was not an attempt to put myself in their shoes; but it was important to repeat someone's path, to follow step by step; here, on the narrow path on a steep climb to where the ends of rusty rails hung over the emptiness, rails from which rocks were thrown, rails that called you to jump down, here something happened through me, the way I had been, something that was supposed to happen in this place.

The sun suddenly shone on the slag heaps of the adits; the shards of mountain crystal that filled the heaps sparkled in response with icy glitter that falsely refreshed the eye. The mountain looked so strange, the pure glow without any color admixture was so beautiful, that I stopped: that ideal clear light embodied the inanimate life of nature, the action of its laws, which in their tested majesty rejected all that was human. The slag heap had rock that had absorbed the mortal efforts of men, the blows of picks, blood and warmth of hands wounded by the rock, and now that rock was coolly sparkling in the sun; its beauty did not weaken or dim and therefore seemed dangerous, freezing, like the glow of thin spring ice beneath which is the dead, airless winter water, filled with the decay of fish.

To break away from this impression, I turned. The sun had filled the lake at the foot of the mountains with light; convex, like a drop on glass, its contour struck me in the eye. A mean trick of nature, a joke that had waited several million years: the lake looked like Lenin's profile, which was imprinted on us by medals, badges, stamps, statues, paintings, and drawings in books.

The lake with its thick, almost pastry-like icing of sunny light seemed like a monstrous monument, monstrous because the natural forms easily and willingly took on the features of something man-made, and this acceptance, without coercion, clearly evinced the meaningless, memory-less existence of nature, which we had anthropomorphized much too frequently.

Seeing this betrayal of matter—betrayal of the men who climbed up to the heaps every day from the barracks, looking at the profile of the dead leader in whose name they were forced to labor—I rejected the feeling of closeness with these mountains, from the line of imagination that had anthropomorphized them. A different, older feeling arose: the possible humanity of nature was just a mockery, a devilish joke; man can count on no one in nature except himself.

Soon after—the expedition was continuing work in the area of the abandoned camp—I went out on a solitary hike. Two days into the trip rain clouds settled over the mountains and it rained, the wind blowing the drops horizontally, parallel to the ground; I was wearing good weatherproof gear but still I felt chilled. The bad weather was here to stay, the mountain tundra was soaked, and everything that was good for the campfire—old logs, reindeer moss, and switches of polar birch—was damp; a heavy front was coming from the west, and it was clear that by nightfall the rain would change over to snow, a northern summer blizzard, and the rocks in the mountain passes would be icy.

I was about to turn back when I noticed an awning of boards and tar paper over an old test tunnel, one of many such holes made all over the slopes for several kilometers around the camp; the prisoners opened up the ground and rubble to reach the indigenous rock for testing. The canopy had been made recently, otherwise the wind and snow would have destroyed it; someone without a tent was sheltering from the weather.

A fugitive prisoner, a *zek*, lay beneath the awning; the pea jacket, tattoos, everything gave him away; the soles had come off his tarpaulin boots, tied with a cord, and his feet were bleeding; he couldn't go on without shoes, he had torn pieces from his jacket and wrapped them around his feet, but the fabric with cotton batting fell apart in the rain; he saw the snow clouds over the top of his tunnel and he probably knew he would die that night.

I knew what he would have done to me if he had found me asleep in my tent; the fugitive was very skinny, his face was overgrown with hair with bits of moss, leaves, wood chips, and dirt in it: he had been wandering in the taiga for a month or more, having decided to run not toward the railroad but over the mountains to a different region where they would not be looking for him. He huddled in the hole, bent over, holding a three-sided shiv made from a file, no longer human or even humanoid; he was a wood spirit crawled up from underground. If I had had a rifle, I would have shot him and covered him with stones—out of fear, out of the sensation that this really was an underground creature that had killed an escaped prisoner.

But I didn't have a rifle; I went down into the hole. The fugitive pushed the shiv aside; he was too weak to kill me with any benefit to him. I could simply go away, as if I hadn't seen the canopy, and the fugitive would freeze to death; who knew why he was in prison, how he had escaped, if he had comrades and where they were; what he ate, mushrooms or human flesh; I went down, turned on my gas stove and started some bouillon cube broth. I realized that I was probably saving a murderer, maybe a rapist, robber, cannibal; he had been in the taiga too long to have had enough food in his pockets for that period, he was giving me too wild a look—as if he saw me gutted, freshly butchered. I should have left, gone back to our camp, radioed for a police helicopter, but I couldn't do it; I tried to imagine his victims, whether they would have been prepared to kill him in revenge—but that had no direct bearing on the hole, the icy rain, the approaching snow front. It could be that the death awaiting the fugitive was just retribution, and that most likely he deserved it; but the idea of retribution was coming from my mind, wondering how to get out of this hole clean, without getting involved or taking anything on. "This is retribution, it is just, go away, and let it happen," I told myself but kept cooking the broth. It turned out that there are situations from which you cannot make an exit without soiling your morality and the point was not in a choice of a number of evils but in the fact that once you've gone down into the hole, you can't pretend you're still standing atop it.

The fugitive drank the bouillon from the edge of the pot;

the tin should have burned his fingers, but it didn't: they had toughened, covered with layers of horny skin. We had nothing to say; he knew what I would ask, I knew how he would lie.

I left the fugitive my climbing boots, the pot, food, matches, two packs of cigarettes, my change of clothes, and my medicine chest. I knew that if he survived he would laugh over the idiot he had met and regret that he had not met me sooner when he was strong enough to rob and kill me, so that I would not turn him in. Calling for a police helicopter was my most frequent thought, and I sometimes imagined hearing the propeller blades through the rain, that it was passing by and would land, and that others would make the decision for me and drag him onboard. But for me to go through the pass and tell our radioman to call for a copter—here, near the former camp—it all took on another meaning; here the echo would have responded too readily to the barking of guard dogs and shots, if the fugitive tried to hide; here it was fundamentally wrong to appeal to the authorities, to the state, its court and justice; this place had its history, and it very strongly defined what was allowable here and what was not.

I climbed out of the hole to see how far the clouds were; behind me I heard metal—the fugitive was opening cans. I turned; the broth had given him a little strength, enough to use the shiv; I couldn't jump into the hole, he would kill me, he thought I wanted to take away the food; all the same, I jumped in to get my backpack, and he threw a rock at me; I tried to pull him away from the cans, but he poked at me with the shiv, growled, kicked, grabbed me with his free hand and held me down with his knee; I hit him, I was stronger, but strength meant nothing here—he was frenzied, he was guarding the hole, guarding the food; I knocked him down, but he rose and threw himself at my feet, biting down on my trousers, and tore deep into my calf with the shiv; I got out of the hole, and he began tossing out the pot, clothing, shoes, bandages—everything but the food; he no longer knew what things meant, and his mind still only recognized food as food. I bandaged my leg while he growled and choked down tinned meat, drank evaporated milk from a perforated can, and gulped down crackers with the wrapping paper; he was killing himself, after a long fast he would get twisted bowels, but he couldn't stop.

He died in an hour; even in convulsions he wouldn't let me approach; even dying, when I tried to press down on his belly, stick my fingers in his mouth to make him vomit, he hit and bit me; in his jacket pocket I later found an empty matchbox and three fingers smoked over a campfire; the meat was preserved and did not rot.

My mind was so debilitated and my emotions so drained that I actually wondered whether the fingers should be buried separately or with him in one grave; then I realized that the second, eaten fugitive was already inseparable from the first; I piled stones over the dead man and added some soil with my sapper's shovel; I did not try to remove the empty cans and wrappers—I couldn't go down there again.

It was snowing; the low front had scattered the small foggy clouds and behind the blizzard, still quiet, transparent, I could see the ruins of the camp; a sunbeam broke through the clouds, illuminating the ruins, and it seemed that they were swallowing the cold glow of the snowy sun, the way light falls inside the rear of a sandstorm; in that space of distortion and loss, the human does not function, there can be no care, or gift, or compassion—the distortions pull them into their orbits and swirl them into unwilling collaboration with evil.

That is how I see that camp and lake in the valley; there I understood everything that subsequently served as a guiding light.

Back from the expedition, I learned that the housekeeper had died; the apartment passed to me by Grandfather II's will. I delayed a long time before going there; I knew it wasn't a question of the apartment itself; I could not accept those square meters, they did not belong to me, nor could they— life was returning me to what I had left: the personality of Grandfather II. I sensed that nothing good would come of it; the camp barracks, the fugitive who had lost all human semblance—sometimes you look back and see how life is bringing you toward understanding, how nothing is random but is interconnected, and if you live with an ear for that causality—not to mystical perceptions that are an imitation of direct conversation with life, but for perceiving what is given to you and how—you cannot select a path, a path and time select you; there is nothing messianic, or being chosen, or fatalistic about this; it is a very hidden, profoundly private sensation: your turn, your time, your deed.

I eventually did go to the old address; on one hand, I felt uncomfortable entering the empty apartment; there was a sense that it was a bit too easy, as if the apartment would have gotten used to the housekeeper's departure, gotten over her death—and only then, carefully, without touching anything, could one go inside. But on the other hand, I was prompted by the feeling that at a moment when death is still nearby, when all the objects are exposed by the departure, you may be able to see and sense things that evaporate and settle down later; the objects will be objects once again, they will shut down, and you won't hear anything, only the given state of mute objects.

As a child, I liked to eavesdrop on objects; I pretended to be leaving the house, fussing over my shoelaces in the entry, opening and shutting the door, so that the objects would think I had left—and then I would hide among the clothes and shoes. Never quite separate from the people who wore them, by virtue of their predestination they were forced to be double agents, my secret helpers; cut to fit the human body, they made me invisible to the vague vision of the object world, for which the main thing, I thought, was the silhouette, the contour.

I often imagined what went on in the apartment when no one was there, and I thought that after a certain time—in case one of the people returned for something—the objects, like crabs on the seafloor exposed by low tide, scurried from place to place, peeking up from below, planning, conspiring, hiding something under the shell of their usual ordinary appearance, and always ready to pretend to be the obedient, weak-willed things that my parents knew.

Upon entering Grandfather II's apartment, I remembered my childhood game, which was no game; I crossed the threshold of his possessions as heir, belated, awkward, having lived a different, nomadic, life, feeling burdened by property and not knowing why I needed a one-bedroom apartment in a luxurious Stalinist building, where the telephone was a relic, heavy black plastic hanging on the wall, as if the words that might come through the receiver should be heard standing at attention; I picked up the receiver like a shell on the beach—to listen to the hoarse breathing of a time past.

In the rooms where Grandfather II's housekeeper—she lived the way petitioners sit, on the edge of the chair, as something second-rate compared to the objects—lived after his death, Grandfather II's life manifested itself in the placement of the furniture seen anew with a fresh view, his habits, his domestic routes, his imperious character: the furniture was sturdy and heavy, on the shelves thick shot glasses on skinny stems shone dully, and I didn't want to touch them with my fingers or lips—what had people toasted to with these, with what thoughts, with what in their hearts had they drunk from them? I found a vodka bottle, closed with a twist of paper, in the sideboard, but the paper crumbled into the lightest brown flakes and the vodka must have evaporated, leaving tasteless water.

Things looked at me—there was only one piece of furniture from the last half of the century, a nightstand made of particleboard; I pulled it away from the wall and on the back plywood panel there was a yellow label: "article, nightstand, 24 rubles," and I sensed that this was my only ally here, and if not an ally, then at least not an enemy; "article, nightstand" was a word combination that had something familiar from the time in which I was born, a time of plywood and particleboard, particularly pathetic materials without pedigree, as if all the more solid and significant things had been used up mindlessly, leaving only sawdust and splinters from which people had learned to make furniture and partitions in their houses. But the cupboard and sideboard, the couches and shelves came from the 1930s; generously lacquered, they were more solid than me, they got you with their weight and bulk, their glass dimmed by innumerable reflections that left particles on the glass, while I was a balloon, something weightless and insignificant in this preserve of other times.

There wasn't a single book in the house and there wasn't any place to put one, not a shelf or a nook, just depositories for clothing and dishes, and beds wide and high—such beds are good for loving a woman, joining blood with blood, crumpling and bunching up the hot sweaty sheets, and for dying unfettered on those same sheets, hot and damp from fever. There were mounds of bed linens in the closets, enough for a large family, and this warehouse of sheets, blanket covers, and pillowcases revealed a time when clean linen meant more than just clean linen; there was the smell that a hot iron gives off when it's filled with coal, the smell of plain soap, the ribbed washboard, running water and wooden mangle. A clean white tablecloth, one without a spot or pulled thread, starched, made a color pair for the main state color of the times—red. White was the mainstay of home; for some because they had come from dirt and remembered it all too well; for others because they sensed the impurity of the times and not seeing a way of staying clean themselves, sought external cleanliness. This drive for cleanliness remained throughout life: the closet had mops, buckets, rags, brooms—the housekeeper had scoured the house until her final hour.

Besides the blatant hostility of the furniture, I felt something else; it was like a message, a letter that lay in the "For Pickup" nook at the post office for ten years. In leaving me his house, Grandfather II considered it a message that only I would understand. Somewhere in here, either in plain sight or under the wallpaper, in the seams of his clothes, in the design of the parquet floor, there was a sign, a sign in invisible ink that had to be heated or wetted or held up to the light at a certain angle; the apartment was not empty, the message awaited its hour—a sleeping seed, a grain of an instant in which fate slept.

I started going through things in the sideboard and cupboards, random things tossed ashore by the tide of life; keys to unknown locks, no longer existing doors, forks and spoons, survivors of sets bought two-thirds of a century ago, lost in moves to various towns; I found the handle from a broken cup—that cup was valuable, memorable somehow; I found bent or broken frames for eyeglasses and pince-nez; coins, kopecks from forgotten years that were somehow selected from the rest and settled in the sideboard; buttons, rusted hooks, single cuff links—one with mother-of-pearl blackened like a damaged fingernail, the other homemade, carved ivory with Grandfather II's initials; it was like the rubbish in a magpie's nest, or the stuff that scatters on the asphalt after a crash, unremarkable, usually found in pockets and the bottom of bags and briefcases, but here taking on the significance of unused punctuation marks: everything is said, the sentence is complete, and the excess commas are strewn on the ground.

What is left when nothing is left is this clean nonrubbishy rubbish, arrayed like evidence on a policeman's desk; what's left despite our vain hopes is evidence of minor mishaps—broke my glasses, cracked the cup, lost my cuff link—as if life was intentionally collecting them, giving us back our unworthy agitation in the face of trivial difficulties; what is left is the biography of objects, which shows that essentially nothing happens to us, nothing really happens; the dry residue that remains are these mementoes, penknife notches on a school desk.

There could be no special testimony, no secret message among these scattered things on their own, away from the hierarchy of objects, the order of things, where there are pairs, dozens, settings, and sets. Sometimes such trifles can form a rebus, but here there was only one uniting trait: all these things were cracked, broken, bent, or spoiled—the sideboard drawer held three watches that had stopped in different decades—and whatever evidence they bore spoke of only one thing: no one slips out of life unbroken, and its effect is mechanical and automatic but inevitable and irreparable. Broken connections, disrupted unity, lost community; interrupted events, vague, having lost their own name; a hole in the pocket, a rent in a raincoat, and everything falls out, and you can catch only a few things in your fingers. It is not a mystery but the negation of a mystery; the apotheosis of ordinariness, the manifestation of mass consumption.

Well, this merely proved (things are the most impartial biographers) that Grandfather II, whatever his past, whatever he had hidden behind his blindness, had in many ways lived the most ordinary life; his things were as harmless as rattles, teething rings, and baby bottles, while I had expected in accordance with my childhood memories for them to at least partially take on his scale. But there was no real scale either—he was not great, but small, a blind old man who knew how to do only one thing—elicit fear, not fright which we often confuse with fear, especially as children, but fear—the oppressive living essence that forces the psyche into an unnatural state and forces a person to stifle himself; fear, the optical lenses of fear increased Grandfather II's figure, gave it a demonic, creepy glow. The real horror was in the useless keys, the saucers from beat-up tea sets, in worn coins—in the anonymity of existence, in the impossibility of learning anything morally from these remains, which could have been caught in an archaeologist's sieve, about a person who seemed to blend into the general background of an era, lost amid the trifles, who had taken on the quotidian as a scheme, or even more accurately, had always lived by it; a person about whom you sensed great evil but whom you could never call great or even having scale in that evil. Not minor, not great—average; his personality had lost the element that gives the potential for the grotesque, for playing with scale, for the chance to turn into a dwarf or a giant. He was like the monuments that filled the country, not big, not small, but which won by repetition, the power of the commonplace.

Time passed, and I understood that as an adult I would not find anything in the apartment; everything that was visible I had examined, and not a single object replied to my silent question. Going through the closets, methodically opening drawers and boxes, searching—the very thought made me want to wash my hands, scald them with hot water until they turned red, until they burned. I had to return my childhood perception—I had spent a lot of time in Grandfather II's rooms—go through the paths of that perception, which drew its own map of the apartment in sensual relief, to notice which objects remained themselves and which ones were slightly blurry, shimmering iridescently, showing that something was hidden inside; remember which corners, dark spaces behind furniture, and secret places behind the drapes called to me; the answer was there somewhere, in the past, in the view I once had from my height as a child.

I lay down on the couch, this position equalizes adult and child; a spring poked my side through the cushion; I lay there a long time, twilight came, the velvet curtains softening the light, and soon the room was dusky, so dark that I could not tell the color of the dark blue vase; the color was gone as if the vase was the usual glass dipped in water. I was getting sleepy but the couch spring, no matter how I turned, bothered me, poking my body, not letting me relax, not letting me sleep. I felt that something was missing and I wound the clock—an old alarm clock with an arc between two nickel-plated bells, resembling a snail that had a clock face instead of a shell. The clock started up, it had a special sound, a tinny dry click, which made me think as a child that it was counting its own separate time, the time of coming events that no one except Grandfather II was supposed to know about. Now it all came together, the clock, the blue twilight, the spring in my side, and I remembered how once I caught a cold visiting my parents, and they left me to spend the night at Grandfather II's; I lay on this very couch, covered with two blankets, and I couldn't fall asleep, the clock and spring kept me in the brittle space of half-awake and half-asleep, the room had already undergone the nighttime transformation, it was inhabited with shadows swaying like underwater grasses, and the objects had huddled in the corners, vaguely rising from the darkness; shadows and corners—the room turned into the combination of dozens of blurred templates, alternating stripes of curved and straight lines; its volume decreased, it contracted from a cube into a sphere, movable, breathing, like the lungs seen from inside.

I recalled how Grandfather II walked through the room that night; he suffered from insomnia—it was only in his dreams that he could see things that went beyond the framework of memory, but he slept badly, went to the kitchen for a glass of water, then a second and third, trying to fill some hole in himself, and only then slept, full of water, bloated like a bedbug; blind, he moved like a sleepwalker, reading the apartment by touch, and I thought that he might forget himself during these nocturnal walks, remembering that he was not always alone when he was awake, and do something that he would not do in the daytime; open a door, get something he did not want seen. And this time I was right: on the way back—the faucet was still dripping in the kitchen—Grandfather II came over, tucked in my blanket, and checked with his hand whether I was asleep; the corners of the eyes are relaxed when a person is sleeping, while they are tense in an awake person who shuts his eyes, and he knew the places to touch lightly to see if someone was asleep; I truly was dozing, I was almost asleep, almost no longer felt my body which had grown alien and heavy, like winter clothing. Having ascertained that I was asleep, Grandfather II went to his room.

He started bustling in there; if I had risked getting up and stepping on the floor, Grandfather II would have heard me immediately; but he had not shut the door and I could see what was going on in the big mirror of the chiffonier opposite the door; Grandfather II opened the top drawer of his desk and rummaged in it.

I knew that drawer; a child remembers every area where he is not allowed and tries to figure out ways of getting in; that drawer was always locked, it had a special lock, unlike the others in the desk, and I never saw a key on Grandfather II's key chain that might fit it. I had tried pushing in a heavy fishing line to move the things inside and guess what was there from the sound; I shined my flashlight through the keyhole, I studied whether I could remove the screws and take out a side of the drawer; all in vain.

Grandfather II closed the drawer; the key was in his hand but he made a fist and I didn't get a look at it; Grandfather II got in bed—where had he put the key!—and that was the end of the incident in the night; in the morning I found a moment to look around his room, but I couldn't see where he could hide the key.

Now two decades later, my old interest in the drawer was the hottest clue I had recalled; I went to the desk and tugged lightly at the drawer. I expected it to be locked, but it submitted to the tug with a creak; the apartment must have been examined for valuables more than once over twenty years.

In the drawer was a bundle of well-worn letters tied with a colorful ribbon, probably tied by a woman, a box of pen nibs, and a few razor blades for removing ink splotches and errors; a calendar with an announcement of elections to the Supreme Soviet of the USSR and a round candy tin filled with paper fasteners; there was a smaller tin, for caviar, which held teeth, with crowns and without, canines, incisors, wisdom teeth—the dental history of Grandfather II's life; he must have collected them out of some strange whim, a madman's eccentricity—something like a belief that you have to show up at the Final Judgment with all your bones, turn yourself in with all thirty-two teeth accounted for; but even the gold and steel of the crowns could not connect these teeth in the box with a human image—they seemed to belong to some animal like a wolf or dog; strong-boned, powerful, big, that had passed many other animals, fat and skinny, it didn't matter, through its jaws; a magnitude—a mathematical magnitude— of the consumed flickered before me when I looked at those teeth; a long line of living creatures eaten so that the jaws could swallow another one.

Grandfather II had saved his canines and incisors as if preparing for a new life where they would come in handy. In the same box, wrapped in wax paper, were my milk teeth, tiny, pathetic, like those of a puppy or fox kit; I wanted to throw them away instantly, there was something nasty in the existence of a part of myself that was separate from me; I was engulfed by the old, forgotten sensation that he was following an instinct and collecting everything that could bring me closer to him, everything through which he could own me, literally and figuratively; the answer to why, or rather the start of the path to the answer, was somewhere here in this drawer; I sensed it as I went through Grandfather II's pagan amulets.

His dental bridges were there, too—pink plastic with smooth ceramic teeth and a special powder to clean them. There were four pieces—Grandfather II started losing his teeth early, either because of some long-ago starvation and his exhausted organism, or because his body was matching his desire to appear to be a little old man, a lisping, gray granddad with teeth-in-a-glass. Grandfather II, he was a grandfather, a mighty word charged with a radical power, traded his body for the signs of aging, even though he was in good health, and it helped him, let him hide behind age, although not completely.

The false teeth, the elderly lifestyle, the insistent use of baby words—puddy cat, yumyum porridge, jammies; walking stick, medication schedule, milk toast instead of soup—all a mask to fool people and cunning to fool death, self-deprecation, marked impotence; here I am, I'm blind, harmless, and weak, I am like a bug in Your hand, do not squash me, Lord. But he wasn't a bug, he was a scorpion sleeping under a cold damp rock on a hot day; the drawer, which gave off a sharp smell of turpentine and furniture shellac as chilling as the touch of a centipede's legs, seemed to be a den of toxic creatures, they had hidden and run off, but the sense that they had been there remained; I knew that feeling from Central Asia, where the deceptively pleasant air always carried the presence of the sun's stinger, the cheery crippling poison dissolved in it, the bite always near.

There was yet another box in the drawer, creamy yellow, for vanilla fudge. This fudge had been my favorite sweet.

Grandfather II knew it and whenever I visited he treated me; I even thought that if I opened the box I would find hardened honeyed grains of the candied fruits that now contained only the memory of their taste. Grandfather II would give me one, sometimes two, but never more, not out of stinginess but as if he knew the final number of candies not given to someone else, and he was in no hurry to hand them all to me at once, so they would last longer; I would not have accepted the candies, even though I liked sweets, for the candies from his fingers seemed oversweet, but I was afraid; I had the feeling that if I refused he would force it on me, shove it in my mouth.

The fudge box was a signal, a sign; only Grandfather II and I knew about the custom of treats; inside the box were strange handmade toys: a rifle two matchsticks long, with a sharp bayonet made from an awl; a horse covered in real horsehide I think—the hide was moth-eaten and straw stuffing fell out of the belly; a German shepherd made of glove leather, with sharp claws glued on; several human figures, as anonymous as tailor's dummies—wood, screws, smooth rounded heads; their arms and legs moved, and there were clever notches in their hands, where the rifle fit perfectly. The toys were very old and too real for toys; it was clear that they were just a small part of some set and I could feel that you didn't play with them the way you do with plastic soldiers—wood, iron, leather were not of a toy nature; the objects in the box were too heavy, too carefully detailed—they lacked the abstraction of toys that left room for the imagination; on the contrary, they seemed as if someone had the idea to depict a specific horse, dog, and people in this crazy way—except the people had no clothes and only one of them had Lilliputian leather boots the size of thimbles.

I had never encountered anything like this; I did remember that Grandfather II had said several times—in a roundabout way, vaguely, and perhaps even making it up—that when I grew up he would give me some very special—and he didn't say toys, he said playthings, games. There they were—rifle, horse, dog, and then people; they could not belong to a child, they were handmade souvenirs for an adult—and at the same time they gave off the aura of madness, a neurosis, a wild concentration on details that came from the inability to capture the whole, the morbid detail of a mad concept, the same kind of paganism as in keeping the teeth. The little figures could have belonged to an aged military officer replaying old battles, but ones in which the wooden soldiers led by the will of the blood-maddened marshal die for real, die the death of things—which is why they had to be made of simple, elementary materials, wood, iron, leather.

I was stunned; the sun's sting, the poison, it was like a blow, a snakebite; I wanted to find a document, evidence, and instead I found Pandora's box.

If he had been alive, Grandfather II would have given me the figures and explained something, told me their provenance; a story or a fairy tale, an anecdote—and they would have been turned into amusing marionettes or cute things from the past: here's what little ones had before there was the Detsky Mir children's store in Moscow. I would have taken them, depending on my age, as toys or as souvenirs; I would have kept them without feeling everything I was feeling now that I was alone with them.

The figures were scary—I didn't want to hold them. It seemed that touching them had its dangers; that they were a connection with the dead people they depicted; yes, the figures were anonymous, devoid of concrete features—but in each of them I sensed a person, just as devoid of traits, ruthlessly dehumanized, rolled smooth by time.

The spirit of the times was fully realized in them: not the general and superficial one that is in the air and forms an era's ambience—fashion, slogans, speeches, technological innovations—but what is deeper and closer to the heart: the concepts of good and evil, the concepts of human and inhuman, the dominant note of relations, what one man can do to another—and the times will accept those deeds as a matter of course.

The spirit of the times—what is a person in those times, how free, or unfree, is the human in people; the figures belonged to a time when a person wasn't even a toy, for that image allows for fate, which is varied and enjoys fickle games, but a unit deprived of fate.

The figures in the box—horse, dog, and three featureless "people"; they had that clumsy solidity that distinguishes a peasant harness or homemade scythes, pitchforks, and shovels; they were obviously not made by Grandfather II, he wouldn't know how, his fingers did not have such tactile precision; some parts showed that the maker lacked needle files and chisels, everything was done with just two or three tools: knife, hone, and boot needle; old leather, old copper wire, waxed thread—the figures were meant to last a long time, or perhaps, the maker didn't know how to work any differently.

There was nothing more in the box; I untied the pack of letters. I didn't remember Grandfather II writing letters often or receiving many; not New Year's or Soviet Army Day cards or telegrams or parcels—Grandfather II lived almost without any connections, friendships, family; his telephone rang only once when I was there, and he spoke shutting the door to his room, and I listened to him apologize and ask the caller to call back tomorrow—I'm not feeling well—as if he didn't want to reveal the real reason, that a boy was visiting him. The letters must have survived because the housekeeper didn't find the key to this drawer when she was burning his papers; the drawer had remained locked for years, and then, when the key was found, it seemed silly to burn a few remaining documents.

The letters, which the sender must have assumed would be

read aloud to Grandfather II by the housekeeper, had wishes for good health; every letter mentioned seal blubber and bear fat sent to Grandfather II; asked if it had helped; seal blubber and bear fat—it was all about the fat, the writer explained how they caught the seal, how they shot the bear; the correspondent was a clumsy writer, words did not obey him, and he piled them on, one holding up the next so the sentence did not fall apart. But as soon as it came to hunting, the cold will of the shooter organized the rhythm of halting style. Seals and bears, bears and seals, the resident of a northern town exterminated them, made the long trek to the sea, went out hunting in the winter, and I don't think it had to do with Grandfather II's needs; the writer did not hunt in order to send parcels to the capital. He talked about hunting as if he did not do the shooting but simply observed the carbine fire the bullets; this removal of the weapon from a subordinate role and ascribing its own significance to it showed a certain restrained reverence. The man had found a support, had found an object that was different from other objects, that had power over life, which other objects lack, and he'd clung fast to it ever since.

He leaned on the rifle, carbine, gun, the way people of superficial faith lean, figuratively, on the church; the weapon became his religion but without all the emotion that usually surrounds it; the smell of the oil, the smoke, the machismo of a man with a double-barreled shotgun, ammunition belts, gunfire, hunting stories—none of this seemed to matter to the writer. He believed strictly and almost chastely, believed in the higher wisdom of the mechanism, in the trigger, firing pin, percussion cap, shell, and barrel; he believed in the laws of physics that made the shot possible. The seals and bears he killed died because the shotgun has to shoot; because the sight seeks a target; because the bullet wants to fly; he was a barely literate arbitrary poet of shooting who saw the world as being flat—a target does not have a third dimension—and that made reading his letters even more frightening; any murderer fixated on destruction was more human than this connoisseur of bluing gun barrels, direct and reverse threading, different gunpowders and types of sights, in love with his gun because it was soulless, which made it seem lofty, impartial, and just.

You could say that the letter writer had discovered a new unity beyond nationality and beyond culture—the unity of people with guns, the unity of pure force, and he enjoyed embodying pure force with no ideological coloration. He must have been pleased imagining arsenals growing and weapons rooms filling up; pleased reading about a new missile or new cannon in the newspaper—they were all merely forms of force, a force without content, force per se, and he had decided as a youth to be part of force—the most imperceptible part, the most impersonal part, without ambition and in that sense safe for the integrity of the force.

Obliquely it was clear that the writer was once very close to Grandfather II; this was obvious from the missing details and information that sometimes made the letters unclear and which Grandfather II apparently knew. Judging by the postmarks, the letters were around thirty to forty years old; the penultimate one came a few months before his death and the last one after Grandfather II had died; that one mentioned a meeting with Grandfather II and it mentioned me, too, as if the writer had seen me. Try as I could, I couldn't remember anything; all I had was the return address—a street in a small northern city that had a huge mining complex, which I had heard about when I worked as a geologist.

I reread the letters in case I had missed something; seal blubber, bear fat—I imagined Grandfather II taking spoonsful of smelly jellied fat, too natural, untamed by cooking; the fat smelled of musk, subcutaneous glands, meat, blood, fur, smelled of animal, and in order to eat it you would have to overcome disgust, one which was greater than ordinary disgust: it expressed human prohibitions and crossing them brought you closer to being a wild beast.

I remember the time on an expedition after a long period of hunger we shot a deer and started eating the fresh liver; after a week of bad weather the sun was flickering in the leaves, and I felt the same warm flicker inside me of the life force, how the fading life of the deer was directly passing into my muscles, and the muscles were responding with readiness to race, grab, tear apart. The sun illuminated the river bottom, and the smooth deep water gave off the power of the current, the wind bent the birches, and I felt the current of natural forces passing through me, I was one with the water, the wind, I was a cluster of desires, translucent and thick, like the sunlight of August in the taiga. I was running and grabbing—and a minute later, I got a cramp, not from the raw liver, my stomach had accepted that, but because I had fallen into an animal state and now my humanity was being painfully restored.

Seal blubber, bear fat, the secret of Grandfather II's longevity smelled of ancient blood, the letters smelled of blood, and I no longer wanted to know what was in his past; just to leave the apartment, throw away the keys, let it stay there like a forgotten mousetrap, locked and sealed; if it had been a house instead of an apartment, I would have burned it down, like a plague house. Once again I sensed Grandfather II's blood circulating in me, I could feel the short animal hairs growing, the too-hard nails growing; I wanted to gnaw meat from bones, ooze blood, suck out the marrow.

I recalled how once at the dacha an old woman from the village, who did not like the dacha owners for parceling out their garden allotments on the best berry and mushroom spot on the edge of the woods, in the most damp spot where she gathered St. John's wort, chamomile, coltsfoot, melilot, bur-marigold, clover, raspberry leaf, and linden flowers, the old woman once met Grandfather II on the forest path. I was creeping after him and saw the look she gave him, with his folding chair, jug, and fishing reels, neat, with a handkerchief in his pocket, she looked at him and said loudly, "Werewolf!" Grandfather II unexpectedly replied loudly, "You're demented, old woman," and went on; he replied rather aloofly and rather disdainfully, the way a cranky old man might have responded to a nasty old woman he knew—she'll wear you out with her nagging—but the old woman was neither nasty nor a nag, she was known for her silence, and she and Grandfather II had never exchanged a word before; I sat in the bushes, so the herb woman would not see me, Grandfather II walked on, and she watched him go, whispering something to herself.

Later I tried to get into her house; someone was sick and I offered to go get some herbs for a cold. The old woman let me into the house, too spacious for her alone; the timbered *izba* dwelling was big, made of logs you could barely embrace, and you could see that it had been built by a big family. In the middle stood an enormous whitewashed stove, which had spread like a woman of a certain age, cosmic in sensibility—everything rotated around it, it was the axis and the support, inside its womb buckwheat porridge stewed, soups cooked, and bread was born—*karavai*, a loaf as round as the fruitful sun, peasant bread; but the stove just made the emptiness of the rooms more pronounced and bitter. Through a hanging I saw a wall of photographs in one of the rooms—dozens of male and female faces, with the peasant gaze, concentrated and severe, as if having your photograph taken was hard work to be approached with full cognizance; for an instant the photographs made the izba full of people, talking, eating, coming in from the gardens, the fields, it filled up and emptied. While the woman went through her herbs, I searched for my knowledge of the force that swept all those people away, leaving the old woman to maintain the house as a memory of the departed; she gave me the herbs, dried, prickly, and explained how to pour boiling water over them; I wanted to say something consoling but realized that there is a deadline for sympathy and condolences, there is a deadline for commiseration and compassion, and it had long passed; my words would have no effect, because nothing had been said earlier, and not by me.

The old house was hopeless, the stove was hopeless, it took so many logs, the crooked fence where the bottles dried, and the lame cat that warmed itself behind the stove; I left thanking her and promising myself to visit the old woman again, but I did not keep my promise—everything I could have felt fit into that single impression, and it could not expand or even repeat itself; there was a precision in the singularity of the meeting, in the fact that it did not turn into a kindhearted caretaking; the old woman did not need it the way a praying person does not need encouragement, and after a few years I forgot her, immersed as I was in the well-being of childhood which avoids problems of the old.

And now years later—life sometimes anticipates our questions by decades—I remembered her, remembered her cry of "Werewolf!"; it coincided with my insight, my sensation of the thick impure blood; I fled the apartment, I locked the door and threw the key in the river, choosing that route intentionally; I went to my parents' house with the firm determination not to accept my inheritance, to have nothing to do with that apartment, to sell or exchange it—let it be, shut, empty, lost among the other apartments, buildings, and streets, let it recede to a dot; I had understood something, and my history was over.

I was alone then in my parents' house; when I came in I started seeking support in books, as usual—you pick up a book, open it at random, and get into the plot to break up the whirlwind of your thoughts; but this time I intentionally selected a book to be as far away as possible from the present and not get the least echo or coincidence from the text; I chose *The Epic of Gilgamesh, He Who Saw the Unknown*, a dark-green, swampy colored volume; I took it remembering the description of Uruk, the humanization of Enkidu, the expedition against Humbaba; but the book did not open there at all. I read:

The Scorpion-Man opened his mouth to speak, said to Gilgamesh:
'There never was a mortal, Gilgamesh,
Never one who could do that.
No one has travelled the mountain's path.

For twelve double-hours its bowels . . .
Dense is the darkness and there is no light.
To the rising of the Sun …
To the setting of the Sun …
To the setting of the Sun …'

Gilgamesh said to the Scorpion-Man:
'Whether it be in sorrow,
Whether it be in pain,
In cold, in heat,
In sighing, in weeping,
I will go!
Let the gate of the mountain now be opened!'

"Let the gate of the mountain now be opened!" I repeated; I thought about the Yakut tales of mammoths living underground, and if the tundra buckled from the ice freezing in the soil, the Yakuts believed that mammoths had walked deep underground; if they found a mammoth carcass in a precipice, they thought it had died by accidentally stepping out into the sunlight. I sensed that this imagery was right—

going through land, through mountain, through accumulated ossified time; but I did not yet know what I would have to do, how to act.

Nights were dreamless, but close to dawn dreams came, three dreams; they repeated in the same order. Sometimes a dream extends into the deepest layers of consciousness that lie beside the main well through which we dive into ourselves; it is they, and not the popular ideas of the moment, that in many ways determine our belonging to a certain historical time.

Military brass bands have different sounds in different years, and depend not only on the hearer; there is a silence on the eve of war that can be torn by the sound of a single bugle, and there is a silence after a defeat in which the sound of an entire band will be muted and lost.

There are times of light and times of darkness; the general tone changes, the illumination changes, and the same color looks different as if in different optical media: the red banners of the Civil War, which had more scarlet, and the red banners of the thirties, which had more crimson, look the same in black-and-white newsreels.

It turned out that the portion of the past that is extant and unnoticed in the present, diffused in it, is very great; it was the voice of grains, the argument under the bench, the voice of random people, chords of random melodies through the rasp of the loudspeaker, the voice of boarded-up windows. Sand, dust, ashes, remains, bone meal, salt, sugar, kerosene, soap, matches spoke; old houses, river bends, rotting sunken ships, coal burned in furnaces, gunpowder pushing bullets out of barrels, and the greenish metal of casings all spoke; everything that vanished, disintegrated, was drunk, eaten, lost, and used up also spoke, and it was lost, it echoed in the dream gathering strength; it would not yield to daytime consciousness, only to sleep.

The first dream started: I saw the springtime river ice,

mushy from the weakened inner tension, and still solid only in one place, a strip across the river.

There was a ford there in winter, the trampled snow hardly melted, and the ruts made by wheels, runners, horseshoes, boots, and children's shoes stood out more. They took on additional meaning: the people were dead—that was the knowledge of the dream—but their footprints accidentally survived.

An archaeologist finds a declivity in hardened sand, a footprint, and in the unimaginably distant past, where you can't even imagine human existence, a notch appears for counting to begin, a sign of affirmation: I was. This phenomenon, which has a dual nature of fact and symbol—one reinforcing the other—graphically approaches the pulsating point in the middle of the page, without any neighboring points; the starting point.

The footprints on the ice also pulsated, but they were not just points: voluminous letters of set type, forming words, lines, text. It seemed that each had been left deliberately: people could have walked without a trace and in general life is such that no traces are left if you don't make an effort—but the ones who had walked on the ice had stepped intentionally so that the wet snow of the thaw would accept the body's weight and take a cast of their soles.

The words frozen in the ice were bitter; every print meant a step, and the step brought them closer to vanishing, which the print resisted. They were repeated—thus a desperate person keeps repeating the same thing, and a recitative appeared composed of many repetitions.

Hasty, overlapping, overflowing, like a lament, the prints joined up a multitude of fates and the single path. It seemed that an unremitting threat had accompanied the travelers, pushing them from behind, keeping them from turning off.

Later—the guess arose one night and then kept appearing

every time—I realized that somewhere in the snowy mush were prints of the guards' boots, who were unlikely to have walked on the untouched snow, but they were no longer recognizable: they were lost, blended into the whole. This indistinguishability of prisoners and guards—when you can't tell which was which—elicited horror, even though there was a hint in it: it was not the convoy of guards that pointed out the direction, for the threat that forced people to walk on the ice hovered over them as well.

Here the dream changed; somewhere so far away that its small universe barely accommodated such a distance, something collapsed, the concussion accelerated time that had been imperceptible until then, an icy crashing roar grew—and a crack zigzagging along the line of the river channel broke the ice of the ford in two.

The crack expanded rapidly, turning into an ice hole, foaming water bursting from it; the ice fragmented, chewed up by the ice holes, tearing the solid picture of the ford into shreds; floes tumbled and the water pushed with greater strength, inundating all the traces, all the prints. This was water of the bottom currents that avoided the ice holes, that had settled in the deep holes beneath the steep banks, oily and stale, as if the drowned had decomposed in it slowly—because of the cold—it was like the emptiness of an undiscerning gaze in which things, phenomena, and events are lost and cease to exist.

Suddenly in a single movement, the weight of the ice as yet untouched by cracks in the channel moved forward, which revealed how wide the channel was. What had seemed to be a sloping bank turned out to be ice hummocks, while the banks were so far away that they could not be seen by the eye or captured by the mind. The movement of the ice knocked me off my feet and then the ice holes moved out beneath me.

This is where I woke up, but I woke from one dream into

the next. Both—and there is still the third—were related to each other like several spheres with a single center. Moving from dream to dream you were always in the heart, in the epicenter of events expressed differently in each of the spheres of the joint three-part dream.

I was on a train platform, seeing it not with the vision of an eyewitness, but somehow from inside the event. And so the dream began: a train approached the platform; two dozen cars seemed insignificant compared to the steam engine. The smoke, imbued with soot, was stifling; the dull cutting edge of the wheels, their red spokes, the grease like a bodily discharge oozing from the pistons; the ruby star at the end of the headless torso was like a brand on a powerful animal that consisted only of muscles, branded by a five-pointed cut, and the power of the muscles pushed red meat through the wound, creating a mark that was a convex star—this all overwhelmed me and deprived me of will.

I—the me who existed outside the dream—naturally knew how the old steam engines looked: I'd had a childhood full of technology, of enormous machines made to scale as toys. But in my time steam engines were different. The imperfection of construction—the way dinosaurs are imperfect from the point of view of evolution—made that mass of metal seem alive somehow; technology and primal force.

The steam engine gave rise to a time whose aesthetics looked to industrial labor for inspiration, a time of the triumph of mechanics; mechanics gave poets metaphors, it was entrusted with the setup of human life, and they tried to take humans apart and put them back together in a new way, to create a homunculus of steel and aluminum with a motor for a heart. The steam engine became a marvelous symbol, the triumph of creative power—but now, as I sensed in my dream, time itself feared it, the way the ancient gods feared the hundred-armed giants they created.

In its furnace, the unbelieving martyrs of the revolution burned as if in a fiery oven, the steam engine brought the body of the leader assigned to be immortal to the capital, and the steam engine itself became one of the minor gods of the new pantheistic religion. Now at the station the arrival of the train spread a sense of dread: the steam engine seemed to have its own understanding of where to go and whom to take, and the trip turned into anxious anticipation—you can never tell at what moment you are traveling at the will of another, elevated above everything else.

The train stopped at the platform and people came out of the cars. The glass dome of the station, the iron beams, all the rivets were covered in the cold sweat of hoar frost on the foggy morning that settled on the smoke particles. Something stuck in the works of the station clock; the minute hand froze, trembling, and the face resembled the round window of baggage scales.

At the very end of the platform, near the steam engine, a few men in uniform appeared; the color and style were not important: amid the overcoats, sheepskin jackets, raincoats, and quilted jackets the essential detail was the uniform itself, identical, anonymous, and severe. It was an image—the image of power, universal, like the law of gravity, so all-encompassing that it has no recognizable features.

The proximity of the steam engine and uniformed soldiers was not accidental: its red star made the stars on the cockades of their caps all the more visible. When they appeared, blocking the exit from the platform, the people who came off the train already belonged to the kind of crowd that appears briefly when a large number of people forced to spend a long time together start to move. This vaguely friendly crowd where the weak attraction of accidental acquaintance was still maintained, moved in a businesslike and almost joyous fashion—the long anticipation was over—and simultaneously each person was separate from his fellow travelers, walking in his own rhythm, and the farther from the wagon, the less this community of people could be called a crowd, for each person was individualized, walking his own road for which the train station was only the starting point, and the law determining the behavior of a crowd did not govern him.

But as soon as the soldiers appeared, the people coming out of the train first slowed down imperceptibly, then each person turned, stumbled, lost his rhythm in order to hide from the soldiers behind the person walking in front. It looked as if a number of targets set at various distances had sidled along in order to hide behind one another. A person walked, hidden behind another's back, and did not see that behind him someone was walking in his footsteps, and behind him, another, and behind him, yet another ... The raucous, cheerful crowd that had filled the platform suddenly squeezed itself into many uneven chains, as if after a chemical reaction that made human atoms combine into extended weaving molecules.

I waited to sense the fear of all those people—it should have erupted, transforming the station air, which had been turned into a trap. However, instead of a sharp eruption I sensed a sedative; there was fear, but it was usual, ordinary, only slightly elevated; there was no tension, it was as if people were rejecting themselves, bidding themselves farewell—and carried themselves to the exit like a pile of folded clothing in an army steam bath, or a prison.

Even though people hid, there was no more intelligence behind it than in the movements of a worm chopped in half by a shovel. Real fear comes in expectation of direct loss of life—here the separation seemed to have taken place much earlier than when the people came out on the platform or even got into the train; it happened almost at birth. Their lives had been taken away from them and returned in the form of a peacoat from naval supply, for temporary use; now, on the platform, their lives were being demanded back—perhaps unexpectedly but with every right to do so.

A separate corner was created next to the soldiers: huddled together were the ones pulled out of the crowd; by its density, the group made an island in the relatively uncongested human sea, but there was no impression of an island at all; you immediately registered one peculiarity—it was as if these people were not there, and only later did you understand why.

Everyone else—many hundreds of people—avoided looking at the prisoners; the prisoners did not look out beyond the limits of their circle, and so the group completely fell out of the entire field of vision.

I tried to hold my gaze and keep it from veering off— but like a compass needle following a magnet, it chased the directing vectors. To break out of the current of gazes that carried me to the exit, past the prisoners, I gazed through the station windows at the freight lines, and there I saw a steam engine that was the twin of the first engine, to which heated freight cars with barred windows were being coupled. At that moment I remembered—remembered in the local "induced" memory of the dream—that I had lived through this already the last time I had this dream, and I swore to watch the freight tracks, the areas of the dream that remained outside my view— swore because this second steam engine, this second train, was intended for the prisoners on the platform.

They began bringing people into the freight cars and I realized that the ones who'd been arrested at the station were taken in order to fill the spots of people who hadn't been arrested in the city. With the view beyond the borders of the station dome I saw the reason for this anxiety which had seized me when I first spotted the steam engine. The prison train was already in place when the train approached the station, the track curved, and for a period the passengers could see the freight cars from the windows; two different times, present and future, passed very close, like oncoming ships, but the present did not, could not, recognize the future, and the future seemed indifferent to the present. For the passengers, the freight cars were the last meaningless shots in a film of their journey, and if you were to ask any of them a few days later what they had seen when the train was pulling into the station, at best they would recall that there was another train nearby, but nothing more definite than that.

But this particular, this meaningless detail—a prison train on the side tracks, a row of gray-green freight cars—became like cancer cells for those who were arrested, multiplying, devouring the healthy flesh of the universe, growing, blocking out the narrowing horizon, and turning into a single rusted jaw of the freight car.

Along the same tracks that had brought them there, the prisoners would be taken back in the direction from which they had come. But although each of them had arrived as someone with a name, who could say I am so-and-so traveling from here-to-there, now they would become no one, they would not even know where they were being taken.

I saw people moving from the clear bright station, whose dome of glass cells formed a network of coordinates on the platform, drawn with precision, as if in a math workbook, by the sun that had suddenly started to shine above the city's morning fog, moving into the shadow of other buildings on the freight tracks, for the shadow of the twilight of the night still held sway, detained by the light frost.

I saw the station, I saw the clock still resisting moving the minute hand to the next division, the enormous mosaic panel on the far inner wall of the station which was not yet completed and which made it look as if the headless red gigantic soldiers it depicted were building themselves, and that the construction scaffolding helped them stand up straight—I saw it all as one frozen instant.

The border between light and shadow clarified the meaning of what was happening: people were being led out from the present tense; its territory ended where the encirclement began, gray soldiers stood with rifles and bayonets over their shoulders, and two convoy soldiers with a canvas bag took away the prisoners' watches. The bag looked as if it would start wriggling, filled with puppies to be drowned, but no, it was just getting heavier and the soldier could no longer hold it with one hand.

The watches fell into the bag and the days of life they measured vanished down its dark gullet. Next to them, soldiers removed wedding rings, breaking marriages; if the ring had grown tight, they called the field doctor; he had smelling salts in case someone passed out, but his bag also held oil and soap. The doctor greased the finger and twisted and turned the ring, which he gave to a special guard. He had a small plywood box with a slot hanging around his neck, and if the ring did not fit through the slot, the guard left it on the lid of the box, so as not to keep unlocking it, and the precious stones set in gold or silver, two or three diamonds, a ruby, a sapphire, looked like colored glass: their value meant nothing now.

But this merely prepared the prisoners; the main thing occurred on the border of light and dark. The watches and rings were taken away in the daylight, and after that the person had to step into the semidarkness, knowing he would vanish in it the way the ones who entered before him had vanished.

This was the most tormenting part of the dream: people did not die but they ceased existing in the present. The present went on quite well without them, every new moment pushed back the previous ones, in which those people still *were*.

I sensed that oblivion does not come in gradualness, extension, or postponement, but that it is an integral part of time itself, whose unreasoning force makes it happen here and now; blind Cronus is continually devouring his children, and every new moment does not try to add to the last one but to destroy it. Only memory can resist forgetting; of course, not always.

Deprived of names, deprived of liberty, torn from their families forever, people do not stop being people. But they vanish, the way a crashed plane vanishes from the radar, both for their families and for the generation of yet unborn descendants.

The prisoners would be remembered the way the dead or those who moved to another continent are remembered: the memories are not added to, and consequently this break in memory is unlikely to be filled.

As for us—we can judge the past only by the evidence that it preserved about itself.

I had time only to see the faces, the most ordinary faces without beauty, or significance, or sharp features of breeding. In essence, the faces, despite the varying ages, were like the ones in their distant or not so distant youth: time had transformed them, compressed, stretched, wrinkled them, and the changes that were too easily noticeable made it difficult to see that if you were to remove all the wrinkles and signs of age in reverse order, like stage makeup, the faces would return precisely to their youthful images.

Time had fallen into their facial features, but mechanically, like erosion that changes the shape of mountain chains; the events of inner life, which irreversibly change and mold the face and keep it from going into reverse aging, were not manifested here.

And now when disaster came, people helplessly sought support within themselves—and could not find it. Past years came off, unpeeled like sunburned skin, to an age in which everything that happens is still perceived with an eye to the immeasurable duration of the future and when it seems that there will be enough time for a whole new different life, and more than one; an age which has no experience of finished and irredeemable events.

People were lost—as if a person had been asked to show his papers and he reached into his pocket only to find that there were no pockets, no coat, no memory of where it all had gone. They did not dare seek sympathy from one another, as if suspecting the same loss of self in others.

Perhaps if they had known of the arrest beforehand, some of them might have found the courage and will to resist, but this—coming off a train and seeing a soldier's finger pointed at you—this was greater than just being caught unawares: it was an evil mockery of fate in general and of each individual fate in particular.

The prisoners' lives were smashed at such a quotidian, unremarkable moment that the very contrast between the event of the arrest, which sucks up the person whole, and the fact that it was not a link in any chain of events, was not preordained or predicted but happened out of nothing without reason or cause—this contrast did away with individual fate per se.

The point was not the fatal injustice of the arrest; that was only one of the consequences of its gratuitousness. The soldier's finger, randomly pointing at people walking past, became its presentation, embodiment, and symbol; this was not that seeming gratuitousness when you wonder why it happened this way and not otherwise; the absolute absence of explanation elevated gratuitousness to the status of the sole reason for everything in the world; from now on any event in this upside down world occurred not by force of causation but by force of arbitrariness, and thus arbitrariness and violence became universal law.

The red gigantic soldiers on the mosaic panel, their red bayonets scraping the station's dome, headless guards, were an expression of that law; the fragmentation of the mosaic made it seem that they lacked human anatomy and consisted of cells of well-fed flesh; the panel was so huge that the red soldiers barely fit under the vaulted station roof, and the enormous building, full of air and light, was suddenly turned by association into a decrepit and vile cannibal's cave.

The last arrested man stood where they were confiscating watches. The train engineer and his assistant and stoker were walking that way to the train, accompanied by soldiers. And I knew—this knowledge had been incorporated into the dream but it did not appear right away—that the prisoner was the engineer's younger brother and that they had not seen each other in a long time. The guards had turned the younger brother to face the wall, going through his pockets, while the steam engine whistled and began backing up, distracting the engineer's attention, and the two brothers did not see each other. The engineer climbed into the cab, threw off his jacket, and while he was pulling a sweater over his head, his brother was led past the steam engine to the freight cars.

Even in my sleep I was stunned by the ordinariness and ease with which this non-meeting transpired; events avoided joining up, they existed separately, unconnected, and what could have been a tragedy—brother recognizing brother at the fateful moment—did not become one.

At that moment, a band set up on a far platform; they were rehearsing a welcome for some delegation. The music wasn't coming together, it wasn't that they were playing false notes, they just couldn't elicit the melody. Then a boy came out, who was supposed to read a greeting from the Pioneers; but the rhymed speech staggered, too, it was as if he had swallowed half the text.

No music, no poetry; for some reason, the poem caught my attention. I understood that the words were supposed to echo each other like watchmen through the rhymes, to *see* one another, and that it was the total vigilance of words, their mutual vision, that created the special cognitive optics of the text, the poetic insight.

I knew that the engineer would never learn whom he hauled in the prison car, and his brother, exiled to live in a place where the transcripts of meetings of the regional party committee were recorded on birch bark and where paper was more valuable than nails, would never send a line about himself.

The train started on the siding. As a child, when you went out to the railroad tracks to count railway cars and guess what was in them, you sometimes encountered a train so long it seemed never-ending, the only one in the world. The train extended and extended beyond the turn, steam puffed, semaphores glimmered; eventually the cars ended, and your eye was caught by the locked door of the last car; it seemed that it was slightly ajar, and that opening was the last chance to do something, to force the dream to change its course; but the train was leaving, and the door remained before your eyes: this was the beginning of the third dream.

The door at first retained its look, then it became just a door, then it changed—it was different every time I had the dream; the door to a bedroom, living room, office; wood, metal, knob, lock—everything changed. Only one thing remained—it was ajar, as if the instant when the door was almost shut was plunged into subjective time that did not have the duration of a dream for the sleeper, and it lasted endlessly. The door was no longer open but not yet shut; and I knew that if it did close it would never open again, it would vanish leaving an impenetrable wall.

I reached toward it, looking for a wedge to hammer between the door and the jamb—and I almost managed, but I didn't; if only to save what was beyond the door with my gaze, I looked through the keyhole—and fell into it, flew through space with a multitude of other doors, shutters, gates, hatches, and well covers. Everything that could be closed was shut—desks, coffers with letters, mailboxes, safes, oven doors, notebooks, textbooks, stamp albums; the whole world was folding up like a big book that would be wrapped in iron strips, padlocked, and placed under a bushel.

There, behind every door, things left behind by the people taken away in the train were dying; lenses in eyeglasses cracked, the thin wire frames of pince-nez bent out of shape, the amalgam came off mirrors in black cancerous spots, the images of faces once reflected in the mirrors faded and dissolved, wallpaper peeled from walls, twisting like ribbons of paper streamers; corroding the corks, iodine evaporated from dark yellow bottles, the belts in sewing machines fell apart, pencil lead crumbled, records shed black powder; wood and cement expelled nails and bolts, glue holding pages of photo albums dried out, elastic failed in underwear, buttons fell off clothing, and fur collars shed; the letters wore out on typewriters, piano strings burst, keys and pedals stuck, and pages eaten with the rust, like blood, of paper clips, released the faint aroma of handwritten letters as the ink faded.

Not a single room in my dream had people; rooms, corridors, stairwells, attics, cellars, entryways, and cupboards alternately formed into a dizzying sequence and fell apart like shards, then joined up again, threaded onto the trajectory of my movement; but I did not encounter a single person. Their absence was the kind that happens only in dreams or in recollections of early childhood: it seems that people had just been here, had just left, hiding from you, and the more clearly the air holds the residual warmth of life and the echo of voices, and the floorboards remember recent steps, the more tormenting is the inability to understand where they went and where to look for them. In childhood this inability makes you bawl, for it is perhaps the first experience of despair:

your mother and father are so obviously, so definitely *not* there, their absence is commensurate with the collapse of the universe; without finding them you cannot believe again in the world, you cannot acquire the strength to live, because *not* means that there is a hole in the world where people vanish— and you could vanish, too.

Things did not die silently; almost every sound a thing makes comes because something is being done to it, but here things had their own voices; their speech is a thousand times slower and more protracted, and usually we do not hear the faint rustle of newspapers wrinkling, the quiet cracking of aging porcelain or glass, the mosquito whine of the filaments in lightbulbs. But in the empty rooms where time was rapidly running out, all these creaks, cracks, and rustles combined into a primal sound.

Sometimes a dying person's death rattle sounds as if the human and animal no longer live in him and only the third component of his being, unknown to him, is left, related to inanimate nature: this is the way clay in mud volcanoes pulsates and bubbles up in bursting blisters. And then, just before the end, speech returns to him.

The objects also screamed at first, as if they had become feral, and then, on the contrary, acquired something human in the unity of their sounds; they had absorbed the voices of their owners, their intonations, and now, dying, they tried to speak in the rhythm of those intonations. A strange speech ensued: to the human ear it sounded like interjections of a pre-language that directly expressed emotion in sounds—be it a moan of pain or an exclamation of joy—without mediating it in words. The fourth string on a violin is closest to the human voice, and every object seemed to have discovered the gift of the fourth string; it seemed that silent tension had lived in them and it could become sound only through dying.

Now it seemed that the things were falling into an abyss,

bumping into one another, spinning, and screaming in horror almost like humans; the rooms and other spaces replaced one another infinitely, this sequence had no exit and no end.

Suddenly, I recognized the cacophony, and at the point of recognition the movement through rooms slowed and soon stopped. From my childhood memory, from the recollections of the same age as that of the apparent loss of my mother and father, came an image: a suspension bridge across the river, stretched on thick ropes, and the sinews of those ropes are severed by a saw with tiny, angry teeth like those of a mouse, the ropes break, but the bridge remains suspended in air as if by the power of habit of those who walked on it, and falls into the water only after a few seconds.

Creaks and squeaks, a crackle and the long, feminine tender singing of the burst ropes extending in an arc over the river water as if in an attempt to recreate the bridge in sound, in the singing arc. And my internal cry, because I could not understand why they needed to destroy the old bridge in order to build a new one, and the firm conviction that the new one would not be better, even though there was no scarier trial than stepping onto the rotten boards and swaying over the rocks below the crossing in rhythm to someone's heavy steps—would not be better because the ability to be better was taken away, just like that, in one instant, with a knacker's ardor, with the desire for definitive change, by dumping the old bridge into the water, when they could have taken it apart, found a use for the wood and metal.

My memory of the demolished bridge extricated from memories of long ago resembled a bush torn out of the ground with a ball of soil hiding the roots: the demolition of the bridge was the epicenter of the memory, and everything else moved into the shadow: the village houses on the riverbank vanished, the church vanished, and even the banks lost the contours of a strictly defined place, turning into an image of riverbanks in general.

The river had risen, as if there was flooding; it was no longer water flowing in the river channel, but the entire world palpable in memory became the channel and the overflowing banks and the sky all became a single current in the midst of which the river was a chute, rapids that gather before a waterfall.

The movement halted by the memory of the bridge began again, but in a different iteration; the river, which was part of the dream, suddenly became bigger than it, as if the place where dreams are unfolded has images that cannot be seen awake, that exist only as abstract concepts; images all the more reliable and expressive because familiar real objects serve as their base but which in dreams are perceived not visually but sensually, not as symbols but as forces to which you and the world of the dream are subject.

My consciousness—the consciousness of the sleeper, sensed as light that makes the dream's reality visible—contracted to a nutshell; the current seized me; it was a strange current, a current in place, as if the source and mouth were both here; the current carried me not away but deeper, a current without distance. However, the current did not only disembody. There was a hint in it, as in rain or wind, of another presence; there was a vague yet clear sense that "someone is there."

Someone fought the current wordlessly, did not want to yield to it; someone's exploit was taking place—long ago, forgotten, but still continuing. I understood that there were people there; the ones who left the emptied rooms, to whom the dying things addressed their scream; the bridge—a road to them—had collapsed, but I had managed to cross it.

Thus, through dreams, a person gets the insight of memory: he senses the ominous presence of shaded areas of the past untouched by the light of consciousness; there, in the prison of time, are people, events, and knowledge of oneself that is excluded from the sphere of inner life.

The clairvoyant of memory—that's who I became in my sleep. The flow of the river into which my dream had turned divided me from myself, tore all the threads that connected consciousness and memory, which allow you to know who you are at any moment in the details of the past; having become no one, devoid of the selectivity in memory predetermined by a personality, I acquired my memory whole all at once.

The power of the water receded; and I learned that the memory of a single man is not a fragile boat. Memory—the way it was revealed to me—was an ark.

In the current, in the movement of water that had seemed empty, islands appeared, banks arose in the distance, and the river became a river again; I had reached the very bottom of the dream where images had no concrete features and now I was returning, moving closer to being awake.

The islands, flat and sad, resemble the islands of northern rivers; consisting of gravel, sand, and soil, they are washed away by every flood, and they wander along the riverbed, cursed by pilots and buoy keepers. These islands are big sometimes, but people don't even put fishing huts on them; sometimes, if the island has been around a long time, held by river rot, grass runs riot greedily, and tempted by the thick grass, people carry haystacks on wide boats, like wagons, down the river. But cattle eat this grass reluctantly, as if sensing that the stalks and leaves came from empty water, that the grass is extremely hungry and will take away strength without giving a drop, it will not sate them; it will dilute the blood and make watery milk. The next year you won't be able to find the grass meadow, only shoals instead of an island; islands like this are not mapped and only the villagers near the banks remember where they were.

I noticed that the water was carrying some islands—huge peat floats; somewhere upriver the water was washing away peat deposits; old, darkened wooden crosses stood on one of the peat islands—the river had torn off a piece of a cemetery.

The other islands did not move; their banks seemed to be held down by boulders, fortified. When I got close to one of them, I saw that it was a shore of human faces; people were close together, the first row in water up to their throats, the next stood higher on the sloping bottom, the next even higher, and many rows were only faces for someone looking from the river.

The water did not reflect these faces: the power of regeneration seemed to have been exhausted by the river, and it carried old reflections, blurry and unclear, in which you just make out a cloud, or the blue and white side of a ship, or the rain-gray pine forest on a cliff.

The river water flowed without urgency or pressure, like blood in the veins of a sleeping person; if it were possible to transfer this river from dream to reality, to separate it from the vague banks of dreams and insert it, as into a frame, into the hills and cliffs of any known valley, from a distance it would look like an ordinary river. But on its bank, a person would suddenly sense that it was yesterday's river; it merely flowed in these parts but no tributary would feed into it, no spring would break through its bottom sands.

The faces of the people in the water and near the water were dark; the current suddenly picked up one or another of them, and his place was taken by the one who had been a step behind him; this is how the river washes away the shore, quietly undercutting the ground beneath the stones. The faces were so dark that it seemed the people had walked underground, not in a tunnel, but through the ground, and particles of dirt had eaten into the skin; there was dirt in their mouths, in their stomachs and lungs, all the body's spaces were filled by it.

The people were buried alive but did not die in their graves, wandering underground until they reached the riverbank and opened the ground like a door. They came out into a world where a note next to their names on long-ago faded lists asserted their nonexistence, and now death was completing the postponed work in just a few seconds. They saw me, they were all looking at me, and the combined force of their gaze created a vision inside the dream: sandy shoals, fog and smoke, a tall iron boat, the splash of water, huge iron gates open on the hold of the barge, a gangplank with ropes above the water. Up the gangplank in a single file came prisoners, guards, officers, sailors, and engineers—they walked without turning and vanished in the hold, where only the bent metallic ribs were visible. Then the metal doors began to close—on their own, no one set them in motion, neither people nor mechanisms—and they looked back, prisoners and guards together, but there were fewer of them—the others were blocked from my view by the meeting gates. Once again I wanted to stop the gates, insert a wedge, reach out—and woke up, my gaze not recognizing the house because my gaze—like an ark—was full of faces seeking salvation in it.

The dreams came for three days; on the fourth, I realized I had to go to the city where the letters found in Grandfather II's desk were written, I had to find the one who sent them. That this was the only way to find out something from the past was already clear, but now I sensed that this path had opened; we were mutually ready, I to set out and the path to let me pass.

Part 4

When you wake up in a train that left a big city in the night, you are surrounded by only vast, expansive things: power lines, rivers, roads, fields. The country comes to the embankment to watch the railcars with the kindly mockery of the permanent toward the transient, and hills and forest edges learn how to be the view from the window; the triangulation towers on local heights—points for attaching geographical coordinates—look like Martian tripods after a failed invasion, but the crosses on churches give optical axes and space is formulated from these buildings; a cross here is not only a symbol of faith but a land surveying tool.

When I opened my eyes we had already passed the central zone and reached the taiga; the train was climbing up the globe, north, along the great canal; somewhere there, beyond the pine forest, waters borrowed from lakes flowed in wooden sluices, the water traveled across granite watersheds; the ships in the narrow canal seemed to be traveling on dry land, the masts high above the trees, and the ship horn chased a long echo; the towns and cities near the railroad stood on the edges of lakes, threaded on the line of the canal, and crane booms and tall trees loomed above the low houses, and it all seemed too big for village life; but the lakes saved everything—spread out with hilly shores.

The canal led to the northern sea; its predecessors were ancient portage routes, the old river paths that were perhaps walked much more than dry land. Probably there was more unconscious symbolism in the creation of the canal—let the water through, let it flow rather than stand—than actual necessity; the locks with their added columns and arches, the temples of cargo delivery, the tabernacles of river ships—the life of the big country was supposed to flow into these parts through the canal, as if through a catheter; a cellulose paper plant was built on the shore of one of the lakes: the trees were cut down for the sake of the word, and power over these regions shifted from timber to paper.

Now the villages and towns were situated on two sides of the road—of the tracks and the canal; ships went past, trains went past—two flows, two directions, two currents bearing away; life gradually took on the features of platform and wharf, wharf and platform, depending on which way you turned; the residents were not fed by the land on which their houses stood but by the water and land roads; sometimes loaded, sometimes empty; the canal and railroad tracks were surrounded by zones of alienation, and the residents were icebound between the two zones.

The train reached a big station; twenty minutes' wait and a locomotive change. On the low platform, shin-high, sellers bustled, knowing where the car doors would be; most were female, old women and kids; paastrees, paastrees, cowoldbeer, cowoldbeer, fish, fish, fish, kefir whowantskefir, berries, berries, hotpotatoes, hotpotatoes, getcher chips, chips, chips, mineral water—dozens of selling patters, pattering sellers, hurry-hurry, hurryitup, mister, wheresyourbag, costsmore withthejar, swallowing letters hungrily. But each face, every figure that had acquired the platform whirl and bustle suggested another face and figure—the real ones they would be back home; God knows what awaited them there—an old woman's corner with a view of the empty vegetable plot, an apartment in a boarded-up two-story barracks, where everything is in everyone's face, and the yellowed sheets of a bedridden man hang on the same wash line as the yellow diapers of an infant.

The locomotive was coupled, the conductors were hurrying

people to get in, the sellers were rushing to the next track, the express was approaching from the north, its high beam and red double whiskers appeared around the turn, while I stood, finishing my cigarette; for some reason I always need to use up all the time allotted for a stop.

An old woman walked along the next platform; she carried a bouquet of peonies, the stems already fading and losing their firmness, but the flowers were still living, deep claret and fully opened. I knew those flowers—I had dug them out and rinsed the tangled roots in a pinkish manganese solution, the tubers like knotted flesh—and by early July the tight glossy buds exploded in a single day into large purple petals, tenfold folded, crumpled, and now falling apart like a pomegranate shattered by its overripeness, almost vulgar in its lack of restraint in proportion, but gorgeous because of that lack of strictness, lushness, loss of form, reduced by the glowing darkness of the depth of its color.

Peonies like that—I knew this—brought from the dacha were now flowering on Grandfather II's grave, their sensitive leathery roots going deep; they are death flowers, which are not only appropriate in the face of a death, but somehow crown and attenuate it; the ones whose vegetative flesh is closest to human flesh and can therefore stand in for it in the funeral ritual, grow in the soil of the cemetery, which does not tolerate random plantings; claret peonies—tiny black ants often crawled into their buds; a dark spot on the green, a herald of future decay.

The old woman's fingers clumsily held the flowers bound by a scrap of ribbon; the peonies were falling apart, bending in various directions, and it seemed that the same thing was happening inside the old woman: her life was about to fall apart, and the old woman was just trying to get into the cover of her house and be alone with the hardship of dying. The unsold flowers were in the way, her hands could not contain them, the hands were almost dead, life had gathered closer to the heart, to the belly.

I realized that I could not get into the train leaving her on the platform; I recognized her the way you recognize people who appear to us only a few times, and they are different, but in relation to use they are the same person—confidante, wordless advisor and comforter.

I had seen her only two times before—in the underground passage of the metro near my house. She healed me from the self-love of grief and self-reliance of insulted injury; they were late evenings of a hot and dusty summer and something was fermenting in people, flaring up in meaningless fights, or cursing, or broken glass; the air was stifling, flowers faded quickly, leaves drooped; I was coming home, wrapped up in my grief and injury, so furious that I was stumbling—everything was in the way, not handy, rubbing me the wrong way—and both times late in the metro passage the old woman was there dressed in a child's knit cap and a very old dress, in the fashion of her youth, threadbare from washing. There was something of a fastidious mouse used to living with people about her; the gray hairs on her lip, the worn fabric where threads held other threads at a third of their power, her poor vision, her weakness, her clarity of mind in the tiny area, about the size of eyeglasses, of her daily cares. She stood there neither meekly nor pleadingly, but without catching anyone's attention; before her on a cardboard box were seedlings of houseplants in plastic cups and separately in a jar the claw-like feather of a century plant.

She had meekness before God; we think that meekness means being ready to bear everything, but that is our pride speaking, our accountant's concept of justice and revenge; true meekness is where the contradiction is gone—bear it or not, put up with it or not, where there is an equal possibility of one or the other—but you do not raise your voice against God.

And meeting that old woman you knew that nothing would befall her in the nasty nighttime metro; all your injuries, anxieties, and sorrow were shamefully tiny in her presence— they became insignificant and nonexistent; just before you had been suffering, a cold, slippery, poisonous lump had filled your solar plexus, and now it was all gone.

"I'll get there myself," the old woman said on the platform, guessing my intention. I bought the peonies; the southbound express hid her from me, the step of my train car began to move.

It happens that an accidental meeting, for a short second, creates a nearness that does not occur in ordinary life; you suddenly learn that there are no distances, no defenses—they are illusory—there is only the most profound kinship; no risk is needed, no overcoming obstacles or going beyond your boundaries to meet another—the meeting has taken place; it is greater than any of us, we live inside it, we have already met; meeting is not an accident, it is a law, a means and an environment for existence: it is not between us, we are in it.

The train had left the station; the flowers were on the table in my compartment as a greeting and sign of farewell simultaneously in saturated colors of purplish claret.

The flowers breathed; their excessive sweetness reminded me of the cemetery, Grandfather II's grave; evening was descending and the train flew out onto a bridge, and the bolted steel girders stood along the sides of the tracks like enormous letters. Below was the broad river, and the river was still, the current could be felt only near the bottom, under the tense smoothness of the water; the train moved for several minutes in emptiness, the bridge itself was not visible, only the supports and the river, and my heart beat harder, feeling this interruption. The river was turned to glass by the sunset and a long fishing boat powered by a single rower moved across the current, slowly, heavily, as if the oars were scooping mercury.

I recognized the boat from the mosaics on the vault near Grandfather II's grave, the long shadows of poplars that seemed to have fallen once and for all and could not get any longer; but there Charon transported a shade wrapped in a long shroud, while here the ferryman or fisherman was alone.

The near bank was still illuminated, molten in the sunset, while the far bank was hidden by the dark, and it was where the rower was headed; a deep ravine bisected the darkened bank, and a tongue of blackness fell from it into the river.

The train rushed ahead and its speed made everything outside seem slow; the rower could not turn, the wind could not ruffle the water, the ray of light could not chase away the dark, and we moved to the dark bank, and we moved through the foggy water meadows, where everything was as velvety as a bat's wing, silent and immobile; people in the last cars could still see the river, the rowboat, the light, but the head of the train had plunged into twilight, into the winged silence of birds circling above the meadows; a few oxbows shimmered, giving off the heat of the day, and it was only these rising mists that showed that *this* light was still here, that the cold of night was not eternal here.

Sensing night, the flowers by the window began folding up their petals; the scent also fell asleep, its discharge ended; the glow of the river, the dark spot of the boat and rower, and the long shadows of the trees remained only in my eyes until I fell asleep. Wherever I looked, everything was blocked by the golden river and the movement of the oars, the world moved into the background, something you remember only through another memory and which moves away like the shore for someone on a boat; and through the water's glow I could see my former life, suddenly very distant and less palpable than the funnels left by the oars on the smoky volcanic glass of the water.

I got off the train early in the morning, dark with rain;

the passengers—and there were quite a few—vanished with amazing deftness. They were just there, coughing, grunting, swearing, with clumsy travel gear, boxes, backpacks, bags, carts, always more than there was room for, traveling hard, in stress, spitting every minute, working their muscles and elbows; they were just getting red in the face, bending over, carrying, dragging, pushing things somewhere, and suddenly there was no one, just a few taxi drivers without passengers smoking by their cars and watching dogs snarl in the empty lot near the station.

I went into the station. Sitting at a table in the café were two policemen and two guys in leather jackets; all four were the same. People who start growing quickly at the age of thirteen or fourteen have faces like that: physical grace cannot keep up with growing muscles and for a year or two the teenager turns into a lout. Their faces still had that expression of adolescent dullness—as if each of them, because of an excess of flesh, felt only with his stomach and penis; the table was covered with plates of shashlik and fried potatoes and a bottle of vodka, the waitress watched from the doorway.

The four sat like gatekeepers of the world I was entering; the waiting room stank of belching, of sour saliva dripping from a snoozing drunk, and then of smoke; people accustomed to sleeping rough—on the floor, on trunks, on the luggage rack of a train car, on dormitory cots, on plank beds in holding cells—lay on the benches, heads covered; everyone was bent over and rolled up for warmth, but it seemed they wanted to look as if they had already been hit, no need to hit them anymore. I knew how to sleep like that—sensing not my heart but my wallet in my sleep; I had slept in worse places, but here, walking through the station, I was still *off the train*, where you're a passenger and think you have some rights—and for the four men at the table I was also a *passenger*: criminal slang is precise in its aphoristic scorn for those who think they are going somewhere and not being taken there.

The bus to town had already left or had not yet come. By the bus stop, painted tires were used for flower beds; I had laid out similar ones on "volunteer Saturdays" in school. I recognized the familiar poverty, the second life of things that substitute for needed objects; flowerbeds made out of tires or upside-down bottles dug into the ground, a feeding bowl out of a cardboard milk packet, ashtrays out of food tins. Born and bred among them, I now wondered: Does that happen only with things? What if my feelings and thoughts are also a forced substitution for something real? What if my love isn't love at all, but another flower bed of tires with spittle-covered marigolds?

A car pulled up to the bus stop; a black Volga with an antenna—someone's driver was making money in the morning. The door opened; the inside of the Volga was like a den: slipcovers of dark, fuzzy, fake fur, tinted windows, everything slightly worn, slightly unclean, smelling stale from the heater; the driver was like that, too—in a wooly vest that left his elbows bare, corduroy trousers, fat, with gold teeth, unshaven, with squinty eyes in the rearview mirror, clearly just barely awake but quick, the kind of guy who likes juggling—flicking a cigarette out of a pack and catching it in his mouth—thinking that was cool; these kind usually become taxi drivers rather than personal chauffeurs, they huddle together meeting trains in small towns, but you think twice before getting into the car. A taxi like that doesn't drive you, it takes you away, and even a familiar road seems slightly unfamiliar; the driver gives off a sense not of danger but of unease—maybe he ran down someone on a rainy night and drove away, maybe he robbed a drunk passenger, maybe he's selling something—and the money he gives you in change will always be ancient, greasy, wrinkled as if it never had a chance to lie in a wallet but kept making the rounds, over and over, folded, crumpled and greedily stuffed into a pocket. The bills—one torn, the second with a drop of blood, the third with some numbers written on it—will also smell of something pathetically forbidden, drunken conspiracies, hangover disputes, called-in debts, the worn oilcloth on a store counter spotted with herring brine; and you will imagine that for half the trip the driver kept deciding whether to drive you where you needed to go or to turn off into an alley or lonely spot you don't know, tell you he has a flat, and see what you do …

The Volga flew up onto the railroad bridge—rail cars, cisterns, floodlights, squat cargo cranes flashed by—and raced down the potholed streets of the city. We had to press ahead, go some thirty kilometers, and arrive in another city, the one in the letter to Grandfather II; this town was low, the farther one arose in the distance with the smokestacks of a mining plant and beyond them gray sloping mounds enveloped in smoke and cumulus clouds.

The forest tundra began outside the city, but there wasn't a single green tree there, only cliffs, stone rubble, and dead tree trunks; the prevailing wind was from the direction of the mining plant, and the smoke from the stacks precipitating with fog and rain had burned and killed every living thing over the decades. There should be no life in these places and they should not be seen—their picture has nothing to do even with the sight of natural catastrophes: just as a criminologist can tell murder from suicide, you can see murder, whether direct or indirect, in landscapes mutilated by humans, you can tell because in nature death is swift and not ugly, while murder done by people is marked by protracted deformity.

Then came warehouses, fences, fences, fences; in the distance there were mountains, night sky, and unfettered expanses, while here everything was fenced, separated by walls; barbed wire covered everything. There were barriers everywhere, warning signs, "no entry" symbols, guard booths and outside them, strays who rushed to bark at the car. Then suddenly, like an abyss, came an empty lot retaining only the start of work—here they excavated a hole, there they abandoned a pipe, there they set up strips of wood to mark out something or other; the lot was as dark as the dirt and you could dig into the darkness with a shovel. The car flew on, and once again there were fences, floodlights, workshops, pipes, smoke, steam, and light—and then another plunge into emptiness. Man defended himself, barricaded himself, he was not master of these lands, and the guard booths were the architectural descendants of prison camp guardhouses; this land was infected with a *fungus*, the fungus of the watchman, and all of this, the fences, wire, barricades, was like a single never-ending shout: "Stop or I'll shoot!"

The car flew and it seemed that we lived on our land like occupiers; that we looked at one another through a prison door peephole; there was music, the singer rasped that all his friends were bulls, fists ready to fight, gun ready to blaze, there was no salvation from the bulls; when the driver switched stations I could see that he had tattoos on his fingers—amateur, pale, perhaps somebody had tried to remove them—and the music, jerky and undisciplined, and the words were strangely suited to the locale. We were racing through a prison camp zone, even though these were not prison factories; the zone was everywhere, its mark was on everything—three rows of barbed wire. It seemed that every object here had to be locked away from thieves, and the locks multiplied, locks, bolts, hasps, the next set of locks, in case the first ones are defeated, and so on; oncoming cars did not turn off their high beams, blinding me, but the driver did not turn away, he was used to it; the gun ready to blaze, no salvation from the bulls, the speakers roared, and we flew, senselessly fast, as if in a hurry to fight with someone, break bones, knock out teeth; the dark, the fences, the empty lots—everything chased after us, everything showed that you could not stop here, in a plague-ridden place, and that gave a sense of daring, a ruthless readiness to live at odds with everything, to chomp onto life like it was a tough piece of meat, with sinews and fur; I had frequently been in such places, but this was the first time I realized that the criminals had won, the camp had beaten the not-camp; the camp was not gone, it had smeared itself into the landscape, cut itself into parts, and each part settled in, changing everything around it, in the milieu of human habitation.

The toys I found in Grandfather II's apartment suited this area very well—faceless figures, rifle, German shepherd, horse; they came from here. A bridge flashed by, the fences were left behind, and the town's narrow streets wound around hills, signs, store windows, kiosks, bus stops, railroad tracks crossed the road several times, beyond the hills factories appeared then disappeared, and the mountains came closer, squashing the town into a hollow, with only one exit, across the bridge we had taken.

To the right appeared another abyss of darkness; but I could make out a big building. The driver explained that this was a train station, that previously commuter trains used to run here, but the branch was abandoned during perestroika and only freight lines were left; the station was unsupervised and there had been a fire. The road twisted up a slope, and the car flew right up to the station; the building was typical, with arches, columns, and very wide windows—a railroad temple from the forties or fifties, an altar of schedules. The fire had merely blackened the walls, and the station had the desecrated majesty of an abandoned church, as if the locals rejected a religion; I could not tell from his tone whether the driver was sorry or on the contrary was proud of the arson, his speech betrayed both.

I came back to the station in the daytime; I had a similar experience only once, in Istanbul by the Golden Gate; I saw what happened to a former crossroads of history, saw how the once-ruined is ruined a second time; at the fortress walls of the former Constantinople, vendors sold cell phone covers, broken kettles, bolts, nuts; here's a defroster (the plastic yellowed by time or smoke), here's a bent microscope, here's a package of syringes. The users of the syringes had moved inside the walls, campfires sent up smoke, ragged bums, who gave off a vibe of cowardice and violence, wandered amid the collapsed battlements.

Depression hits you by the Golden Gate; a new horde, the nomads of the new world, traders in fake leather jackets huddle in the ruins, unable to take them apart completely and build something different; they have grown accustomed to disarray, to accepting crevices in the old walls as living space; to the fact that you can live without looking back at the past and assuming that the shade of ancient walls is convenient shade on a hot day and nothing more.

At the station I saw the same kind of abandoned crossroads, a silt-filled mouth of fate; the city cut off its own path to the outside, destroyed the window to the big world, and now lived like a blinded Cyclops deprived of its train headlight eye. But the station was burned, and the city was forced by the landscape, by the hollow in which it was situated, to shut down on itself; the place exerted a kind of terror against its populace, and people responded in kind: the walls of houses and garages were thickly covered in graffiti, curses addressed to no one in particular but directly at the environment; the scrawls were written over rectangles of fresh paint—the swear words were painted over—abundantly, fluently, and monotonously; evidence of petty revenge—knocked over garbage cans, broken streetlamps and windows, rubbish tossed on the side of the roads—showed that the residents were fighting a partisan war with the town.

Dropping me at the hotel, the driver left, and I started

looking at the ads on the lamppost covered in white drips of glue; most were about apartment sales and exchanges, there were many, and they were glued on in layers, the lamppost was covered with a clustered fringe, and it seemed as if no one was comfortable living here, everyone wanted to change something, move, find a new view from the window even if it's still within the same city limits.

In towns like this above the polar circle, the hotel is called either "North" or "Arktika"—this one was Arktika. These hotels have a special kind of discomfort; most guests are there on business, there are no insouciant vacationers.

Here dreams are laconic, like a still life of a pitcher and two glasses, but you still have to bring dreams, like food for the train, from home. In your room, you find yourself on the unfurnished margin of life. There are too few objects—tray, electric kettle, ashtray—the distance is too great between them, like in the desert, it takes a half day to get from one to the other, and they are all not quite real. In a room like that you can lay out your things, toss a book on the nightstand and cigarettes on the table, but it still feels as if you've stopped in some uninhabited area. All around, as in nature, only monotonous surfaces; out there—hills and valleys, here— horizontals and right angles; it's a kind of new wilderness, a new wildness; the best reading here is a geometry textbook.

The hotel windows opened on a blank wall of the building next door; it was about ten meters to the wall, and there were no curtains—why bother, when the brickwork was so close?

Forced to live with a view of the wall, I read it like a book, the book of the wall. It's good to look at a town from the point of view of buildings; from the point of view of bricks; then you are not an observer, you are one with the spirits of the place. But this wall did not allow me to mentally move into it, it repelled my gaze; the brick was not laid evenly, the lines were crooked, and the wall wavered; all you could learn was how gradually it was laid and how the people worked on the construction.

It seemed to me that the intention to build was missing from their actions; each brick was laid not even automatically but with a thought that was as far from construction as possible—a thought about home or about the evening's pay packet. As a result, you could not say about the wall or the whole house that they were actually built; you could not say that the house was solid on the ground. The wall before me blocked my view but at the same time was not convincing; it seemed that it could collapse at any moment because they had not put in that something that holds a house together along with brick and mortar.

I saw that a great force of compulsion had erected the town, cleared the forest, laid the roads, dug the canals, and built the factories; but it turned out that compulsion is incapable of one thing: the effort a person brings to work freely chosen. Without that effort, without that bit of spiritual labor that merges with physical labor, all the roads, bridges, cities, and factories were held up only by the will of the state that had them built. When that will vanished, when its time has passed, people were left with a legacy of great construction in which spiritually they were not involved; they were left among houses, stations, and streets built under duress.

Sleeping in a room with a view of the wall was good; dreaming was a way of leaving the building. The dreams—the three dreams I had at home—did not come anymore; they could not exist in this hotel room, they were too personal for this commonplace setting; the dreams I had after the train were not even dreams but just preparation, clean sheets of paper for dreaming on which light, unrecognizable shadows flitted; I could not expect more than that for now.

I had decided ahead of time that I would not go looking for the man who wrote to Grandfather II right away; I wanted to see the town first, see its present—and only then disturb its past.

The town was named for a Bolshevik killed in the mid-1930s; the name of the town communicated nothing to the place, or the place to its name. They spoke different languages and avoided each other.

The area's mountains bore names given to them by local ethnic groups; these names left the sensation of raw meat and gnawed bones in your throat; reading a dozen names in a row from the map was like drinking thick blood that was steaming in the cold; the names were redolent of campfire smoke, fish scales, rawhide, canine and human sweat, they were long and the syllables joined up like reindeer or dogs in harness.

The town name—two syllables, with an *sk* ending—gave away its alienness, the Bolshevik's name looked good on a big map of the country where the names of his comrades formed a toponymic constellation, a lifetime and posthumous pantheon, but up close the name seemed ridiculous, a random collection of letters which the residents got used to and considered themselves dwellers of Abracadabra-sk.

All the original foundations of the town lay outside it, first it appeared in a plan, on a map, and only then in the area. No matter how it grew, how it developed, it remained a papier-mâché town. There were houses, stores, streets, trees, intersections, and streetlights—but it was inherently ephemeral; the town existed as long as the ore lasted next to it; of itself, without the ore, it meant nothing. It did not arise at a focus point of historical fates, or at the crossroads of trade and military interests, but near a giant pocket of land from which riches could be mined; it was created according to the will of the regime that moved thousands of workers to the north, it grew out of barracks, temporary huts, and that spirit had not dissipated; stale, uninhabited, the spirit of a new construction, of a workshop, oiled rags, and rotting pipes.

I left the hotel in search of the library; I hoped to read something written by regional historians and then to go find the city museum, if there was one.

It was too dark to read in the library, damp and green; there were flowers everywhere in pots, vines, sharp-leaved plants, and the books seemed to get lost in the jungle; the librarian, who did not see me, walked past with her watering can, and the pots stood as if she was watering books instead of flowers, adding the water of words to old, dried out volumes. The wall calendar was from two years ago; charts with letters—*A, Б, B*—stuck out from the shelves into the aisles, rabbit ears of the alphabet; it was classroom-like, pathetic.

There were no works on the town history in the library; instead, the librarian showed me old editions, prerevolutionary and from the 1920s, with half-erased ex libris inscriptions; books were taken away from those sent here, and that created the first collection for the library.

Local history could be learned only from the newspaper archives. The pages, as fragile as dried seaweed, kept the hieroglyphs of the past's daily news; photographs turned into black-and white underwater photography; you could barely make out a few details—the corner of a house, a man's silhouette, but that was all—through a murky substance, like water at a silty river bottom; the view into the photograph was the view through the glass of a diving suit—you expected a deep-water fish to swim by, a bottom angler with glassy beads on its whiskers. I realized the substance was time, and I was a diver who could speak only to himself—the deep diving suit does not let sound escape.

The newspapers lay before me, but they did not let me inside; they joined up in columns of letters, bristled with names, details, dates, decrees, announcements, and holiday editorials; Dumin's brigade overfulfilled the plan for skidding logs, excavator Rutin got a state award, the separation line was started up in Mine 3a—the newspaper pages reported only ancient news, news, news; news items crowded, chatted, hustled one another, there were so many, as if everything done was done for the sake of creating news, and even better, for creating two or three stories, news that the previous story, just a day later, was obsolete and here is something even newer; the newspaper pages flashed by like an express train you couldn't jump on to from the platform. The surnames and names also flashed by, unless it was an article about some production worker; the thin sheet of paper—a vertical slice of time a micron thick—was stacked with others just like it, the newspaper lay in thick piles, but there was no temporal volume; I needed a book in three dimensions, a book as a collected, repackaged rethinking of time, but no one ever wrote a book about the town. "There isn't enough of us for a book," said the librarian. "We haven't accumulated enough, we're too thin on the ground, too thin."

The library as entrée to the past did not work. The museum was even more hopeless; it was too new, that museum, and its creators were too concerned with having a good, trustworthy past; so the whole thing was a stage set, newly minted: the way restaurants are decorated in "olde time" fashion. In the middle there was a reconstruction of an earthen house in which the first settlers allegedly lived—they called the prisoners "settlers"; the house was made of first-class logs, with glass in the low windows, the roof covered with even sod; this was a historical attraction, an attempt to amend one's genealogy.

A glass case displayed a kettle made out of a can, an explorer's rubber boots chewed up by rats, a rusty lantern, and some other objects, real ones, not fakes, but placed under glass and brightly illuminated, they appeared to be frozen lumps of mud from a tractor rut exhibited in a museum for some reason. The past did not come closer, on the contrary, it was moving away, and the exhibits were presented as evidence of a civilization—earthly or not—to which we now living had no relation; "Look, they also had a life" said the glass cases, and the respectable present, ashamed of the rough past (which is why the earth house was made of the highest-quality wood) showed them in their best light and rushed to announce that the past was in the past and shoved it deeper away, into the stifling sack, the sleeve, the cellar.

Next to the cases representing the history of the town were cases with archeological exhibits; a spoon hand-carved out of wood, a lighter made out of a shell case—and nearby bone arrow and spearheads, sharpened cutting stones, fish bone needles, clay beads; it was strange to see that, despite the difference in intention and materials, both types of objects lagged behind us by an immeasurable period of time and were closer to each other than to us.

The prisoners of the 1930s and 1940s lived in foxholes before they built barracks; the fishermen and hunters of the Neolithic period who left drawings and petroglyphs in the nearby mountains, hunters of the sun and pilots of the moon— they were related by the dark of the cave, where the first rational feeling was pain; and I thought of an old acquaintance, a professor of archaeology who studied Neanderthal culture and was then arrested and sent to the camps.

We met in the region where he had been exiled and later remained; there he studied the history of local tribes inhabiting the long and narrow sandbars in the thousands of kilometers of swamps. In times closer to our own, an epic was being created by people's lives, and big events, wars and revolutions were woven into its pattern and reinterpreted as a mythological scene; Nicholas II, Lenin, and Stalin were turned into heroes of the middle world, Bolsheviks were born out of the ground; battles and clashes reached them like a wave striking a distant shore, the receptive myth reworked them without destroying its own wholeness; the GOERLO plan for national electrification was turned into combat over the sun, collectivization into a clash between the spirits of the land and the spirits of war who destroyed all the fruits of the earth for the work of death.

The professor studied these tribes without scientific detachment, rather, he did not separate his perceptions from those of the people whose minds created the myths; the professor said that he tested the effectiveness and saving power of a mythical perception of reality, turning it into a battle of the ancient polymorphic forces of good and evil, a struggle without distinction of warring sides. In this consciousness, good is not yet separated from evil, they grow out of the same life root and easily flow into each other, they are close and fraternal; for instance, what is really evil is presented as good and what is seen as a victory of good is actually the triumph of evil. This is how the mind protects itself, the professor thought, extending the spectral presence of good through mythology, when facing the totality of evil without the distorting lens of myth would destroy you.

Yet the professor did not forget his prior scientific interests and liked to tell me that since he had been in the few caves with Neanderthal remains and had studied their skeletons in order to establish what the creatures looked like, in the camps he had the feeling he was surrounded by those he thought had become extinct tens of thousands of years ago.

The discovery, in the final years of the professor's life, that Neanderthals were not ancestors of man, but were an independent subspecies and warred with humans, confirmed his unscientific hypothesis, which was nevertheless exact in a different way: the ancient anthropoid races did not vanish, they learned to coexist with humans, grew to look like them, but their cannibalistic nature remained the same; when the human qualities in humans are abused, that nature is revealed and manifests itself: the cannibals openly practice their cannibalism. However, the professor used this hypothesis metaphorically as well: "It's easier this way than accepting that everything I have seen belongs to human nature."

The town also had a geological museum; the main exhibits were the local ores used to make fertilizer and the minerals with rare earth metals.

All were ugly, here was one homely stone and oddly, a whole city, tens of thousands of people, arose just to mine that stone, so ordinary looking; when you look at the minerals cerium or scandium, you understand that they have an admixture of metals that are extremely expensive, but their value is profoundly conceptual.

Of course, you are judging like an ordinary person expecting an obvious depiction of value that would justify the massive expenditures—processing plants, quarries, mines—but at the same time there is something very true in the ordinary view; it was telling you that labor here has a specific meaning and there is no point in judging it by its fruits.

Even coal extracted from a mine is a compressed form of the fierce sun of the Jurassic period, the sun of gigantic creatures and vegetation, it remembers the shimmer of scaly skin, the heat of the sun that was younger by hundreds of millions of years, coal—and there is a reason why heat and food is calculated in calories—seems to be the food of fire, and the ancient respect for fire makes coal the bread of flames, a significant presence in the business of life. The rocks and minerals in the museum did not speak to the heart, they could become valuable only in a chain of chemical transformations, traveling along several conveyor belts, and it seemed that a miner who cut out a rock like that with his jackhammer should ask himself why he's done so and should have to persuade himself that his work has meaning and is useful—for the distance is too great between a piece of gray dull rock and the extraction of a useful substance.

After the library and museums I decided after all to visit the street where the man who wrote to Grandfather II lived; not drop in on him, not ask about him, just walk down the street, as if by chance; bring the future a little closer, but not enter it; see what that man sees—or saw—every day, his store, his tobacco kiosk, his bus stop, his front door; take a good look—for now as a casual stroller—at the street that would irreversibly become *that* street, look at it freely as one of many streets, and maybe it would tell me something, warn me.

I wanted to ask for a map at the newspaper counter, but realized that the town did not need to see itself from the outside; they would hardly publish a map here, it was all known, all the corners, intersections, alleys, and courtyards; people don't look at maps here, they ask the way; and so did I.

No one knew the street indicated in the letter; people tried to remember, stopped others, one even called home—there was no such street; of course, it wasn't hard to get mixed up: it was called Red Kolkhoz Street, and the town had many other streets with red in the name: Red Army, Red Partisans, Red Lighthouse, Red Dawn; none of them had anything to do—by name—with the locale, creating a parallel system of ideological cosmogony in which Red Dawns rose above the country and the Red Lighthouse lit the way for the Red Partisans for some reason; people were trapped in this net of non-reality, and they lived in it, pronouncing the names and extending the existence of this hassle. I remembered a village outside Moscow where I was visiting friends in their dacha and I awoke in the morning with the horrible realization that I was in a place called Lenin's Precepts, and the very possibility of living there, of saying "We live in the Precepts" or "The population of the Precepts,"—it was detrimental to sanity to live in something that was doubly fictitious because Lenin never left any precepts. Now I was dealing with the topography of an entire town that was deprived of its own voice, drawn on a grid, and the streets intersected like footnotes in articles of the latest mythological dictionary.

At last someone recalled that Red Kolkhoz Street had existed but then the old buildings were razed, they were some of the first built in the town, and the Rainbow neighborhood was created, and the street was now called First Rainbow.

Hoping that maybe Grandfather II's correspondent had been given an apartment in one of the new buildings, I went to First Rainbow. They were multistoried houses painted in bright colors copying one of the big northern cities; orange, pink, and violet nine-story buildings. They were no longer new—it was fifteen or twenty years later, but the cheerful colors denied the possibility of a man from the past choosing to live here; there were no old people in the courtyards, they apparently did not manage to live here among walls the color of fruit-flavored gum.

For this place, the local past did not exist; the residents were not miners but factory managers, they had forced out the former owners on Red Kolkhoz Street and planned their own, separate neighborhood free of mine dust, and the times were such that you could change the name from the straw and manure Red Kolkhoz to Rainbow. Actually, you could gauge the attitude toward the past by the name change: moving into new apartments—this was during perestroika—people were moving into the future, they called it Rainbow, and even though they couldn't get paint in the entire rainbow spectrum, they could set themselves apart, legalize their caste, and probably no one saw that the neighborhood looked like a dollhouse in a filthy wasteland.

Beyond the last buildings there was one more, a village house, low, its shingles blue-gray with lichen; it had not been torn down for some reason. I went there—the house was from former times, it was the same age as the letters that were dropped into a mailbox around here by the man who wrote to

Grandfather II.

An old woman was hilling potatoes in the garden; there are old woman like that—eighty, ninety years old, who lost their husbands a long time ago at war or in the mines, so long ago that others manage to live an entire life, from birth to death, in that period of time. The past—marriage, motherhood—is so distant that either the person or the past has to die, and if the person lives, the past dies. These old women are a special breed—they don't get tired, life to them is a daily chore—dig, water, hill, weed; they harness themselves habitually and probably only for themselves, without hope, without expectation, without haste. After all, you get tired when the work is hard and rest is far away, but they truly do not understand the meaning of rest, and no work is hard for them because in order to sense its difficulty you have to know the meaning of idleness, which they have never experienced. They are not inspired to work—people like that eventually tire; they work like abstract forces in textbooks—they press, haul, accelerate, move; there is horsepower and there is human power—and that power alone is what keeps them alive.

I said hello; the old woman yelled at me to go away—she wasn't going to sell the house. I replied that I didn't need the house, I was looking for the people who lived here twenty years ago, before the new neighborhood. She unlatched the gate and led me into the house; she didn't quite believe me and kept expecting me to start talking about buying, to name a sum, but there was something else as well that made her mood change so readily.

The house was a kingdom of hand-knit rugs, coverlets, and curtains: a sewing machine, an old Singer, stood in a prominent place and it seemed that the old woman had gotten a magical spool with never-ending thread; she sewed, spun, knitted, and never ran out of thread, and she did not know what to do with it, but she was afraid to turn off the machine and spindle or put down her knitting needles: What if the thread was her life?

A framed newspaper clipping hung on the wall, wreathed in paper flowers, an atheist shrine; that clipping—the woman started telling me about it—determined her fate. There she was in the photo, a young weaver, the only one in the entire town to have ever personally seen the Bolshevik in whose honor the town was named, and she was even photographed with him; he received a delegation of shock worker weavers and they brought her, a girl, as an example of youth labor; then the Bolshevik was killed, and she moved to the place bearing his name—and in this town the newspaper clipping served to ensure her well-being. While the town bore that name, the authorities—both Soviet and the ones who came after—took good care of her; the old woman—I was told this later—gave talks about the Bolshevik in schools and kindergartens, at municipal meetings and anniversaries; her own life was insignificant, she had become something like a film strip or a gramophone recording that captured the image and voice of the deceased; she did not embroider or invent things; she toiled as an eyewitness.

Yet no one thought to find out how she felt about the man for whose posthumous existence she had stifled her own life; it was only much later, in the new times, that they learned he had sent her parents to the camps; but she had continued talking about him, witnessing those eight minutes she had been next to him; first the newspaper clipping saved her from being sent away and turned her into a visual aid for schoolchildren; then she became an eight-minute segment of newsreel, and then she no longer could change.

Telling me about her past life, she spoke as if she sensed the time was coming when her newspaper clipping would mean nothing, no matter what the town used to be called; her house was standing thanks to that clipping, she was the only one who hadn't been moved out of Red Kolkhoz Street, and now the framed newspaper wreathed in flowers looked more like an idol of a forgotten deity; the face, the font—they were all too long ago and it kept moving away, not forgotten but losing its meaning, turning into a curiosity, and if people learned that she had seen the man for whom the town was named, they were only surprised that she was still alive.

When she heard I was looking for someone, the old woman hoped I would bring changes, that an old relationship would be rekindled, time would turn back; but seeing that my interest was not in that, she seemed to regret letting me in; she said only that people from Red Kolkhoz Street were resettled in various places, these had been the oldest buildings in the town, and some had gotten good apartments in the center, in the Stalinist houses; apparently the managers of the factory had enough power to move out the former owners but had to humor the former higher officers of the camp guards; basically, that was the plan—to divide the town's past from the town's present, to separate so that it would be easier for some to forget the others.

I asked her some more about the town, where I could look for the people who moved, what they lived on now; the old woman told me to go the quarry—I would understand everything there, about the people who moved and the ones who didn't; the quarry for her was an answer that obviated the very possibility of a question.

She, a former weaver, the guardian of someone else's memory, who had lived a life different from the rest, protected by the newspaper clipping on the wall, replied as if I had asked her where her peers where, where her husband and children were and whether she had had any; where was her generation, what had it left behind, where were the survivors, the last ones, what could they tell me; "Go to the quarry," she said and closed the door, then bolted it.

I walked through town again; I was just strolling, keeping the general direction in mind, and realized something I had noted but had no words to describe: the town was planned for people walking in columns and turning at right angles; a single person, a single dweller with irregular routes was apparently too minor for the planners' focus, they lacked the vision to see the human figure through the plan; as a result, the city was divided up by plants and factories and the person—an ordinary person—seemed to be there illegally.

I saw how "zones," walled off by fences and barbed wire, whether a prison camp or a closed, restricted enterprise, entered the public and private space and distorted it. In essence, the town as town did not exist—there was a territory on which private interests were permitted selectively, stores, schools, nurseries, but this was a necessary concession; things were not intended for humans here, and thus the locale resembled a beam chewed up by a wood borer; everything was illegal, crooked, roundabout, and under the table; cut this corner, move this board, go through the dump; across the lot, in the hole in the fence, and back alleys, alleys, alleys.

You couldn't get to the quarry just like that, it was guarded—including against people like me, simple gawkers, who could be hurt in a blast; but the higher the fences and the more guards, the more varied the loopholes; I didn't even have to search—any spot used frequently gives itself away, by a path leading to it, or clothing wrapped around bars that are just a little wider apart so that a person can squeeze through; or by signs of useless fortification, soldered strips of metal, piles of concrete beams, "no entry" signs; but there was a path that disappeared inside the labyrinth of beams; these people who erected these barriers also lacked vision with the correct resolving power, so there was always a crack—sidle in, losing buttons, pull yourself up, and get through somehow.

I met tramps collecting metal; old men going into the

tundra for mushrooms—the road to the best mushroom places crossed the quarry; workers who had hidden something on their shift and now were back to retrieve it; kids—they were on their way to play at war; a couple looking for a trysting spot; they all squeezed in habitually, clambered, pushed, dragging in a basket or some bottles; the tramps were hauling a spool of wire; I used their path into the quarry.

I had seen quarries like this in Kazakhstan; but there it was hot, the air over the enormous pit boiled, turned white and opaque, and even the sound of the blasts were drowned, muffled by it. Here in the North, the pit opened all of itself at once, pulling you inside, into the five hundred-meter depth; the quarry was a mirror reflection—in terms of the earth's surface—of the Tower of Babel, molded out of emptiness; the spirals of the quarry road, circling down from level to level, went to the bottom, so deep and narrow compared to the top of the quarry cut that there were only a few hours of sunlight a day down there.

The gray quarry cliffs were covered by a coat of very fine stone dust that had been wetted and then dried; this coating, with pulverized minerals weakly reflecting the sun, gave the quarry this color; dust covered the dump trucks, huge Belazes, excavators with toothed jaws; here, where there was no soil but only solid rock, the sophisticated human mind discovered its predatory nature; the technology was ready to bite, chew, dig in, crumple, blow up; this mind—I thought of the museum—was close to the mind of the Neanderthal but on a new spiral of development; a mind that combined the jaws of a saber-toothed tiger, neck of a giraffe, and body of a woolly mammoth to create a hybrid, the excavator with gaping jaw; a mind motivated by an insatiable, hopeless desire to devour.

My brain refused to recognize this five hundred-meter hole in the ground, these stalking excavators that embodied the stupid assiduousness of metal, as the work of humans. They must have been created by semirational animals or insects who preferred scale to accuracy or grace; creatures that did not know individuality and functioned only in quantity. The gigantic hole and the enormous trucks had a challenging but unarticulated manifesto, a heavy symbol; the practical meaning—extracting ore—took a backseat in this picture: human effort multiplied by mechanical power created inhuman effort and the quarry showed the volume and measure of that effort.

There must be proportions that keep things made by human hands commensurate with man and when violated turn those things against him. It was not that you feel like a grain of sand or a dust mote at the quarry. The violation of the principle of proportionality separates people from what they are doing; it deprives them of significance in terms of labor. In fact, labor as such vanishes, if we understand it as a living connection between the worker and the result of his work, a connection that is mutually enriching and ennobling.

The quarry boomed, thundered, and clanged metallically; the dump trucks and bulldozers bellowed, diesel exhaust floated in the air, water pumps rumbled; but the result was ephemeral: tons and percentages, units of measure.

The whole city—streets, windows, bread and vegetables on a counter—was covered with a coating of gray quarry dust, giving it an aspect of death, like the cheap powder at the morgue, for the excessive scale of labor here left its trace on the residents.

This was particularly noticeable in late August, on Miners Day. The whole city drank; they drank without abandon, ardor, zeal or the ordinary pleasure of drunkards. Time, as colorless as vodka, twisted like a filament in a bottle; the colorless day hung horribly, unnaturally long. Colorless people lay in the streets and others walked past; the connection of words fell apart, the alphabet fell apart, and people shouted and muttered vowels, clumps of words; the collapse of reason manifested in those sounds reached a peak. Then the final last silence settled over the town.

On the day meant to celebrate their work, their labor, people vented on themselves what they couldn't vent at the quarry, workshops, and pipes; on the day of legal and even approved drunkenness people felt an outburst of definite, collected, and predetermined self-destruction; this kind of suicide is not tried by healthy people but by legless cripples already a third dead—they only need to kill two-thirds of themselves, death had done part of its work, and they set to it with determination and facility, knowing that the mortal path is a third shorter.

This was the ultimate rebellion, stifled almost in embryo; dozens of kilometers of tracks, hangars, pipe, factories, precipitation lakes, the quarry, the transporters of enrichment plants—it surrounded and divided up the city, it looked like a car after an accident in which living flesh is squashed and mutilated by metal. Only the quarry kept increasing, growing in width and depth, and all their labor went to using their own lives, the effort of the muscles, and the wear on their hearts to magnify the gaping hole in the ground. This was the most monstrous part—the extracted ore was broken up, turned into fertilizer, freight trains took it south—because what they saw, continually, daily, was the growing hole sucking up their work.

The slopes of the mountains around the quarry had been blown up and it was called the "avalanche zone." You could see the thrusting chunks of cliff flesh from every point in the town, the twisted, unnaturally smashed rock, moved by the centrifugal energy of the blasts; the avalanche zone took up three sides of the city horizon, the blown-up cliffs huddled on the slopes as if beyond the point of equilibrium, frozen in midfall.

There are pictures, a combination of lines and angles,

that humans should not see: looking at them is like chewing ground glass to see what flavor it is; they painfully damage the sensory foci of perception; the view of the avalanche zone was one such picture. The world after a catastrophe; the world cracked open, disjointed, with no possibility of bringing it together again; I was amazed to understand that the raw material extracted from the quarry is for fertilizer which is then sprinkled on fields; I saw the joyless cereals growing on those fields—as if sprinkled with ash from a crematorium.

The gray bread of my childhood, the loaves of bread on the bakery counters, people lining up an hour before opening, the line darker than twilight; women in gray scarves, men in gray coats, faces gray with lack of sleep, and the gray salted urban snow; I understood now where that bread had come from, delivered in vans that looked like Black Marias; where that ubiquitous gray came from—not in a belittling sense but grayness as the absence of color or as the color of dust.

You stood at the quarry edge and told yourself this is how hell looks; but the image of hell, the circles of hell marked by the spirals of the quarry road, came from culture; you were using it to save yourself from what could barely be described in artistic language, because the quarry was an anti-image, the negation of imagery as such.

It was *gaping*; they say a gaping wound, and if you can move away from the details of the flesh you can see in a wound not the outline, not the shape, but the incursion of destructive shapelessness.

The quarry sucked up your gaze, where it was lost; it encountered nothing but emptiness, traces of the work of emptying; it was impossible to deal with the absurd, to let your mind think about the *volume of absence*.

Something was done in this place that should not be done; some line was crossed that should not be crossed in human nature—the hole of the quarry gathered the city around itself, pulled in the region.

The view of the quarry materialized the hopelessness of life, verging on despair, translated this sensation into a visual one, existing in the world as a thing; the quarry did not threaten to swallow up anything, did not beckon with fatality, it simply was—in the dull steadiness of a hole, the most immutable thing, and that man is transient compared to its immutability was almost unbearable.

I left the quarry, but I could have stayed; distances meant nothing here. The quarry was carved into my consciousness; before I did not know how the human world looked without humans; now I knew.

At the bus stop—a shift had just ended—I heard that the rock in the quarry was deteriorating with every year; they were working with an ore content per ton that would have been considered without prospect in the past.

This was another point of view—the impoverishment of the rock, the impoverishment of the urban environment, as if the two processes were connected, not directly, but connected. Old theater posters hung at the bus stop, two months old, and no one was putting up new ones; the city was as washed out as these posters and had nothing fresh on offer; its fate was covertly intertwined with the basic activity of the residents—extracting ore in the quarry in the mine that opened veins leading away from the main mass of ore. The rock was being depleted, and the city was being depleted, for it functioned as a factory, unable to create an urban environment on its own, and people were lost within it.

It was evening; I walked along the outskirts of the town, past warehouses and garages, built close together, clinging to the neighboring wall, as if the building would fall down without it. There were rubbish heaps and packs of stray dogs, shaggy, with dried mud and burdock in their fur; each garage and each shed was built differently, but they had one thing in common: the garage and the shed were built while looking over the shoulder, with an uncertainty, with a sense that the construction was not quite legal—did you have to get permission or could you get away with it; and the sensation that the building did not quite trust the ground on which it stood combined with another sensation: that all the construction materials had been either blatantly stolen or picked up along the way. The combination of the two sensations created a third—the sensation of a life that did not look at itself, that had shrugged itself off.

The garages and sheds had been built thirty or forty years ago; the five-story buildings of the town had moved right up close to them, and the balconies on their facades—as if by an airborne architectural virus—had turned into the same dilapidated sheds, slapped together and glassed in sloppily; the houses had looked at the sheds for so long they took on their features; people lived in the concrete boxes as best they could and they increased their living space by an extra forty-three square meters, and those balconies poking out of the building facade presented a pathetic, almost illegal private life, ubiquitous and unseen, like mold; life resembling something base, self-sowing, all-penetrating.

People here bought cars to have a garage; in a city that did not know about beaches, in a city you could cross on foot in an hour, a car was just a form of winter clothing, fur-on-wheels. The crowded apartments, where men's clothes and women's clothes had to squeeze into a single closet, where everything was dual purpose, served two functions, like a double bed, and every spot always had more than one person—the crowded apartments got additional space with the garage, something that in the general asexuality of life, with the exception of the kitchen, had a gender specificity. Men visited one another in the garage; the garage was storage for everything that would not fit in the apartment, it was storeroom and cellar, for potatoes and pickling; a creature of the housing deficit, an appendix of lifestyle—a garage, a shed.

The town's five-story apartment houses were ugly in their anonymous similarity, while the garages stunned you with a different ugliness; monotonous and extremely functional—walls, roof, door, that is, simply useful cubic meters—they still differed a bit; every builder tried to create a distinguishing detail: make it stand out, different from the others, add a stovepipe, bending it a special way, attach a small overhang above the door, weld an iron corner over the lock so the lugs couldn't be broken—and these small changes became unbearably noticeable. Accumulating in your view, they repeated as attempts to be different somehow, with no possibility of doing so. I sensed that boredom was more usual here than yearning, because yearning refers to something that does not exist in a given life, while boredom asserts that there is nothing to yearn for: there is nothing anywhere, every place is the same as here.

I grew up in place just like this; it had a glue factory, and trucks from the slaughterhouse, carrying bones covered with a red-stained tarp, drove there along a pot-holed road. The trucks bounced, bones fell out, and all along the road dogs lay in the bushes waiting for a windfall; sometimes a clumsy old dog, perhaps wounded in the melee, slipped and fell under the wheels; dark wet tracks remained on the asphalt.

In the winter, the trucks going to the factory were joined by others, carrying snow to the melting station, which was under our windows; snow fell, now was beautiful—but there, behind the fence of the snow-melting station, it lay dirty and splotchy, piled up like defective hides at a slaughterhouse, and all winter I watched the absurd transport of snow to be melted, another sign of quiet, habitual madness.

Trucks carried snow, trucks carried bones, dogs, which lived in the winter by the snow-melting boilers, watched for the trucks, and everything around was waiting for something.

This anticipation, like a secret ballot, selected two genii loci, two of its permanent residents.

The old woman who came to the store with her old cat in a purse and showed him—as people came out of the store with their purchases—what she could have fed him if they increased her pension; and the old man who collected bottles in the morning and then used the kopecks he got for the movies, watching the same film a dozen times; everyone waited, everyone hoped silently; having read a lot of spy novels I hoped that a plane would accidentally drop a bundle with clothing, money, gun, and documents, a package with a different fate.

There were a lot of poplars in the area, and in the summer the wind chased balls of dusty gray fluff along the sidewalks; later, in the Kazakhstan desert, I saw balls of tumbleweed and I learned that the infinity of boredom was the indifferent repetition of life. I understood that I had experienced that sensation before—it was the background of my childhood: trucks with bones, trucks with snow, stray dogs by the road, clumps of fluff in the gutter, carried by the wind.

It wasn't that nothing new ever happened in the neighborhood of my childhood; worse was that there was nothing old in it: its houses, built to depopulate the dormitories, communal flats, and rooms with eight people in eight square meters, started falling apart the moment they were built; they lacked the dignity of age. Life did not expand, it limped along, going nowhere.

Now in this northern town, it was like returning to my childhood; I recognized the twisted backyards, delineated by laundry, the roofs over domino tables, the sandboxes—and right there, the garages and sheds; everything was so mixed up and stuck together, growing into one another, that I thought: it's no wonder that the most attractive place of my childhood was the shooting gallery—a blue trailer behind the movie theater. There was always a long line, and from the number of people waiting—five kopecks a shot, moving targets attached to the ceiling, rabbits, boars, and wolves—you could guess that the shooting gallery served a special need; people lived among fences, alleys, dead ends, and went to the gallery for a gulp of straight shooting, to see the clarity of the goal.

I went back once to my old place, where I had not been for over twenty years. Streets, houses, yards—everything seemed extremely small and miserable; you could imagine that I had grown up and what had seemed enormous to me was now in its normal size. But that explanation left something out, it was based on dry mathematical calculation; I thought that sometimes a child is forced to see not the geometry of space that exists but the one he creates in his gaze, increasing perspective, adding volume where it does not exist in reality.

I realized that I simply could not have lived as a child in that courtyard, among those houses—they were too spiritually and visually insignificant even for a nine-year-old, and the exaggerated metamorphosis that I imposed on them was a question of salvation and self-preservation.

I walked past sheds and garages; I needed to find out, to see the town from the inside out, walk the paths and tracks that its residents used, to re-create the drawing of their movements— that is how a place becomes familiar; on Friday nights they drank at the garages, spreading a newspaper on the hood of a car or on a crate; there was music— persistent music that I had already heard in the taxi; its essence wasn't in the melody but in the cheap voices, male and female.

Cheap voices—men and women sang about love, separation, meetings, long sentences, prison, they sang as if the night before moving they'd heaped everything into a single pile without separating the rubbish from the essential. People drank and ate to those voices, cooking shashlik somewhere;

the garages and sheds came to an end, the trampled thin woodland began, and on every meadow a bonfire burned.

And suddenly, in the woods, I heard different voices—people conversing, how much to pour into whose glass, who wants the hotdog, give me a light, and this simple conversation was without the empty intonations that pretend to add some meaning.

I turned from the road and saw five men sitting on logs. One, quite old, sliced up a sausage and then stuck the knife in his leg—no one winced, they all knew it was wooden; another, also an old man, sat aloofly, leaning on a stick made out of a bus handrail, bicycle reflectors sewn onto his faded overalls; the third, with a scar across his whole face covered with rough stubble, was pouring vodka into the glasses, the fourth I saw only from the back and he sat too still, as if paralyzed, and the fifth, on the contrary, was shaking, a subcutaneous tic ran all over his body, and his features winked at one another, made faces, and his left eyebrow teased the right.

You could see their miners' past in them; the horizon, or plane, is a work term for a miner; in order to reach the horizon—one of many—you have to go down into the mine, and often miners work on a single horizon for decades, limited for them by the end of the pit face; their horizon is a dead end, and people fight the rock in that dead end, but it merely retreats without ceasing to be a dead end, and labor in the pit face—even if the ore is hauled up to the surface—is labor that has no exit in itself.

The horizon of life, underground, dark, the daily descent into the mountain strata, where it is already warm from the heat of the depths, a descent along a long vertical; the people working in mines seem to hold the sky on their shoulders; the body remembers the pressure of the stone strata sensed by the spinal cord. Heavy muscles, heavy tread—they are like lead and platinum in the table of elements, they are compressed by pressure, they are nurtured by darkness. Underground walkers, receiving a miner's headlight sturdier than a human body every twenty-four hours from the lamp room—they were people who live in two worlds, this one and that one, people whose daily path on the ground is shorter than their path under the ground—the side drifts are often several kilometers long, and the miners walk beneath their houses, the city, the suburbs, walk though stone, where there are only the mole tunnels of the drifts and the vertical conduit of the mine shaft—its throat, the only way up.

All five had been miners, laborers of the underground; all five had been in accidents at different times. Now they stuck together—half-crippled, too strong to die; the mine tossed them out like slag, but there was enough power in their bodies for a long life—life after the collapse—and they gathered here in the woods, where they could see the quarry, the mine yard, the building of the shaft, the waste banks and refuse heaps; it seemed that the mine attracted them, lured them to this place.

They noticed me and asked for cigarettes; I gave them mine and they offered me a drink. The vodka slid down to my stomach like a warm slug; they asked me who I was and where from—without curiosity, I had two legs and not one; I told them I was searching for at least a trace of a man who was long gone—and named Grandfather II.

They were silent, the combination of letters did not move or upset them. Of course, I did not expect random people in the woods near the city limits to know Grandfather II's biography, that the mystery of his life would be solved so easily; however, I kept still: for the first time it occurred to me that perhaps it was no longer possible to learn something about Grandfather II, that I was the only person who had part of the information about him and the rest was lost for good, dissolved, or else existed without any connection to him, for example, just as objects who knows from where, things among things; a photograph in somebody's dresser drawer, a book on a shelf, a cup in the cupboard and no force of will, no insight could combine them, make them recognize one another and give evidence.

I said nothing; they asked me what I wanted with this man who had died so reliably and so long ago, who was I?— grandson, great-grandson, distant relative, journalist, just curious? I replied that I hoped to understand what I wanted with him when I learned something about him; I repeated Grandfather II's full name—out of hopelessness, because I saw myself then: behind the garages, among the thin birches, with a view of the mine, in a random place with chance acquaintances, at the end of a cul-de-sac; the man with the scar called to the legless one—try to remember, you know everything; try!

The legless man seemed to wake up and gave him a sly look: first you tell me to forget everything and now I have to remember; the others began persuading him—it looked as if this was a favorite pastime, like spinning a top on a map to see where it lands, asking him to recall something, feeding their general interest which found no nourishment in their quotidian lives.

As I later learned, the old man with the wooden leg was in charge of the mining office archives. "The archive is like the pit," he told me, "except there's paper instead of rock." Every ton of ore extracted from the quarry and mine gave birth to numbers, ore demanded ink for the typewriters—and paper; pages of maps, work plans, reports, transcripts of thousands of meetings and thousands of committees settled in the archive, thickening, baking over the decades into boulders of paper; people rarely looked into the pages, but regulations required they be kept, and paper took up most of the room in the archive basement, the paths among cupboards and shelves narrowed, the light from the ceiling lamps could no longer reach the lower shelves or distant corners; the archive really did resemble a mine.

The head of the archive received new documents once a quarter and the rest of the time he waged war against rats; the rats, apparently attracted by the smell of decomposing paper, crawled into the basement through pipes, chewed through wooden covers and doors, tried to jump into the pocket of his overalls when he went down from the common space to his work corner; the rats must have been lured by the warmth of the basement, the warmth of paper scraps, so good for creating a nest and bringing up baby rats, but they seemed to hate paper. Creatures of disasters and sorrows, wars and revolutions, creatures of the timeless times, they sensed that the archive was a warehouse of the past, even if the past was only data on ore excavation, and they tried to destroy, befoul, and shred the paper and bring up equally gluttonous progeny.

The old man blocked entries with concrete, sprinkled poison in corners, set up homemade traps; he was afraid—said the miner with the scar, laughing—that the rats would chew his wooden leg if he fell asleep in the basement and would never be able to get back upstairs. But that was a funny fear, and the old man laughed, too—the battle with rats gave meaning to his life and maybe the other envied him. Upstairs, in the mining offices, there were engineers, geologists, surveyors, management; they passed around test ore, argued about spare parts for the Belazes, ordered carloads of explosives, made plans, and drew schemata—while below in the basement a mining engineer with a wooden leg, caught once in a mine collapse, was fighting off rat attacks, and he believed that the upper floors stood only thanks to his struggles. The administration building was set on a foundation of paper, and the old man who retained the reverence for paper that came from the olden days when it was a rarity, no matter what was written on it, and its appearance in some village almost meant a change in destiny—the old man, who knew the value of income and expenditure, selflessly protected the archive; the stamps, signatures, the lines of extractions let you re-create the architectonics of fates and the march of time.

I told the old man Grandfather II's surname again; he pondered, as if trying to remember on which shelf the documents could be.

"He was the warden of the camp," the old man said after a pause. "There was no town here yet, just the camp, the quarry, and the mine. He was in charge of it all. Fifteen thousand people. Two thousand guards and employees, the rest were prisoners. He was in charge for a long time, around ten years, from the first barracks to the first houses. Then something happened to him, I don't remember what. I wasn't there, I know this from documents and stories. I have very few papers from that time, they are all kept by the ministries."

"They called me in *there* once," he added with a snigger. "They needed some reference about the factory. You know what's *there*? The same kind of archive as mine, just bigger. Massive deposits of paper. It lives a long time, paper. And they sit there, pulling their dirty tricks, not human beings, just identification badges, but there they sit on that paper, on old files."

I remembered that building; the town had secret manufacturing plants, and that's why there was a branch of *that* organization; I hadn't gone there to ask about Grandfather II. The building was in the Constructivist style—a gray cube with an inner courtyard and a rectangular hanging arch; the cube seemed to be endowed with a special unloving life, and if it were fed, the building would grow, expanding to the size of the House on the Embankment, the warehouse of fates in Moscow, and then it would give birth to smaller cubes. There was something about that house, with its small inner courtyard shut by cast iron barred gates—something that exuded both prison and crematorium at the same time, two places where a person no longer belonged to himself; but that was the architecture speaking, the intention of previous times, but now—the old man was right—the building's strength was only in the paper stored inside it.

Of course, now, two decades since the former regime had ended, there was nothing shockingly new among the files in the cardboard folders; but the point was that none of the cases had seen the light of a uniquely precise moment of history, at the only time when they could have changed anything; not necessarily, in fact probably not, but still it was possible. But now it was only dead paper; no demonic spirit, no aura of horror surrounded the office—just dead paper; the archives held what was left of people, there were pages with sentences, and the office even let you look at them, let you make photocopies, but kept the actual papers as collateral; even in death the office controlled those people, otherworldly serfs; the office turned out to be—without irony—the only owner of the assembly of souls.

All five former miners looked at me; now I couldn't just up and leave, even if I had wanted to. What had happened to them—accidents, wounds, the life of a cripple—had happened to me; it was no longer the fact that the blood of Grandfather II who had started this place was in my blood; I had come here to rid myself of the shadow of Grandfather II, had come with an approximate idea of what I would learn, even though I had not imagined that Grandfather II was warden of a prison camp; I had come with an inner isolation from the place and its people and I had regarded the residents here only from one angle: what they could tell me. But here was the hellish hole in the ground and cripples damaged by a mine collapse, and I couldn't learn anything dispassionately, first I had to reply to the question of who I was, before asking about Grandfather II; I had to stand beneath a mine collapse, call it down on myself, stay here—and only then something would be revealed to me, because I would become part of what was revealed.

In the morning—for I spent the evening there in the woods, going out for a bottle a few times as the youngest one, drank, and listened to stories of how the mine grew and the quarry expanded—I went to look for the new address of the man who had written to Grandfather II. On the street someone told me that the city had a lost and found office, which included an address bureau.

It was located in an old pump house; red brick with a pointy tin roof painted dark green, the pump house had been built by the steam engine depot, where there were garages now, and the water tower was given to the police for some reason. With narrow windows and brick crenellations, it looked like a fortress tower lost in geography. Inside it was cold—the cold water from the deep well had seeped into the bricks.

The lost and found office and the address bureau were run by one man—a police captain with the manner of a pickpocket, skinny, tall, all cartilage and fluidity, unable to sit still, able to be in two or three places at once; he did well among the lost wallets and long narrow drawers with address cards: the town lost things, people got lost in the town, and they came to him with every loss, and he sat there looking as if he had stolen the items, had lured away a person, and then, befitting his job, was also involved in the search.

The captain led me down a spiral staircase to the former pump room; now it was a storeroom for items and address files. Along the way he managed to complain that the lost and found wasn't what it used to be—pronouncing "lost and found" with a special intonation; before, the captain said, people turned in more, whatever they found in the street, but now they would turn in a purse only if they'd found it on a bus and had called in the police to check whether it was a bomb; otherwise, nobody turned anything in.

Of course, the captain was exaggerating: we walked past piles of unclaimed items, dusty bundles, gutted wallets, attaché cases, ladies' bags; I saw cosmetic bags, a roll of roofing felt, a picnic cooler, drafting tools, baby carriages, downhill skis and even ice skates; a plastic horse on wheels, milk cans, pails, carts, a bag of cement. It looked like the antechamber of the world to come, which people reached after a long journey, accumulating stuff as they went, and then had to leave it all here. The objects stood there, huddled in bunches like sheep without a shepherd, and it seemed that if anyone whistled to them, the carriages and carts would roll on their own and the rest of the stuff would climb in, and the canes and crutches would hobble and the skis would slide. The things were afraid: they were abandoned and now, aged and old-fashioned, they didn't know what would happen to them; I saw the captain with fresh eyes: Did he understand what service he was doing? The losses of the entire city were gathered here and there was something bitter in the fact that they were unnoticed; it was easier to accept, to just pay no mind to the loss, even though the lost items could be found and returned.

While the captain rummaged in the drawers for the address of Grandfather II's correspondent—if still alive—I thought about those things; once, when I was with a woman, I realized that we were both tired people who looked with pity upon our own bodies, and our embrace had a taste of that pity; we had lived so long that the only object from the past we had was the body: another city, another apartment—the body lives longer than contemporary objects made to be replaced. I wanted so much to tell it: here we are all alone, pal; here we are alone … I thought about things and the loneliness of man among them; of the fact that a person can be described as a selection of his important objects—but when someone else comes to this selection, what is he going to do? Create a puzzle out of a wristwatch, a cigarette case engraved *From your coworkers*, a wedding ring, and a validated ticket? And here I stand among lost objects when all I need is a person—one who might know and remember; I do not trust objects.

The captain told me the address; the person I sought had moved from Red Kolkhoz Street. Then he suggested I take a look at the finds—if I liked something, I could buy it; sort of like a pawnshop, said the captain. I said no; he kept trying to interest me in a fishing rod left on a bus; he spun the gilt-edged lure and triple hook, showing me how the fish would swallow it; the pole was pathetic, homemade, but the captain took that into account, making up a story about how tackle that doesn't look like much is really the best; the captain was a bullshitter, he spent the day among rubbish, trying to sell it and waiting for success—what if some fool brings him something truly valuable; at the door we ran into the next visitor with something under his arm; the captain bustled and rushed me out the door, these were probably stolen goods for sale. I gave the captain some money, he perked up and stopped rushing me, the money received as a bribe equalized me with the rest of his visitors and created a relationship—I gave, he took—and he probably wanted to introduce me to the petty thief, out of boredom, to see what would happen.

It was sunny. The city authorities had started the fountains six weeks late and the pipes were not yet cleared; rusty, murky water rose to the sky; I bought an ice cream and then the captain caught up with me. "Lunch," he said. "Shall we have lunch?"

We went to a café; over lunch the captain asked me in a seemingly confused way but actually quite cautiously why I was looking for that person; seeing that I did not understand where he was going, the captain spoke more clearly: in this town many old men have a lot of money; if someone, for example, had a good job in the business sector, he retired a millionaire; kickbacks, accounts, faked documents, construction materials sold on the side—there were plenty of ways of getting rich, the mining plant was too big, too dark and convoluted even for the people managing it, and "many, many"—as the captain repeated—managed to use their jobs to their advantage. And if I, say, were looking for that kind of man, being related to him in some way, and having expectations of money, then I should get myself some friends first.

The captain told me as an aside the story of a young city slicker who asked him for an address, he had come for his inheritance, but, alas, he never got it—something happened to him. "I gave him the address all right," the captain said, "but he refused to have lunch with me."

The captain was probably lying; he lied the way he ate— not concerned with the taste, hurrying to get it into his gullet and take another bite; in essence, he was chewing price lists, swallowing rubles, he wanted to have an expensive lunch at my expense; he was cowardly, the captain, used to looking over his shoulder and making do with small change; I noticed that the suitcases and bags at the lost and found had their side seams undone—the captain had sliced the stitching with a razor in case something was sewn into the lining. He was giving me a similar once-over; but it was clear that the captain was not alone, he could get in touch with others and make it seem that I really was a future heir.

It was too late to tell the captain I was only looking for someone who could tell me about the former camp warden; too late to pretend to be a historian or a journalist. The captain believed what he had made up about me, his guesses and fantasies were reinforced, and any attempt to be anyone but a seeker of inheritance would only make him suspect that I was trying to get him off track. The captain had waited so long among the old bags, among the card files, alone in his robber's tower, had spent so much time buying up rags and stolen electronics, all small-time, all secretly, that now he saw me as his one and only sparkly, shiny, precious opportunity. I realized that believing his own fantasy, he would tell his fellow crooks I was a rich heir, not even realizing that he was lying; the captain ate olives, sucking the pits and neatly placing them on the edge of his plate; he was eating me, he was a local and I was a stranger, and he knew that very well.

I could only pretend to accept his offer; I was counting on his greed—he would pretend to have told the gang when in fact he would not because he knew that he would get nothing, being an idle blabbermouth; the captain replied that he would find out where I was staying and come visit me that evening. I got up, put money for both of us under the ashtray, into which the captain, smiling, dropped an olive pit.

I went to the address the captain had given me. In the nominal center of town there was a block of Stalinist houses; in Moscow they're just a fragment of architectural history, one style among others, but here the Stalinist buildings comprised the only architecture there was. Wind, snow, and rain did not spare their excesses: the stucco moldings and decorative balconies were flaking, the white trim of the windows had vanished, and the wall paint had peeled; damp drafts filled the broad and high-ceiling lobbies, wind moved through vaulted arches, the concrete, lime, and brick crumbled, mold the color of pond scum covered the bottom of the walls, and moss spread in the cracks; rust dripped everywhere, and where the stone was broken the reinforcement rods stuck out, and in places you could see that the concrete was reinforced with tightly wrapped barbed wire instead of rods—they must have run out of metal.

That sight—a house built on barbed wire—gave me the feeling that the building was about to shudder, all poked through, riddled, and no surface would hold, no matter the brand of cement. The wire seemed to be breaking the house apart from inside, the way tree roots break through asphalt, and all the molding, the bas reliefs, the vases in niches were not enough to make me believe that this building was meant for living, for people. Animals have a good sense about this, and it was the case here: there wasn't a cat or dog to be seen, a bird feeder dangled empty in the wind, and only rats rustled in the garbage cans.

There was something strange in this neighborhood, one detail—I couldn't figure out exactly what—was disturbing me; something was missing from the sounds of the city, a note in the background noise was gone. I stopped, but the more closely I listened, the more I realized that hearing would not help; the answer was literally before my eyes. Here—the only place in town—the windows were not covered by light cotton curtains but thick, heavy brown or straw-colored drapes, probably weighted by dust, full of heavy folds like the skin beneath an old man's eyes; the drapes covered the closed windows; no sound reached the street from the apartments.

The residents had shut themselves off from the air of the street, locked the wide entry doors; in their apartments, where the sunlight rarely fell, they tried to preserve the air of their dwindling days; in the diffused honey light at sunset, perhaps they dusted the lacquered furniture, enjoying the cognac-colored lacquer, the cut-glass crystal glasses in the sideboard, and the existence of well-crafted things took away the fear of their own impotence.

I remembered the other time I had heard this silence, only once, but I remembered it for its singularity; as a child, one morning in the paleontological museum in the dinosaur skeleton hall.

The museum was empty that morning; I beat my parents to the biggest hall with the tyrannosaurus and other carnivorous monsters, and I was amazed: usually I was afraid of this room, afraid of the fangs and claws the size of my head, afraid of the skeletons that looked like enlarged drawings—they revealed the natural-rational meaning of creation, and I did not know what to think of life, of nature, which creates with equal thoroughness both the tender jay and the predatory pterodactyl.

It was quiet, completely quiet; and what I saw in the gaping monstrous jaws was not the anger and wrath that had frightened me before but instead the distortion from suffering and death; I saw that the room with the skeletons, the entire museum, the entire sunny autumn day—everything, we were all inside invisible jaws that had not yet closed, but in some final sense it had already happened.

And here on the street of the northern town I recognized that silence—the silence of a museum where the vanished creatures of a different era, fierce and horrible, were diminished by the fleshless face of death and became just as harmless as a squashed frog drying in the heat.

In the lobby I was met by the same ocher, rhomboid tile as in the Moscow building where Grandfather II lived; tile, walls, railing, elevator—it was all the same. I was amazed: how many other cities were there where I could walk into a building whose interior would inevitably elicit memories that I considered profoundly personal; even the wires leading to the doorbell bent the same way as in the former building, and I thought that there was really only one building, like the statue of Lenin, and that the differences in the biographies of its residents in various cities was averaged out by this uniformity; that the memorial plaques you sometimes see on its walls are just a mockery because for each apartment many more were led out of it than those who live there now. I imagined what would happen if all those decomposed residents were to return—the house could not fit them all, they would stand on the staircases, in the courtyard, strangers to one another, but each would recognize the sand-colored rhomboid tiles, the doorbells, the little plaques with the apartment numbers …

The ones who survived would stay inside their rooms, afraid to come out, afraid to open the door a crack, because through that crack would squeeze flimsy shadows with black spots, ink splotches for faces, blotted out by the censors' ink.

I started up the stairs; for a second I thought there was no one left in the building, that stale funereal air came through the keyholes, that behind the doors all the mirrors were covered. I recognized the beginning of my third dream that started me on this path; not that it had taken place here, though it could have.

The air on the landings still held—as it holds the smells from your neighbors' kitchens—the febrile, sweat-soaked, throat-rattling dreams of old men; they slept, turning under their eiderdowns, gritting their teeth so as not to speak in their sleep, not choke, like a drunk on vomit, on the unexpected words of a sleepwalker, and their bodies trembled and sweated, and the sweat reeked of death.

Fourth floor, apartment sixteen; the bell jangled, it seemed, behind every door at once, the sound flew down long corridors, striking the glass panes of wardrobes and scattering as bouncing beads on the parquet. There was quiet behind the door; I rang again and waited a few minutes. The lock clicked inside the apartment.

In the dark of the chain-length crack, I saw a face. A woman stood behind the door, a meter and half from me, but I could not say whether it was a person or an image; then I realized that her face was partially paralyzed, only the eyebrows moved, expressing surprise; I couldn't see her features, it turns out a face lives in motion, in the barely perceptible movements of the facial muscles, and when it is motionless, there is nothing to be said about it; my gaze was attracted by the nostrils—two black dots, two entrances into the inner darkness of the body.

I imagined that a lizard or snake could crawl out of those black apertures, like holes in a stone wall or a cliff; that they did not belong to the face, they were openings, dangerous, evil; if I could, I would have shut the old woman's nostrils, filled them with flesh.

To get out of that darkened moment, half inhaled into those nostrils, I spoke; I greeted her and asked for Semyon Vikentyevich. The old woman went back down the corridor, she left so noiselessly, as if she spent a lifetime trying not disturb someone's sleep, sensitive, troubled, imbued with neuralgic pains; she returned just as noiselessly and unlocked the door. She had three dozen keys—probably to all the rooms, cupboards, closets, desk—and they did not make a sound, as if each key had been wrapped in cloth. There was something bizarre in that key ring, in that passion for keys, for their grooves and teeth, in the desire to keep all the keys together; there was a hint here, a key to the woman herself; she made an inviting gesture—come in—and immediately shut the door behind me. I had not noticed but I immediately felt it: the door was locked.

Keys and doors, doors and keys; I understood who she was: a former warder, the wife of some big shot who got her a job in his department; now an aide for the man I was visiting.

The old woman gave me a gentle shove: go. I went down the dark long corridor; two skinny cats were cleaning themselves near their bowls, the walls were bare, the side doors were shut, and only at the end of the corridor weak daylight from the room illuminated moth-eaten bear and deer heads, cotton stuffing poking out, and moths twirled in the sunbeams like animated dust; I remembered the letters—bear fat, seal blubber—the head belonged to one of the bears whose flesh supported life in the body of Grandfather II.

The first thing I saw in the room was a stick, just like the one with which Grandfather II killed the black dog in my childhood, made of polar larch, honey-rose from the resin, twisted like sinews, lacquered, and caught in shiny brass bands; the stick leaned against an armchair, and the vertical line of bright light through a crack in the drapes gave it a long shadow, like a sundial.

"An eternal stick," said the man sitting in shadow. "A larch like this grows two hundred years, you can't chop it down with an ax. A good thing. We'll rot but it won't."

I was looking at the stick; now I saw that it was not just similar to, it *was* the one, the stick that had broken the black dog's back. The stick was repeated, the way, when you go down winding tower stairs, the view is repeated through the windows set one above the other; it was repeated, fixing a spiral of time.

But there was something else besides the larch stick that sent me back to the past. From the almost pre-memory state of memory, from the first five or six years of my life, from the regions which show you to what degree a person consists of blanks and gaps—from there, as if through gauze, something was beating, as if memories could have a heart.

The voice—I knew that voice—but I had never heard it before.

The old man started to speak again; I barely heard what he said because this time his words resembled the sounds vibrating in my memory; I thought I was losing consciousness, falling forward, but in fact it was the liberated memory laying its hand on my forehead.

That's what had happened—a heavy hand on my forehead, hard, bony fingers, a half-awake state, and two people by my bed: Grandfather II and this old man seated in the armchair. They were speaking in a half whisper thinking I was asleep; two aging men by a five-year-old's bed. I didn't know whose hand was on my forehead, whose fingers were so cold—their hearts could barely pump blood to them; their figures rose above me, blurred by twilight, and my body under the blanket got goose bumps: an alarm clock always ticked in my dacha room, but it was silent then—probably it had run down and no one rewound it—and those lost seconds came out as goose bumps.

I had a clear sense of my young age, the childhood of my body—not consciousness, my body—how weak and pitiful it was; the old men stood above me like priests above a prepared sacrifice, and I felt threatened just by our relative positions, increased by the rough hand that caressed me, practically scratching me.

I recalled a taut apple, unripe, that I had cracked open that day, and I saw myself as a soft seed, not yet turning brown; the old men stood over an open bed, showing white in the dark, and the moment was broken like the apple, to its very core.

I recalled Grandfather II grafting apple trees, we had many of them in the garden with knobby grafting scars ringing the bottoms of their trunks; of all the knives of my childhood there was only one I didn't dream of owning—Grandfather II's crooked garden knife, hooked, scary, scarier than a scalpel, ugly, like the beak of a bird of prey. You couldn't peel with it, or cut up a potato, or play knives—you could only slice layers, cut apart tree fibers, leaving a shiny smooth cut. All those things—the white apple, the grafts cut at an angle, the apple trees with twisted trunks if the graft grew together badly, Grandfather II's knife—they combined into a panicked sensation that the two old men were there to do something to me.

That they were just standing and talking was even more eerie, their speech sounded like a spell spoken over a sleeper whose mind was softened and defenseless; the hand kept stroking my forehead, and I felt an invisible mark, a seal, being left by that touch; the old men spoke of their childlessness, Grandfather II said two names and I understood that he had had a wife and a son who died in early childhood; I also understood that now, blind, he was imagining that he was at the bedside of his child and showing him to the other old man.

In that replacement, that substitution, the sign his hand was putting on my forehead was created; it is wrong to put a living person in place of a dead one, even in thought—it puts in place unnatural ties and casts a shadow into the future of the imagined predestination, which will never come to pass, but will tie knots the person will have to untie with his own life.

I must have blocked this memory; I honestly did not remember the second old man; he must have been passing through Moscow and come to visit Grandfather II at the dacha. In the morning when I got up, he was gone, the night was gone, Grandfather II's words about his dead son—the event moved into the distance, as if it had occurred years ago, and soon after vanished completely; dream or reality, the vision was too much for me to handle then, which is why it was hidden by my consciousness and returned in childhood as a vague, tormenting echo in my dreams, where I sensed that my place in life was taken by someone else, a cuckoo in the nest, a monstrous infant who grew along with me but remained an infant. I shuddered when I heard "Who's been eating my porridge? Who's been sleeping in my bed?" I knew who; a blurred white face, as if in a beaker with formaldehyde, looked at me from my dreams, the key to which I had lost, and no one else in our family had ever heard of Grandfather II's wife and son.

And now standing in the room to which I was led by postcards in Grandfather II's papers, I sensed that one of the most significant events of my life had taken place: that which tells us about ourselves exists in fragments, scattered in time and space, and most often we do not know the most important thing about ourselves, though it already exists; I remembered the second guiding dream with the train engineer and his arrested brother, missing each other forever by the prison train, brought together so as not to meet; I sensed that my life was being refracted in the present moment like a beam in a magnifying glass, refracted and reset by this lens of understanding; I learned what I had come for, and that knowledge, it turns out, had always been with me, in my memory.

Essentially, it was the end of the journey, I could leave the room and go home; but I remembered that the door was locked, too firmly locked. Naturally, I could have asked to open it, moreover, that's what I wanted to do; I was eager to get out, eager to think about what had happened; but the door wasn't being opened yet. Gradually I realized there was something else I was to learn and understand, and my being resisted this imminent discovery. But leaving meant leaving, acting arbitrarily.

The right thing was not to leave before the hosts opened the door for me; the right thing was to take from this meeting not only what I wanted to learn but what my mind rejected in foreboding, which promised not a return home but another, new journey.

The old man rose from the armchair toward me; I jumped back. Before me stood an aged child, physically; the concept of thinness no longer applied—he was not just thin, he was desiccated, as if he had been drained and pinned like an insect and kept for years under glass on a velvet cloth. His muscles had melted leaving only sinew, the skin was as transparent as fine parchment, and the inner life of the body was revealed; blue blood vessels, with a pigeon-wing iridescence, were woven into a map of the blood flow and here and there dark areas like squashed blueberries showed subcutaneous bruising. The old man was half dressed, his body no longer could sweat and exude the death that was crawling beneath his skin; he no longer had a face in the human sense, the flesh had melted like butter from a growing fever, and the twitching pupils looked out straight from the skull. The cartilage on his ears had wilted like smoked mollusks, his eyelashes and eyebrows had fallen out, and only a weak childlike fluff, as if it had been scorched, covered his brows; the swollen capillaries on his cheeks had blended together into fine hieroglyphics written in crimson ink; the old man was dying of radiation disease, he had been exposed to a low level dose which was acting on his body only now; the body was no longer capable of hematosis, the blood in his veins was not renewed, and he was slowly being poisoned by the life he was living—and had lived—poisoned by the past, its slag and toxins accumulating in tissue. He was being killed by time; standing before him, I was the embodiment of that new time; he hated me, that was clear from his clenched teeth, he had forgotten that his withered lips did not cover them anymore; his dentures were smooth and white, and I remembered Grandfather II's false teeth.

I handed him his own letter; he read it, nodded to show he understood who I was, and began to speak. He said he knew how Grandfather II had died, he knew that I had received a blood transfusion from him— Grandfather II had told his housekeeper whom to inform if something happened to him and ordered her not to tell my family about it.

The old man waited to find out why I was there, and I asked if he had any papers, maybe photographs; I didn't want to ask him about Grandfather II, the head of the prison camp, didn't want to ask about their relationship, it was all clear anyway.

The old man told me to take the album from the closet and remove the greeting card from the first page; there was a photograph behind it.

Age had removed most of the black and white from the photo, it was faded; it felt as if the photographer had been taking a picture of a memory.

There were people in the photo, they were gathered for an

opening ceremony for something, among them I recognized Grandfather II; there was only one spot that stood out—a spot of blackness in the place where the shovel in Grandfather II's hands had dug out a clump of dirt. The hole was dark, it attracted the eye like a beauty mark on a cheek. I understood that the quarry I had seen the day before had come out of that hole.

The photograph tried to convey the joy of the actions, spectral banners blended with the clouds, officers of the camp guards and engineers squeezed together to get into the shot; a poorly dressed band played horns and there was a sense that not the clothes but the musicians were made out of quilted cotton fabric charred by bonfires in winter, and then patched up, not people but puppets; the band played, the flags fluttered, but it was all done—the quarry was begun and the future was predestined; the future of the town, of all these people, and my future.

I stood there, knowing there was nothing more to ask, it was all there in the photo. Get out, get out as fast as I could; I just wanted to find out where the wife and son were buried so I could visit their graves and thereby complete my descent into the past. The old man told me where to look in the local cemetery; but when I started making my hasty farewells, he stopped me.

The old man talked; he knew that the end was near and that he could "confess," and whatever he said, whatever he admitted, I would not even dare to berate him, so fragile was his health; perhaps this was the first time he could talk freely and he used that freedom to deal with me. "You want to stay clean," he said. "It won't work, I'll dirty you up!"

No, he didn't see me as a pure boy whose naiveté was irritating; he didn't want to prove that everyone is more likely to do evil rather than good, he didn't want to make generalizations; nor did he try to justify himself through a person's total dependence on circumstances. He hated me because I came from a world with mobile phones, foreign cars, Internet, Wi-Fi, trips abroad, bowling; the world had changed, people chose not to remember anything rather than remember with fear or remember with sorrow, and the old man whispered—thinking he was shouting—that he had been head of the execution squad, he had seen a bullet fly through the body of a goner and the goner did not die because while wounds endanger a healthy body, a person in extreme emaciation no longer senses a wound as a wound, he has great endurance in the face of death. The old man whispered, thinking he was shouting, that the abandoned slag heaps of the mine where they tossed the bodies attracted bears for many years; he whispered that he had shot people himself, with a Nagant rifle, he whispered that there are still undiscovered graves near the town, he knew where, he could show me if I didn't believe him; the old man was scared.

He wasn't afraid of what he had done; he became frightened when he realized that he, head of the execution squad, was nothing in today's world; they did not spit in his face but nor were they afraid of him. He, who had outlived not only his victims but those who could have served as witnesses about and for them, was alone; all the executions, all the murders were forgotten, an entire era had settled to the bottom of memory, and he, locked inside it, was trying to prove that he had existed; the old man could not tolerate the fact that the evil he had wrought no longer existed as evil; he had killed, and the world had finally shut its eyes and when it opened them again it was as if nothing had ever happened. The world did not notice, and the old man was deprived of the only, almost otherworldly, perverted spiritual support in a criminal's self-perception: knowing that you have done something irreversible, irreparable, once and forever, that you took the place of God; that your act would not be smoothed over or forgotten.

I managed to escape; the old woman unlocked the door and I ran down the stairs carrying the photograph, which I had forgotten to return. I planned to go back to the hotel and lock myself in—everything around me, everything I had seen and felt came back in one sensation, that this world was born of Grandfather II, that he had touched the ground with a shovel blade and the ground responded, opened up, and now it could not be closed, it could not be reversed; the town stood on a fault, and the past had more power over it than the present.

I didn't reach the hotel; the Volga I had taken from the station came out around a corner and blocked my way; if I hadn't recognized the car I might have gotten away, instead for a few seconds I thought that the driver had also recognized me and wanted something; then three men jumped out of the car, and in the backseat I saw the captain from the address office; I ran, they caught me, hit me in the back, and bent back my arms.

They opened the trunk about a half hour later; it was getting dark, the car was parked at an enormous man-made lake—one of the settling pools of the mining works, filled with greenish acidic mass; nearby a bird struggled in the chemical mixture—they said birds were poisoned by the pool's evaporation and fell into it; the lump of dirt fluttered, gurgled, and only its beak—the sludge of the pool did not stick to it—opened and shut, a tiny bellows filling the lungs.

They made me kneel at the edge of the pool; dried vomit and blood stained the concrete; apparently, this place had been used before.

The captain and the driver stayed in the car; they smoked, the dashboard glowed green, the city lights flickered in the distance, a train carrying ore moved along the tracks, the diesel locomotive had long disappeared around the curve but the train kept going, and I suddenly realized that I was afraid

I wouldn't see the final train car; that fear hid the greater fear, that they would beat me, drop me over the edge and dip my face into the settling tank. I looked over my shoulder: three men behind me, I couldn't tell which one was in charge; the tattoos on their hands were like stamps on the damp linens of *platzkart* railway bunk beds, the hands twitched and danced as if they'd undergone an electrical shock; the three were talking about what to do with me and the one missing the right ring finger was the most adamant.

They had kept an eye out for me, the captain had mentioned something to somebody about the foolish heir, and they were going to torture me about nonexistent money, jewels, and safe deposit boxes; my entire inheritance was the photograph in my jacket pocket. And then I looked closer at the one missing a finger and I recognized the features of the fugitive I tried to feed in the distant mountains by the abandoned prison camp; this was his younger brother or twin, unless I was hallucinating.

I started to talk; I told him that I knew how his brother died, knew the place where he was buried; I saw the stump of the ring finger and I thought that the one who had died nameless had left that notched ring behind.

I was right: his brother really had escaped—that was the last they had heard of him—and vanished; they let me up and asked questions, I told them how I had found him and tried to save him and then buried him. My captors discussed whether or not I had turned him in to the cops and decided they would have heard that he was returned to the prison colony and given an extra term. Had I killed him? I told them to look at me: Did I look like a killer? They laughed.

Things were turned around; the captors weren't all that sure I was a rich heir, they were checking the captain's tip; they drove me to a cheap eatery for me to draw a map of the fugitive's grave; the captain sat next to me on the backseat and regarded me respectfully: he was certain that I had fooled the three men and was probably almost in awe of my cunning.

They asked me what I was doing in the town; and contrary to reason, I gave them a quick version of the story. The adopted grandson of the camp warden—I told the bandits about Grandfather II and they listened with respect; I was one of them, I was related to the camp world and it turned out that barbed wire not only separates, it unites: they even apologized for twisting my arms. There was no distinction between prisoners and guards, thieves and turnkeys—in any case, in the past; there was only a man who had founded their town, a man in whom they sensed a greater, senior power— and they thought they could have found a common language with him. Grandfather II, like them, bent and broke people, and now that the old feuds were becoming insignificant, they missed the arbitrariness elevated into law—they thought they would have found a place for themselves in those days, a place on the side of force, and the reflection of the force would have lent legality and justification to their base passion for torture. "I would have worn a uniform in those days," said one; and I saw that all three would have worked as guards— freedom did not interest them, power did; the fugitive, the big brother, would have killed anyone suggesting it, but these men, younger, would have accepted it as their due; they did serve, in fact, as private security at the plant.

The dead man, almost against his will, protected me; that attempt at humanity had worked. If I had abandoned him, I would not have had the right—for myself—to refer to that incident; but I didn't abandon him and I didn't turn him in— and now I avoided the sludge of the settling tank where the deceived bird was dying in sticky bubbles.

Their mood had changed sharply; I described the way to the abandoned camp as best I could, but I knew that the younger brother would not travel to rebury his big brother—

he would only tell stories about how he grabbed an outside mark, and the mark turned out to be a guy who had seen his brother's body; gradually the story would mutate to the point of unrecognizability—either I would become a traitor punished by the younger brother, or, on the contrary, I would have carried the fugitive on my back; but all that would be later and for now we drank at the eatery—to friends, to the failure of enemies—and the captain drank with everyone, as if he had never ratted on me.

I planned to go to the cemetery in the morning, to the graves of Grandfather II's wife and son, but I changed my mind; I sensed that the trip would be the end, that I would have to return after I did it—and I tried to postpone the end.

I wanted to see the place where the old man who was chief of the execution squad got the dose of radiation. The town had its own radiation—the radioactivity of dysfunction, of strain and fracture; I wanted to compare the sensation of the two places to see if they were similar in any way.

Not far out of town, in the mountains, was the ravine where the prisoners dug radioactive ore.

When they were creating the nuclear bomb, every geological expedition looked for that ore whatever else they were doing. Here in the North, they found it. I imagined tens of thousands of people all over the country, in the steppes, the deserts, taiga, and tundra looking for the decaying substance that was fraught with chain reaction, searching for the yellow uranium tars the color of the spots on the skin of poisonous snakes; I pictured Geiger counter needles reacting when they found grains of minerals surrounded by the brown aureole of radioactivity and the sharpened tips of pencils marked the contours of future sites on faded pages of field diaries in graphite.

Searching for substances whose life span is equivalent in duration with human life, searching for short-lived mineral compounds, betrayers of rock that has it own, long life of millions of years; searching for the key to the forces of nature; searching for the accelerator of decay, in a sense the philosopher's stone commensurate with the philosophy of the new age that seeks means of destruction rather than construction; methods of stopping history, ending time.

Uranium, an element named for the castrated god, the god of time who gave up his place to Cronus and by disappearing made possible the change of generations of the gods—uranium is a sterile creature that cannot give a start to a thing and cannot be smelted into a permanent form like copper or iron; uranium, discovered by Martin Heinrich Klaproth in the year of the start of the French Revolution, the year the Bastille was stormed and the Declaration of the Rights of Man and Citizen was passed—did the German natural philosopher think that the black substance in his test tube would weigh more on the scales of history than all the gold ever extracted by humanity? That for the sake of this substance roads would be built and mines created? Did he hear in the sounds of that year the underground jolts that were predictions of future revolutions—and the revolution that would take up the French revolution's red flag?

To get to the ravine, you had to go past abandoned plants and an unfinished enrichment factory. It was the place where the outskirts of the city joined the mining plant's territory, creating a no-man's land where no one lived, not even tramps and feral dogs; while the ruins of factories and houses along the edge of town smelled of neglect, here it seemed that the space itself was decaying and filling up with caverns.

There were fireplaces and rusted snarls of cord—the metal guts of tires—everywhere; splashes of rust, cisterns knocked on their sides, smashed power line towers, hunks of metal, twisted, bent, hacked by giant scissors; truck tire tracks that looked as if someone had intentionally tortured the earth. Among the skeletons of barracks, like trees chopped by mortars in a military dream, stood wastewater risers; huge fountains of water gushed pointlessly from forgotten wells. None of the usual litter there—cans, papers, wrappers, scraps of food—only the remains of former habitation, warped metal and murdered wood.

I couldn't walk through that space; here at the juncture of the town and the industrial zone, everything that in other places nearby was practically hidden, masked by architecture and landscape, was laid bare; the mutilated space itself did not elicit fear but the reality of the inner lives of the people whose effort and determination, or rather, lack of effort and absence of determination gave rise to it.

Once, several geological institutes had their laboratories here; the barracks frames were all that was left, everything else was looted when the labs were closed. Among the chopped and charred slate were pieces of core samples—long cylinders of rock raised from the depths of holes. Usually they were laid out in special boxes meter by meter, and the meter columns of samples gave a reading of the entire vertical of the hole. Those abandoned core samples, overgrown with weeds, pointlessly removed from the ground, from great depths, showed that people left here as if rejecting their work, tossing it aside casually and hastily, and in the vacuum created by their departure, a different life began: the way bindweed takes over old ruins.

Looking at the core samples, I remembered a story that used to be told as a joke; back in the 1980s, a retired driller applied to the Ministry of Geology. He had a project to make use of some of the old holes, which were usually filled with cement to keep the underground water strata from mixing. He proposed turning the holes into cemeteries: burying people vertically, lowering one on top of the other; there were thousands of such holes drilled all over the country, and his explanatory note stated that their total capacity would enable decades of burials, freeing up, he explained scrupulously, the workforce, the cemetery diggers and coffin makers, for other state needs, the word "state" underlined.

The ministry had seen all kinds of proposals: the era had given rise to wild thoughts, the suppressed energy of restructuring and transformations found a way into apolitical and, in that sense, safe technological inventions. The more slowly time flowed, the more alleged inventions appeared that rejected the laws of science, overriding them out of the inventor's desire, a desire so clearly inept and passionate that it was beyond science; people wanted to change *something*, and the laws of the natural sciences seemed more malleable than the laws of the social order. But the scientist who proposed vertical cemeteries amazed everyone; and now, standing before the abandoned core boxes, I sensed where that man had come from and what environment had addled his brain.

To get around the ruined land that belonged to no one, I decided to follow the railroad track leading to the mine; women's voices could be heard above the embankment; I couldn't make out the words yet, but I could pick up the intonations. The voices did not come from any particular place—the air resonated with them, as if it contained them like a chemical cloud or steam.

Two women were wearily discussing something. From the interjections that arise when vowels are pronounced, lighting a word from within with different emotional tones—a-a, u-u, o-o—you could tell what they were talking about. I got closer and the phrases were clearer. Yesterday Valera said ... ate some hot dogs ... I have to sleep with him when he's drunk .... the kids are in the next room ... he burned a hole in the pillowcase with his cigarette ... started drinking first thing in the morning ... he's trying to get in my daughter's room ...

The words were about human life, but they seemed to be spoken by the area; two women dispatchers sat in their respective booths, kilometers apart from each other, at two sets of crossroads, and now, as there was a break, there were no trains running carrying ore, they were having a conversation over the loudspeakers. No one could eavesdrop because there was no one around; day after day they chatted and it seemed there was nobody closer—among friends and neighbors—than each other.

Maybe these conversations had been conducted for years, and had not changed; in rain and blizzard, in summer and winter, one woman said "he burned a hole in the pillowcase," and it was always the same pillowcase and the same cigarette; and her friend said nothing in response, just listened.

The same ruins, the same gouged earth, lay around the embankment, and the women's conversation did not clash with it, the way a conversation about domestic things would, referring to home—in the sense of walls, roof, hearth—amid the abandoned buildings. On the contrary, this was the only conversation possible here.

The voices carried from the loudspeakers up on posts, and it seemed that the words spoke themselves and there were no people at all, just a recording set on repeat in an empty dispatcher office.

It was muggy in the ravine, low clouds were caught on the mountain peaks; it was raining but it felt as if the drops were already flying and had not yet reached the ground. The ruts of the old road were overgrown, and the bridges across the river had been washed away; a narrow path trampled in the rut showed that people came here for mushrooms or berries. The river water was mountain water, too transparent, too clear— it will never slake your thirst, you have to add salt or acid; bilberries ripened in the thickets; the ulcers of the industrial zone were just a half kilometer away, but nature here was untouched, in another decade the old road would disappear under new birches.

The camp appeared after a turn; some of the houses were built out of river boulders, and now they looked like a parody of medieval architecture: two stories, hunkered down, without roofs, with narrow windows to keep in the heat. The wooden buildings had rotted or been burned down long ago, only the electric poles with crooked crossbeams remained, but the eye refused to see them as crosses, to take in the symbolism—they were just poles; it was the same with these buildings—I realized that someone seeing this without knowing it used to be a prison camp would never guess.

Neither the masonry, not the black spots where they used to dump coal, nor the abandoned carts on the slope, nor the adits, nothing in and of itself was evidence. Even the roll of barbed wire, in which a hare had once gotten caught—rodents gradually carried out the tiny bleached bones, as if they had been dumped from a plate—was just a roll of barbed wire. In order to unwind it, like you unwind a thread from a ball of wool, pulling out the entire past, the entire image of this place six decades ago, and not only the image but the essence of what had gone on here—you needed to know something about it, you needed some sort of guidance.

I went through the camp workshops, the trestle beds were still there, to the compressor room where rusty pipes stretched up to the adits leading into the mine; the only thing I found was a button, a homemade button carved out of a piece of tin can; a comprehensible and simultaneously useless object without clothes. The impression of the place was the same; it was a button: real, indubitable, yet torn from something more important, too small, hopelessly lost.

But the button in my hand reminded me of something; I remembered that I had stood in the mountains on this latitude but a thousand kilometers to the east, and I had seen the remains of this camp in the broad saddle of the pass, and the rusted pipes from the compressor room had stretched along the slopes.

The button had two holes made with an awl or nail; I remember the nail I had held in my hand then as evidence that a trace is always left, what remains is what held together the building of the past, and these things, as a special material, always live longer than the building itself. But now I held not a nail but a hole made by a nail; the situation had reversed itself. I began looking through the button, like miniature binoculars, and its two openings suddenly joined up with two spots, the openings of adits on the ravine slope.

I did not want to go up there; but every dark hole in the ground attracts you, as if it were the opening into the underside of the world, an addition to three-dimensionality. I also remembered the goal of this walk into the mountains: the adits were tunnels to the places they excavated the mineral that then yielded uranium.

The disfigured no man's land, the disintegrating speech of two women on the railroad had not yet become even a recent memory, they were still part of the present moment, and the source of all this impoverishment, destitution, and privation beckoned the way a struck dog on the side of the road, flies in its exposed guts, catches your eye; it attracted your imagination by the honest openness of ugliness. To see not the consequences but the original cause; to see the belly of the collapse—to enter it!

I climbed up to the adits; once, they had been blocked by stones and crossed by welded rails; but the water dripping from them dug out a road, created collapses, and you could gain entry. I expected to find the center of danger, the source of the murk that filled the region; nothing of the kind. At first, being underground made no impression at all; then I realized that I was wrong to look for something noticeable; something else was more important, but what?

In abandoned adits where there are no currents, no drafts,

the immobilized air gradually loses its flow and begins to resemble frozen colorless fog: each breath you take creates an emptiness, a hole, and in order to breathe a second time, you have to take a step.

Disintegrated air, decomposed: your voice sticks in it, light diffuses, and the watery dust from drops falling from the ceiling creates rainbows in the flashlight beam, as joyless as the wing of a dead butterfly.

The blackness had penetrated its very being, corroding it from within, the way rust corrodes iron: it falls apart at your touch. It seemed that every molecule, every atom was enveloped in black, could not see one another; you suddenly feel that the air is blind, the way a person can be blind from internal disarray: the coherence of the world is beyond his ability to see.

What I sought was what I was breathing in: I should have brought a respirator. No one had breathed this air for decades and it preserved everything, like virus strains in a test tube; not thoughts and voices, but the toxin of the era, the exhalation of destruction and decay. I was filling my lungs with something that should not be touched by man; my breath caught, as if I had seen that the meat I was eating was rotten and filled with maggots, even more repulsive than worms: the maggot turns into a worm inside your flesh.

I lit a cigarette, letting the strong tobacco disperse the miasma; no strange whispers, no sense of someone's presence, only the air, empty, preserving nothing but decay, and time, for I realized that this tunnel was a cellar where the air remained from specific years gone by, numbered just like a prisoner.

Time did not stop here—the word stop implies a fixed moment when movement ends; it had never moved here at all, it stood like water in black caves where the movement is from striped fish. I thought that if this adit could be tipped like a bottle, the air and the time would flow out; they would mix with today's time and recognize each other as past and present.

Coming back out into the light, I heard a helicopter. An Mi-8 from the local airport landed not far from the ruins of the stone barracks; people came out—not people, just splotches of color so bright and radiating that it hid the outline of their figures; yellow, red, violet, light blue, emerald, navy blue, and orange jackets, trousers, backpacks, and hats; they moved the way people do with cameras and video cameras, looking for the best angle for a shot and where to best pose for a photograph; they separated, mentally dividing up the valley with their angles, and no one looked at the ground. The wind carried English words; in the city I would have perceived it as foreign, but here in the ravine, it seemed even more alien, doubly strange, as if people who spoke a foreign language decided to imitate tropical birds.

Streams of hot air came from the helicopter's exhaust vents; the foreigners, who had been brought here for an excursion— I'd seen the sign in town for "camp tours"— wore protective footgear and tried not to touch the soil or the buildings, they must have been warned about radiation. I stood on the mountain slope, by the adits, like a savage witnessing the landing of a spaceship; their clothing came from a different, full-color world, and I wanted to shout that you can't come here in a helicopter, you can't land for an hour to take pictures and pick up a souvenir that the tour organizers left for you to find. If I'd had a gun, I would have chased them away with a shot; instead all I could do was watch and understand that despite the spirit of the our times which insisted not just on the equality but on the total conformity of people, there were insuperable barriers, indelible differences deeper than religion, culture, or prosperity; the colored jackets negated the area, protected against its colorlessness, and I saw—through color—that we were born in different times, even though they coincided chronologically. This difference—between those born in the same years but in different times—was so powerful that it elicited denial. The two women at the railroad and the three bandits from the night before were closer to me—it was not that we were surrounded by the same realities of life, but that we were born of those realities, we carried their deficiencies and could speak in the language of deficiencies; but the people in the colored jackets with cameras were whole and in that sense, estranged.

The helicopter flew away; I went down, down, down the stones, the river channels, and it seemed that now there was only descent for me, down the dried channels, the crunchy moss, down, down, down.

PART 5

The city cemetery where Grandfather II's wife and son were buried was just a piece of land in the middle of the tundra. The graves, fences, and crosses unframed by trees looked as if patients in hospital beds had been brought outside; a cemetery without trees, without a brick wall around it, it seemed like a slum repeating the boredom of the garages and sheds. There was also the feeling that the deceased had settled themselves in a new place, and the result was a disorderly conglomeration of graves instead of a regular order; they huddled together like prisoners on bunk beds to keep warm, like people with bundles pushing into a train car until their ribs cracked, they buried others and then climbed into the ground themselves.

A little church was stuck on the edge of the cemetery; its red brick, which hadn't yet turned dark, reminded me of the few big houses where the mine bosses lived, as you come into town; if not for the dome, it could have been yet another mansion, and it was probably built by the same crew of workers; the church was seen—by those who commissioned it, by the architect, and by the builders—as God's mansion; it was strange that they hadn't found a different kind of brick for the church, that they'd put it there like a guard hut without searching for the more perfect place, and so from whichever angle you looked in the cemetery, the church was pushed into the ground, destroyed by the power of the complex's smokestacks, striped like prison garb, belching volcanic smoke, and dwarfing the cross and the gilded dome.

In the chaos of graves there was one section where the

stones were higher and more massive; amid the rusted crosses and the low fences sinking into the boggy soil stood rectangles of black dolerite, brought here by railroad; the inscriptions on the stone were gilded. This is where the bosses were buried; oval frames showed portraits of men in uniform and suits, colonels, chief engineers, PhDs in technical sciences, and they looked at one another, because the stones had been placed in an imaginary circle, and no sightline could escape it.

The low clouds brought a June blizzard, snow blackened by the smokestacks fell on the graves, black snow. It looked like ashes from an old fire falling from the sky; then the stacks belched smoke the color of cinnabar, and the snow turned deep red, melting on my face, spotting the cemetery paths; a man ran out of the guard booth, grabbed me by the arm and dragged me under the roof; cinnabar snow can be dangerous, but I did not care.

The tundra around the cemetery reddened, as if watered-down blood had seeped from beneath the ground; red water flowed down my arms, my face; the color of brick dust, cinder with the bluish cast of gunpowder splashed across the landscape, colored the mountains and sky, and the monuments in the cemetery became islands in the high water of the color. I understood that this was coincidence, a burst of snow that was imbued with smoke from the stacks; but a red polar hare ran in the tundra, looping around, escaping an imagined hunter, the madness of red, and it turned out it was running in circles; the hare tried to escape the red blizzard not knowing what its own color was, leaping aside, trying to confuse the trail, going low and then jumping back up on the graves.

Finally the hare wearied and collapsed in a mossy hole; only its ears were visible. I realized that it was pointless to run like the hare if you were to see red water on your hands; pointless to say that this is just pollution from the complex when in your gut you know what the red snow is *about*; you are called, and you can only experience your own shock, follow its path—without trying to understand it, break it up into its components. Only then will the red snow covering the cemetery become something deeper than an image or a metaphor—it will become an opening door leading to the space of growing destiny; the words of Gilgamesh came to mind, his response to the Scorpion-Man:

> "Whether it be in sorrow,
> Whether it be in pain,
> In cold, in heat,
> In sighing, in weeping,
> I will go!
> Let the gate of the mountain now be opened!"

Red snow fell over the tundra to the Arctic Ocean; the land was red, and the water devoured it, and dark mirrored rivers flowed unperturbed; red drops fell from wires, snow melted on stone in the quarry, and red rivulets ran along cracks and fissures, as if the blood-carrying veins of the earth had been cut here to extract it; red foam appeared on the oil rigs that looked like camp watchtowers and in the mouths of the wells, and the gas torches over the tundra cavities turned crimson; the chain saw at the felling site splattered red sawdust, and the excavator shovel dug into darkness where something slurped viscously; bedbugs under the boards of the collapsed barracks awoke from their half-century sleep, and bears whose ancestors grew fat on human flesh returned to the slag heaps where the executed bodies were dumped; human blood flowed in the wires, the tree trunks, in the arteries of animals, in the emptiness of the land, as if the world had turned into a bleeding tumor, a tangle of blood vessels, and only the rivers flowed unperturbed.

Then the red snow melted completely; there was a light

ringing in my head, as if capillary strings had burst from the tension. We went outside.

The watchman's left arm was artificial, and his uncreased shoes revealed that his legs were also prosthetic; the wrinkles on his face were deep and aged, he could no longer smooth the skin in order to shave, it was baked like skin after a burn, so that uneven gray bristles peeked out; thin, once very tall—any line arranged according to height would start with him—the man was now bent over, and the hump on his back was like an incipient second head; his eyes belonged to a different face, a different body: life had wearied the flesh, but the eyes, their red, ulcerated whites, held something sleepless, remembering, always awake but expecting nothing.

The watchman was not one by profession or calling; he was a watchman without verbs, if I could put it that way: he did not watch, he did not guard, he did not execute the duties of a watchman, but nevertheless he was one, in a different sense.

When the cemetery had been part of the camp, he, an invalid who had been a stone mason and engraver in his past, was sent here to make headstones; for decades he carved out names, ranks, and positions, as if he worked in the posthumous human resources department; he kept his own records of those who had arrested him and guarded him, kept his book of life and death—a pile of pages in a cardboard file labeled "Case No. ... ," in which he listed all the dead.

Later, when the town grew bigger than the camp, his quarter-century sentence came to an end, but he remained; the engraver said he had nowhere to go, which was true, but that was not the real reason: he had merged with the cemetery, gotten used to standing at the gate hunched over, grown deaf from the whine of the saws on stone; former camp bosses retired and sooner or later, with an honorary salute or not, with medals on a cushion or not, the officials were lowered into the unyielding, stony earth, where a meter down the hoe hit the ice of permafrost; the engraver picked up his instruments and chiseled the dates of the life on the stone.

There was not much flesh left on him, a third of his body was metal, wood, and plastic—the engraver had been treated with care; the flesh that remained was imbued with the dust of stone and abrasives, stone dust was in his lungs, he had become almost mineral, the way the bodies of miners who died in salt mines turned into salt formations found decades later. His name was Petr, rock, and he was no longer subject to physiology, he belonged to petrography, the study of mountain ores. Having spent much more time with rock than with people, he had learned its slow power, the power of pressure that bends strata, the power of hidden, seething pressures; he turned the power on himself, overcame the weakness of expectation, and surpassed the strain of patience; he was simply the cemetery stone carver, he lived at the cemetery, and even in his extreme old age he cut the letters smoothly and evenly into the stone.

His vision and sense of proportion established the same precision within him, letters requiring accurate delineation subjected his body to the service of lines; maybe he survived only thanks to those letters, their graphics; he stood on two borders simultaneously—the line between life and death and the threshold at which the invisible word becomes visible, captured in the graphic cluster of letters; letters became his prison camp rations, and he did not depend on meager calories, he was fed by the alphabet both in the practical and spiritual sense. He lived without dreaming of revenge, he lived a solitary and isolated life, and his life went on as long as there were still people alive who had served in the camp as guards; he met them at the cemetery gate the way they had met him at the camp gate; he stood on borrowed legs of metal and wood, while they lay on their backs and their feet were in shoes bought for the burial. He was not in the thrall of vengeance or justice being meted out—he simply watched how they left in a line that extended for years, left as if they had lived ordinary lives, had been ordinary men—and it had to be him, he had to chisel out the numbers, the farewell words of wives and children on their headstones, so that their deeds, almost forgotten, not having become guilt, not having elicited repentance or expiation, would be fixed, confirmed as something that had really happened; confirmed not in human memory, but as something that did not depend on memory, on being "multiplied" in reminiscences, but was just a fact of life.

One engraving, one line, was enough to keep a thing from vanishing. It needed only one person to take on the labor of remembering; remembering means being connected with reality, even being that connection; we do not preserve the reality of the past in our memories, the past itself, having occurred, speaks through human memory, and the speech is exactly as clear as the person is honest, not in the sense of following the truth but in the sense of absolutely allowing it to speak through him.

In the back of the workshop, the engraver tried to make a memorial for his long-dead comrades; but his ability to convey the proportions of the human body was in inverse proportion to the precision of his hand at making letters; he treated the human form like a letter, so that the body was racked, stretched on imaginary axes as if crucified on the letter; unfinished statues lay by the wall like executed bodies, and that probably was a memorial fully suited to the times and events—a memorial existing in numerous attempts but never succeeding; a memorial no one would see.

I told the engraver the grave I sought, and he led me to a small hollow that looked like the earth's lipless mouth. In those regions, permafrost could push out crosses and statues the way it pushes out foundations of buildings, or it could remain indifferent, or it could swallow a raised grave site. I recalled the photograph of Grandfather II taking the first shovelful of dirt at the quarry site and the feeling I had first looking at it returned: the shovel digs into the ground and it's too late to put the soil back, to deny, refuse, say something; events linked up in ways that could not be unlinked, fate could not be stopped. Therefore the location of the grave had a dent in the surface that seemed to repeat—in one of many places—the funnel of the quarry begun by Grandfather II.

The engraver told me that one batch of prisoners brought to the camp were mental patients; the institution where they lived had been turned into a polling place because the village school, where people usually voted, had burned down with the kolkhoz office. The patients were naturally locked up, but they got out at night and tore down the posters hanging in the streets, to put them up in their own ward. One poster ripped and they hid it in the outhouse; it was a portrait of Stalin.

The engraver heard the story from an orderly in the institution, who was sent to serve time along with the mental patients. They could not remember their own names, did not respond at roll call, and the orderly was a valued worker: he replied for them all, combining the names of three dozen people with his own. The madmen were excellent laborers, perhaps the best at laying the foundation of the quarry: they did not know that somewhere outside there was freedom, they were not envious if someone got more food, they did not try to deceive, work less, pretend to be sick; through pickaxes and shovels, through unity of action and form—just as they were taught to use spoons—they acquired a small dose of reason, enough to merge with the tool and become one with it. The shaft of a shovel, the handle of a crowbar became their support, their earthly axis, and they dug, broke rock, made holes for explosives, giving themselves fully to the work, replacing their own existence. That's what people called them—Pickaxe,

Shovel, Wheelbarrow—and they quickly learned to respond to the nicknames.

Gradually the brigade of mental patients was noticed and given better rations—no other brigade suited the bosses as well—and the guard officers even joked that the experience should be extended, all the nuts throughout the land should be arrested: Where else could you find such obedient workers? The other prisoners called them the Psycho Brigade; the bosses had the sense not to hold up the mental patients as an example—the other prisoners would have killed them then—instead, people just took out their frustration on them, mocked them, but did not hurt them.

The officers who suggested using arrested mental patients did not know that all credit was due the orderly: he had understood intuitively that the repeated actions of simple labor with the soil could help those men get back into the world, at least partially, and he had spent years at the institution teaching them to work, first with four hands, the way you teach people to play piano, and then, when they understood the movement, independently. The orderly's brother was among the madmen, they said it was hereditary, and he tried to save his brother and forestall his own madness; he had managed to instill the skills of simple labor in his patients, in muscle memory; but now his plan equated man and instrument.

Some of the patients had no guards—you could escape from here only if you had the intention to escape, it was impossible to get lost or go missing, so the patients were allowed to move freely; they were sent to the bosses' houses to chop wood and haul water—the bosses liked these workers who made them feel even more important than did the usual prisoners; besides which the mental patients did not know to hate the bosses, the convoy guards, and their families, so the bosses could relax with them the way you do with a dog or cat—feeling superior and at peace.

The crazies came to Grandfather II's apartment, too; his seven-year-old son, born near the camp, and knowing nothing but the camp and the camp people, unexpectedly grew attached to them; one of the madmen, whose name the engraver could not remember, used to carve wood and was the father of a large family; he had not seen children for two or three years. You couldn't say he felt something for the boy, the son of the camp warden, for he had lost the ability to feel, but his fingers retained their own memory and carved—with a shard of glass, since the Psycho Brigade did not have knives or razors—a wooden bird whistle. He carved it mechanically, impartially, as if every child—the man knew what short stature meant—was supposed to have such a bird.

Grandfather II's son, who had lived without toys—all the children of the camp guards grew up that way, they didn't even know the usual children's games like Cossacks-and-robbers, they played at the work of their fathers, being convoy guards or soldiers in the watchtowers—suddenly left his peers; the simple bird whistle touched something in him. No, he did not see the world in which he had been born and bred in a different light, he did not come to pity the prisoners or realize what his father was; the toy merely revealed that there could be another life, where the air can sing lightly; there are no songbirds in the tundra and the boy had never heard a lark or nightingale, nor did he know that people had songs: in his seven years he had heard only a few records and thought that singing was the work of a box with a handle and horn; the box knew how to sing in a human voice, that's what it was made for, but people could not sing.

Lips touching the resonant opening, the exhalation giving birth to sound—the boy started breathing differently, certain powers within him, unrequired and dormant, awoke to life; he began seeking isolation, he made up simple melodies and whistled them, as if hypnotizing himself, summoning the unknown that arose inside him.

The way the engraver told it, there was something uncanny about how the boy grew attached to his whistle; the engraver recalled the legend of the Pied Piper of Hamelin and the children he led away with his flute; the crazy wood-carver had unwittingly made him a strange and scary gift. He came from the sticks, from the forests and swamps that three generations of irrigators, Tsarist and Soviet, had been unable to drain; he would run away from the orderlies and collect driftwood, burls and birch fungus, and carve the same things out of them: the mocking faces of forest spirits, distorted as if in a fun house mirror, and you could not say that he was making them up—he was releasing the features already in the wood, as if the forest truly were filled with taunting, beckoning faces, peering at people from behind trees and pretending to be clumsy growths should people turn back to look.

The boy was not losing his mind, but simply spent more and more time on his own; sometimes he mindlessly went off somewhere, as if the whistle of the singing toy extended a guiding thread visible to him alone, and an otherworldliness developed about him, as if he were here accidentally and would not stay long; the appearance of the bird whistle somehow stopped his growth, took away the powers of growth which children have in great abundance, with a reserve; these powers seemed to be exhausted in the vain and repeated attempts to breathe life into the wooden bird, which lived with another's breath.

Finally, Grandfather II noticed that something was wrong with his son; he noticed too late and then acted with great persistence. The boy could not explain to his father—children do not have the language for expressing inner states—and even if he had, what would he have said? That he was enchanted by a toy made by a crazy prisoner? Grandfather II, thanks to the boy's friends, learned about the whistle and took it away;

he learned who had made it and summoned the crazy carver under guard; he no longer remembered the gift or the boy, and his fingers palpated the wood of the boss's desk, as if trying to measure what could be done with such a thick oak plank if you cut it up and used it for various small items.

Grandfather II, given the limits of his perspective, decided that the carver was only pretending to be mad, that he was actually rational since he'd tried to gain the graces of a child who was the son of the camp warden; he became sophisticated in his cruelty: the miserable madman dared to think he could benefit this way, manipulating Grandfather II through his son.

He sent the carver to the distant timber area, where they prepared the beams for future mines. "Let him work with trees," Grandfather II said, knowing that the madman would probably be squashed by a falling tree; he could have simply ordered him shot, but that would have been direct murder, and Grandfather II liked to act so that his sentences were executed by the apparent course of events, the forces of nature, postponed and removed: it was not his personal intention to send the man to his death, but the man fell into the whirlpool of fate, from which he could not escape.

Grandfather II's son did not know what had happened to the carver; when they took away his whistle, he fell gravely ill. For a week the boy had a dry fever, his body tense and ossified; he cried out, struggling with something in his delirium. The doctor said that the child's face changed so sharply and wildly, it seemed that two different people were arguing inside the boy, each appearing alternately in his face. One clearly showed the harsh pedigree of Grandfather II, who was born in a village by chalk cliffs over a river, where the soil was so imbued with lime that only cherries could grow there; the other face was tender as an infant, a vague face, as if he had just arrived in the world without a line of ancestors whose features could have shaped his. The one who had Grandfather II's blood in his veins, thick and as viscous as the sap of cherry trees, was trying to push out this infant from the boy's body, chase it away, toss it like a bird from the nest.

After a week, the boy awoke recovered, thinner and almost without memory; many memories did not survive the fever and had dematerialized, or maybe it was a part of his soul, the finest, purest, and childlike part that had dematerialized; he regained his health and forgot about the whistle, but he had become angular, wooden in his movements, as if the liveliness that gave fluidity to his body had been lost, and every scrape and bruise now lasted a long time on his skin.

He returned to his peers, but it was out of a sense of duty to be friends with boys his age; he played with them indifferently, without passion, and only hide-and-seek responded with his new sensibility: he searched badly, without focus, but he hid so well that it seemed he had not hidden himself at all, had no intention to hide—he simply vanished into a crack, like a coin into the floorboards, and when the seeker gave up, they all went looking for him, finding him only by accident. The boy had stopped *wanting to be*, his inner state was that of an old man; something extremely important had burned away in that illness, when Grandfather II sat at his bedside. He lost the gift awakened by the bird whistle, the gift of his own life, not subjected to anyone else, a life about which the boy had known nothing except the enchanting foretaste of it; the boy emptied out, grew as light as a wrapper, and that is why he did not hide playing hide-and-seek, rather he fell into empty spots, holes in the universe, like a random object that had no place of its own.

Grandfather II did not give up; he saw that the boy was still not himself, and he thought it was because he was taking a long time—an incommensurately long time—getting over the loss of the toy. He behaved as most adults would—he decided to replace the toy he took away with a present, to intercept the inner gaze focused on the loss with something new, significant, and valuable. This is the action of people for whom all life events are basically equivalent, one easily replaced by another; used to dealing this way with people, Grandfather II probably did not know that there were things that were irreversible—not physically, like death or injury—but because the most important aspect of a relationship happens in a single moment, beyond which everything has a future dimension based on trust, or else everything is forever too late.

Grandfather II started the quarry—and everything was too late, the town was doomed to the funnel; for him and his son the moment—everything is too late—had also come, but he thought and thought about what present would please the boy, how to show a father's generosity, and at last came up with a gift with a significance that would define his son's adolescence and maturity.

On Grandfather II's orders, they searched the camp and found another carver, this one in his right mind. For several months he did not go out to the sites, slept only three hours a night, at work on his assignment; Grandfather II looked in occasionally to check up and give advice, leaving enough shag for a couple of cigarettes: he didn't have to pay the carver too much, his life was in Grandfather II's hands as it was, and the carver labored, extending his existence with each curl of wood, with each movement of his knife— Grandfather II could send him to the mines, and the elderly prisoner would die after a month of digging.

But despite his desire to live, despite his desire to please Grandfather II, the work did not go well; the commission was beyond the prisoner's abilities: he was supposed to create the camp in miniature. Use a cobbler's hammer to knock together barracks with wooden bunks, erect watchtowers, make the delousing room, the gun room, the steam bath, warehouse, and other buildings—all tiny, to fit a special base and be placed on a table; he had to carve and paint the convoy soldiers, sheepdogs, cooks, steam bath attendants, all the service people, and most important, the prisoners; make wheelbarrows with buttons for wheels, pickaxes out of furniture nails, shovels out of tin, boilers, furnaces; my new friend the engraver was assigned to help him in the fine work. The engraver used a magnifying glass to model the soldiers' guns, fashioned bits of a broken cup into porcelain isolators for wooden poles using the finest wire which pricked your finger if you touched the end, and one of the free seamstresses sewed sheepskin jackets and peacoats for the guards and prisoners. Snow banks of cotton were placed around the camp; it was meant to be eternal winter, but the electrician made a dull, cheese-yellow sun from a 20-watt bulb that moved around the camp on a special arm the way the sun moves across the tundra in summer without going below the horizon.

The entire camp universe was being created by the efforts of the carver, engraver, and seamstress, but the further they worked, the more they felt they were doing something unseemly, almost forbidden; they were violating some unclear law; the carver and engraver confessed this to each other and even considered burning the toy camp by starting a fire in the workshop, but fear stopped them; they saw how excessively attached Grandfather II was to his idea, he came by more frequently, stayed longer, examining the toy, and it seemed that he had forgotten it was intended for his son. Grandfather II would chase them out of the workshop and remain there alone, they watched through a crack how the warden, illuminated by the flames of oil lamps and the fire of the opened furnace, with a dark face, too tall for the low ceiling, moved the figures of prisoners and soldiers, halting like God above the newly created earth, and deciding something in those moments when he silently smoked, exhaling on the toy barracks, as if their chimneys were smoking, and the draft blew smoke onto the cotton snow.

Three months later the toy camp was ready; Grandfather II organized a viewing of the work. A windup locomotive ran down wire tracks with wagons loaded with real ore, billowing caustic soot: inside it was a boiler with burning tar; the electric sun made its slow orbit; the excavator could bend and unbend, the guards could aim their rifles, and the toy shepherd jaws opened revealing red mouths—the seamstress had used red calico freely; the toy camp was exactly like the real one, except for one missing figure—Grandfather II was not there, even though inside the camp office there was a thimble-sized bust of Lenin, carved from dog bone—that was the only bone there was—and on the wall a poster with Stalin's profile, made from a postage stamp.

Grandfather II decided that the gift had to be a surprise; the anniversary was approaching of the day when the quarry gave its first ton of ore, and they were planning to celebrate. Grandfather II took these production anniversaries very seriously, they meant more to him than birthdays or other holidays like May Day. He usually celebrated in the laboratory where they tested the quality of the ore; however, he decided to betray his habit.

That evening Grandfather II brought the gift into the boy's room; his son, he thought, was sleeping, and he set up the toy camp on the table and covered it with canvas, so the boy could open it himself.

But the morning brought something else: they found the boy shivering in the corner, wrapped in the canvas; the first snowy dawn was trying to break through the thick clouds, a watery, yellow blister of light appeared in the sky, and that light poured into the room through the rectangle of the window, illuminating the table and Grandfather II's present.

The camp was smashed—everything down to the last

connection, nail, thread knot, wire twist; the boy must have worked all night, destroying the toy, putting all of himself into the destruction, and now he trembled with sleeplessness, exhaustion, and fear. His fingers were bleeding, his nails were torn, the canvas was splotched with blood; he had managed to break it all noiselessly, silently, as if performing the greatest exploit of his life—not just the seven years he had lived, but for his whole life going forward; he was afraid, the room smelled of urine, and perhaps he was ready to give up his free will and wished it all to come back together, for the camp to rebuild itself, but the dawn entered the room, and the fluid objects of the night acquired their final, hard, daytime shapes, and not even the specter of desperation could re-create the broken camp.

Grandfather II staggered in the doorway. He would probably have been less shocked had the real camp been destroyed. On the evenings when he came to the workshop and threw out the carver and engraver to be alone with the toy, he enjoyed his own idea so much that he might have kept the toy camp in his office if that pleasure—as perceived by others—did not smack of eccentricity.

This miniaturized, facsimile camp truly did belong to Grandfather II. There was something not in the least metaphorical about the change in scale, in the optical magnification of his own figure, not from pure narcissism but as an expression of the correct proportions in his view: Grandfather II in his own estimation was not a god, not a master, he was himself, a man, and the fact that he was master of life and death over other men without considering himself something more simply proved to him that in fact he was truly greater. He gave his son a toy camp so that he would share his father's destiny, accept his own from his father's hands. Barracks outside the windows, whichever way you looked, barracks on the table—Grandfather II had sent his son to prison camp, excluding everything that was not-camp.

This can be called a crime against reality; a rather naive formulation, but one which accurately reflects the essence and can be interpreted more fully: much of what Grandfather II and those like him did was a crime against reality.

Reality always takes revenge on those who cut it down, who simplify it, who deny its multiplicity; it avenges as implacably as do the laws of nature; we are not always able to recognize events not as random but in accordance with the laws of nature.

With his commission of the miniature camp, Grandfather II had without realizing it overwound a tight spring; before he was a camp warden among others, not the best, and not the worst in those times, where the moving force was a depersonalized bureaucratic cruelty; he was also depersonalized, he did not stand out, his shoulder boards and uniform spoke for him, managed for him, while he was merely the wearer of the uniform, something secondary in relation to his rank and duty. But now—and there was a reason the craftsmen felt they were doing something inappropriate—now he had crossed the line of his work and tied his fate and his son's fate with the camp, in life and death.

Had Grandfather II been simpler and more volatile, he might have beaten his son, expressed his anger, shouted; but his anger was not expressed directly, it was held inside, ripening; the anger went through the coils of his inner being, acquiring a toxic thickness and essentially ceasing to be anger. It was transmuted into the ability to take a person to the most painful limit, force him to confront himself; the ability to make the most extreme and truthful deed meaningless.

Anger openly expressed reinforces the event that caused it; that is why Grandfather II, who knew the fury he felt instantly, as if it was always on a boil under his skin, burning his tongue, blistering his fingers, remained outwardly calm. A person who acted against Grandfather II's will had to undo it himself, as if sincere repentance was not enough: Grandfather II did not believe in words. He needed the action to be overturned by a counteraction, the antipode of the deed; Grandfather II swept away the traces, leaving no signs in memory that evinced his evildoing: the witness destroyed his witnessing, went backward over the path of his intention, undoing it.

Grandfather II said the boy had to repair the toy camp; he would not leave the room until he had done so, he would not go to school, and food would be brought to his room. Grandfather II locked the door with such force that the key got bent in the lock, the lock was broken, and the boy was truly locked in. Grandfather II did not believe that his son would escape through the window: he must have felt his will was a force like gravity which locked the boy up, squeezed him inside the room as if in his fist, and now he decided to wait, without loosening his grip, to wait and let time do its work.

Left alone with the inability to do what was demanded, the boy was supposed to feel time collapsing upon him, bringing no reprieve now or in the distant future; you sit there, knowing there is no way out, and the passing hours exacerbate your condition, exhausting and destructive.

Grandfather II saw his son as a traitor, he would have disowned him had there been examples of that, but in those days it was only sons who disowned their fathers. So Grandfather II did not punish the boy—he was forcing the boy to disown himself.

Seven was no age at all, thought Grandfather II, who was used to reckoning time in prison terms—ten years, fifteen, and you still have time after that to live—so a seven-year-old had to reject himself and curse himself daily, and then Grandfather II would take him, drained, limp inside, and mold himself another son.

His wife could no longer have children, and the barrenness

of her womb depressed Grandfather II, who still felt the desire for fatherhood. Fatherhood he imagined was a plastic process, similar to sculpting, and he wanted to bring into the world not a new life—a living thing while it is alive cannot be molded, it has its own laws—but something meek, suitable for his creative efforts.

That may be why his wife, before becoming barren, had two stillborn children after the boy. She gave birth, and then her female nature died, became insensible, as if her body was horrified by her husband's true desires.

The boy did not come out of the room for two days; he refused food the first morning, and Grandfather II ordered that he not be fed forcibly. He knew that the boy would rebel at first—it came out the way he wanted—and then the arrest would undermine his strength, and the more the boy believed he could prove something to his father, to stand up for himself, the faster his resistance would die out.

In the two days that the door was locked, the boy used his penknife to pry up a rotten floorboard and he squeezed into a space leading under the house. Grandfather II was at a loss for the first time: he couldn't call out a search party for his son. But it wasn't necessary—the boy was found.

The camp quarry, wide and deep, even in those days seemed to tilt the surrounding mountains, tilt the plain on which the nascent town stood. If a man, either drunk, or from joy or grief walked so that his legs carried him on their own, he would end up at the quarry.

The boy who ran out into the night not knowing where to go was doomed to end up at the quarry because of the town's configuration; the quarry was not guarded at night. At that hour it was the eye of the earth for the boy, it saw the boy everywhere, he had nowhere to hide. The quarry was his father's creature, and the fear of his sleeping father was transferred to the sleepless eye of the quarry; Grandfather

II had brought his son there, to the edge of the top ledge, and the boy thought there was a general madness in the stubbornness with which people, obeying his father, dug a pit, and the spirals of the quarry ledges seemed like a reflection of his father's will twisted into a spring. The boy went to the quarry because it was only there, in the center of the pupil, that he could he hide from the all-penetrating gaze; the pupil saw everything but not itself.

The work brigades found him in the morning; a sand bed had collapsed beneath him and he'd fallen; the body lay on the stones in a pile of sand. He had fallen by the wall they were dynamiting to find ore with eudialyte—a bright red transparent mineral; in daylight the whole side of the quarry was covered with red splotches. Eudialyte was called shaman's blood by the local tribes, who believed it to be the traces of a battle with a dark shaman, conquered and secured into the cliff over the lake; the eudialyte now flared, as if the boy's death had strengthened its glow, and it was impossible to chip out all the grains of the mineral from the ore, as the foreman had wanted to do at first, realizing what Grandfather II would see. He was afraid—the stone was a witness, the stone was an accuser.

Grandfather II went down into the quarry; the brigades were led out, and only the doctor was with him. Soon the camp warden came back up; the body was left on the stones, left to the doctor and orderlies. Grandfather II banished his son—the boy had tried once again to go against his will. Grandfather II did not believe the boy's death was an accident, but he himself was the least at fault: he blamed it on impudence, disobedience, stubbornness, not knowing the value of life; now he sought reasons that forced the boy to do that, but he did not seek them in himself: someone had spoiled the boy, set him against his father, confused, bewitched, plunged him into madness; Grandfather II considered the destroyed toy camp a sign of madness, of spiritual illness.

Grandfather II banished the dead boy, returning to the memories of the obedient, proper son he had been just a few months earlier, and when he thought of the boy, he thought of the former boy; his son lay on the rocks amid the bloody shimmer of eudialyte, but Grandfather II no longer could see him. The eudialyte burned his eyes, eternal, indestructible, and he left the quarry, ordering the chief of construction to blow up the spot where his son died. They made vertical blast holes in order to slice off a thick layer, the dynamiters laid the charge, but when the roar of the boulders ceased and the dust and smoke were carried away by the wind, they all saw that the eudialyte vein was revealed as being bigger and more powerful; the fresh grains of it, not yet muddied by the cold and rain, glowed red in the gray rock. Grandfather II ordered a second blast, but the stone would not yield, merely showing deep cracks; after that, the camp commandant never looked at the north wall of the quarry, and even the observation platform was moved so that the place where the boy died could not be seen.

His son died in an accident; his wife died soon after: the two stillborn babies shortened her life, her strength had gone into pregnancies, births, and it turned out that the boy was the only thing keeping her in this world. Her life poured into him at birth, more than usual with mother and child; the boy, firstborn and only son, absorbed too much of his mother—not in looks or personality, but in the ability to live, the life force, and she was an accidental victim.

When he was ill, so was she—her inner state was a mirror of his; you could put two thermometers next to each other, and the mercury was always in the same place, as if only one person's temperature had been taken. The mother seemed to have yielded life to her son; without the intervention of doctors and a caesarean birth he would have died in her womb, and so he lived illegally, on the margin; there was no place for him in life, life did not open for him, welcoming him, giving him a place, and so the boy was defenseless, without the protection everyone has as a birthright. Everything was dangerous and hazardous for him—nails, slippery ice, drafts; every accident, everything unforeseen or unprepared was attracted to him; the boy lived using his life strength faster than it could be replenished, and his mother—his mother depended on him, and when he died in the quarry, she did not survive it.

Grandfather II was left alone; he seemed not to have noticed his wife's death, but in fact it changed him. He had met his wife before becoming the man he now was, sacrificing his son to the camp and the quarry; his wife remembered the former man, and her memory, which he had no control over even had he wished for it, was an obstacle, it held him back; their joint life created borders, limits for his inner changes.

Grandfather II had simply chosen her—in his insensitive male simplicity—and she married him for life until death, and the fact that her womb was dead and she no longer had children by him did not yet mean that their connection was lost; a woman creates a man not through her wishes but by the moral impossibilities that her presence entails. When the connection between a man and a woman is broken by her disappearance, the man can quickly fall apart morally, if his surroundings are conducive to that, because he no longer encounters the honesty of flesh, fidelity, and the woman no longer supports him invisibly, he no longer has the support of even the habit of her existence.

For Grandfather II the collapse was manifested in this manner: he moved entirely into the realm of death, now certain that only death was constant and not subject to randomness; he started testing people with death—will the person succumb or not—as if trying to understand why his son died.

At that time a group of kulak peasants arrived at the camp;

they were not supposed to be used in the works—the order was to send them even farther, to the low reaches of the river not far from the town; the idea was for the kulaks to colonize a wild region, but anyone who was aware that downriver was just forest and tundra all the way to the ocean knew that colonize was just a euphemism.

The echelons arrived when the rivers had opened from the ice; just then there was a collapse in a recently started shaft.

Work stopped in the pit face; the geologists agreed that one more round of detonations would get them past the danger zone, and the collapsed rock could be reinforced, held by steel supports, welded with cement. But someone had to go into the pit and drill openings, five-meter blast holes for the charge; they couldn't reinforce anything before the repeated round of explosions, because it would destroy the reinforcement.

The men who had survived the collapse refused to go; Grandfather II drove to the mine. Everyone thought he would threaten them with execution and wondered which death—bullet or rock—would triumph. But Grandfather II did not send the surviving miners into the pit; he stood at the opening, which even on a hot day sends out a cool dampness, inhaling the mineral smell of smashed shale mixed with the stink of explosives; water dripped from all the cracks, and rocks fell from the vault, and it seemed that underground the mountain's heavy, slow mind moved damply; it did not avenge or threaten—it simply turned over, unable to comprehend its own existence. The growth of crystals, the movement of rock is measured in so many years that the stone would not notice human events; while we, going underground, enter compressed eras, find ourselves in a past so remote that the length of our lives is reduced to zero.

That is why it is so scary when stone separates, crumbles, comes alive, there is something that is not quite a natural catastrophe about it—it is ossified time falling apart, the very foundation of the world, what is supposed to be solid and hold the rest; you have to be a demiurge, a titan, to step into that catastrophe and find what inner resources are needed to withstand it.

I don't know what Grandfather II was feeling as he looked into the opening; but he ordered the kulaks brought there, the ones who were supposed to be sent to the lower reaches of the river. They were brought over, still in their old clothes; the prisoners were as worn as objects can be, as if they'd been rubbed out on the wooden bunks, yet they stood casually, some buttoned up, some not, they stood too freely; Grandfather II ordered the announcement to be made—whoever takes the risk and enters the mine, drills the blast holes to create a second, artificial collapse, will not be sent to the tundra, but kept in the camp.

Grandfather II probably figured that if anyone did accept, he would die in the mine. But ten men headed by the former village elder, who had never seen a mine drill before, managed to move quietly through the shaft, freezing at every creak, drill the wall as indicated on the map, and return unharmed; death did not take the exiles.

Maybe Grandfather II would have kept his promise, but he learned there at the mine that all ten came from the same region as the carver who had made the whistle and had been sent to fell trees; the former elder even had time to be pleased that the camp warden knew their home places, he thought there might be a possibility of leniency in that—but Grandfather II was already in the car giving orders to prepare the next step.

All the exiles were taken along the embankment of the railroad under construction to the river, where they were loaded on barges; the convoy soldiers returned alone and they said nothing—the people were dropped off on an island and the tugboats and barges left; since then many others were sent there, some managed to survive and start a settlement, but no one knew anything about the fate of that first group; where the island was or what had happened.

About a year later Grandfather II went blind. In late spring when there is still snow on the tundra but the sun shines brightly, the snow, icy, sugary, brilliant, reflects the harsh light, and a haze of light hangs over the tundra. It does not envelop the eyes like fog, it burns them like a magnifying glass on wood; the flood of light, anticipating the high water, gives birth to an inflamed day, and the eyes become inflamed by the unnatural whiteness.

In late spring Grandfather II traveled by car to a distant village along the ice road, still unmelted and made by trucks, like a log road through the impassable tundra swamps. A stream undermined the ice, washed out the road, and Grandfather II's car crashed, the concussed driver drowned, and Grandfather II was left in the tundra dozens of kilometers from anywhere.

It was not a great distance, a few days' walk, but the sun was so strong, the snows had still not melted, and the rays of reflected light turned into razor blades; whiteness looked into Grandfather II's eyes—not the blurred, myopic whiteness of snowfall but the morbid whiteness of sparkling ice that steals the color of the sky.

Nature's white is blind, it has no depth or perspective as does black, for instance; white in the North is the profound color of nonexistence, the color of death, a color wall that removes the distinctions of closer and farther, and locks a person inside it. The world turns into a sphere without horizon, and eyes ache because while seeing they do not see, there is nothing to see except the color white, which drives you insane with its stolidity, its indivisibility into shades, its thing-like solidness—it feels as if you could tear it apart with your hands, chop it with an ax. You fall into a coloristic trance, into monotonous color madness; whiteness enters the visual nerve as a blinding injection, and only the emptiness of white remains, smooth and scorching.

In two days, Grandfather II went blind: the tundra took away his eyes. He was found by men sent from the village he was traveling to, they found him by accident: one of the men in the truck was a soldier of the "flying" squads that went out to catch fugitives; a lot of people tried escaping over the spring snow crust, and the soldier knew how to look and still protect his eyes from the sun and ice—through smoked glass; and through the smoked glass he saw a dark dot far from the road in a long declivity; if he had just been looking with his naked eye, even with his hand shading his eyes, the black dot would have been swallowed and dissolved by the glare.

Grandfather II almost died; he dared to test death on others and was thrown into it himself; he was pulled out, as if by his umbilical cord, by the sharp eyes of the searcher, but he paid for his salvation with blindness. His vision returned slightly, he nearly overcame the weakness, but then he lost his sight completely.

Now I knew what he always saw before him, the last thing his memory had retained—the color white; he tried to trick fate by inscribing characters upon the blank background; get back his son, and his vision would return, his past, too, and the years he did not see would vanish, as if they had never been.

PART 6

I still had to go to the river and find the exiles' island—I had to travel the entire trajectory of Grandfather II's fate; I felt that there, in that nook that even he did not know fully, was a limit; I called it the limit of oblivion.

I was stepping into a space where there were no witnesses. The island mentioned by the engraver was a point—a pulsating point where everything begins and where everything ends.

Bidding the engraver farewell, I left the town; I needed to hurry, as if a deadline loomed; I remembered my dream, the island of faces, the barge with prisoners and convoy guards, the closing doors of the holds; the time for wandering was coming to a close for me, the town was pushing me onto the road. The inner state I had maintained since the decision to learn everything about Grandfather II's past was also running out; if you understand "inner state" to mean a readiness for perception, a lasting effort to be open to events, it also has a time limit which should not overstepped, otherwise, it's all artificial respiration, self-inducement, and naked dutifulness.

I did not think about how I would return; the thought of returning would have turned my search for the island into a round-trip. But you couldn't reach the island and then come back the same way—that contradicted its finality, the point's absoluteness.

I headed to the river along the roadbed of the former railroad; I turned off at times, climbing up on the hills to look around: the gravel bed was low and offered no view. The landscape was the work of a demented soul, continually repeating the same word, line, motif; tundra lakes, swamps, and hills were so similar that the concept of continuity vanished: the locale held nothing that the gaze could recognize as new or different, and you could not tell if you were traveling or marching in place.

You could measure distance only by the remnants of camps. The barracks and watchtowers had rotted; the post with barbed wire had fallen. There were only the outlines, which were visible in the distance, but for those inside a former camp, the camp did not exist: just dirt and more dirt, hummocks and more hummocks, except for a porcelain isolator or a shard of brick on the ground. I picked up an isolator; just as a meteorite found in the tundra is recognized by its alienness— cosmic speed cast in metal—a piece of carved white porcelain, looking like a chess piece, was alien here, and the place did not want to hide it, it turned it in the way people turned in fugitives for a sack of flour.

The rails and sleepers had been removed from the embankment; only the bridges across rivers remained. The five-meter earth rampart had been built by the hands of prisoners; the earth lay so densely here that the rampart had taken on the flow and unobtrusiveness of ancient burial mounds in the steppe: they were simultaneously man-made and natural.

"Built by the hands of prisoners …" I said to myself; there was too much in those words of culture and not enough of real sensation; the embankment was no longer horrifying, did not make you grieve. Like any large-scale structure, it commanded astonishment for itself, to be seen as a single whole in which the efforts of individuals could not be found, representing a visible, embodied gesture of superhuman creative will.

I walked along the embankment; it was hard for me to realize that there was nothing in this embankment except the time spent by forced labor, except hundreds of thousands of wheelbarrows of dirt. And if the embankment had any scale, it was the scale of the meaninglessness of what was done.

The fact that the embankment has been abandoned, that there was no railroad, was not seen as a mistake but as the consequence of the original meaninglessness; the embankment was a false path, and all the human effort expended on this path was spent for real but for nothing—the path was made to take away these efforts, devour them, and no more.

I imagined the wheels of the winches turning, the smithies with water hammers, all those capstans, pulleys, cables, blocks, gears, rollers, axes combined into a mechanism wasting real human effort, dispersing it into the wind—the efforts of labor, thought, the intention to be. It could have been creative, could have moved something, aided something, become something in historical time—but it all had passed through the mill in the name of this goal that was detached from human life, and that's what killed it.

I walked; the parts frequented by hunters and fishermen were behind me; I was in uninhabited places. The difference between a place that is visited a few times a month and a place where no one goes for years is marked: it's not in the sense of primordial nature—that is naive and it merely substitutes for another, deeper feeling: the absolute absence of another human being. Where you by yourself are the human race, you feel a strange longing that is impossible in other places: a longing not for warmth or socializing, but for humans in the anthropological sense; a footprint in the sand by a brook can make you alert—you don't know who the stranger is: a solitary prospector, a fugitive, a seeker of peace or revelation in the tundra—but you will follow his tracks because even the possible evil you might encounter will at least come from a creature of your own breed.

It must be this longing that brings people together in a place where meetings as a fact of life do not exist; where it is much more likely to miss each other and almost impossible to meet; where two people is already too many for the rarefied spaces.

One day I went up yet another hill; the cold wind scudded light clouds in fast waves, making the earth even more still. Suddenly I felt a quiver in one of the spider threads your gaze wraps around the visible; a few kilometers away I saw a man walking.

I knew it was a man, even though it was just a dark spot— you couldn't see an animal at that distance; they blend in, live near the ground, feed on the ground, and their every step repeats their gait, which like rhythm in music, exists in the extension of the landscape; an animal lives in the horizontal, its body is extended in it, while a human is a vertical milestone; his movement makes everything around him change, creating a moving axis of coordinates.

A man; I was interested and turned so that I would intersect with him. A half hour later I could observe the stranger.

Attached to his backpack were a large watering can and a strange short-handled rake with very fine teeth. He would stop, move on a bit, then remove moss and lichen from sloping, rounded stones, and then sparingly pour water on them from the can.

He was not young, he moved without quite trusting his body but depending on it; thin, gray-haired, wearing worn oilcloth and swamp boots, weaponless but with rake and watering can; his eyes were focused on the ground.

I have encountered very different tramps in the tundra; some sought precious stones in the hillsides, others rooted around in abandoned settlements for hidden caches; still others collected mammoth tusks in riverbeds, or the remains of an AN-2 which crashed while bringing gold dust from a mine, or just wandering around in the hope of grabbing someone else's find, whatever it was. There were seekers of ancient pagan temples; madmen who wanted to found a state; collectors of meteorites; and free interpreters of history, looking for traces of Hyperborea.

The man I met—his skills, his experience—suggested he was a prospector, seeking something real; the rake and watering can no longer surprised me, they were clearly tools in his search, but I didn't know what he was looking for.

Catching up with him, in a long declivity covered by hills from the embankment, I stumbled across a skull. It is impossible to dig a grave in a swamp, but here, in a valley between cliffs, stony soil had accumulated; in a few places it had sunk in even rectangles, the tundra foxes had burrowed in them, and the entrances were revealed by the trampled earth and tufts of fur; the skull was by one of the dens—the foxes had scratched it out of the depth of their burrow.

The fox burrows went into the softened dirt of camp graves; now, when my eyes knew what to look for, I found a rib, a vertebra, a tibia in the moss and rocks; the foxes had extracted and scattered them; the small rodents that destroyed bones were the foxes' prey, so the bones remained; dirt filled the pores of the bones, which made them dark, primordial, and the rain could not wash them clean. A large orange-cap mushroom grew near a broken collarbone; the cap was contorted by the sun, revealing a sticky and slimy sponge underneath, and this bloodless flesh, which did not know pain, belonging to the lowest kingdom of living organisms, was repulsive; I remembered the mushroom near Grandfather II's grave; white, doughy, like an old man's wrinkled ear; human flesh rotted away, but the flesh of mushrooms was renewed, growing from the tiniest spores, and humans were very fragile compared to mushrooms.

We met at the bottom of the hill; the stranger was smoking and boiling water on a smokeless fire; I was walking, the sun shone brilliantly, but inside me was the darkness of the foxhole; the foxes waited for me to leave and leaped up on the hillock behind me, as agile as ghosts; they froze amid the stones, low to the ground, pointy-eared—not animals but hatchlings of tundra gods that feed on the misery of others, the aborigines of pestilential places.

The stranger was armed, after all; he was clever, people would think he was unarmed if they didn't see a rifle, but he had a handgun, which he aimed at me while shading his eyes from the sun. The gun was no threat; I was in that state I had felt when the black dog attacked me—the man, sensing my weakness, put away the gun, gesturing at the stone slabs. He'd raked the turf and washed off what remained with water; now the water was evaporating on the slabs.

The light stone revealed chiseled drawings; some the size of my hand, others bigger than a man's height. There were rolling wheels—suns with spokes; flowers with four petals, like a cross; large and small fish, swimming in various directions; crooked and straight lines, furrows in the stone; flattened beavers, the way skins are spread out; dozens of deer wandering in a long herd; hunters following the deer and catching them with unnaturally long spears; chains of bear tracks, birds with bony wings and harpy beaks; animals that look like an animated saw with a snail's head; boats and snowshoes; dogs turned upside down as if in space orbit; triangular eyes with oval pupils; a gaping circle—the way the vagina is depicted in anatomical atlases; a round woman with short legs and arms, and inside her, head down, a child floats weightlessly; a man with an incredibly long, snake-like penis that makes him resemble a spermatozoon; axes and oars; animals, people, whales, pulled together by threads like umbilical cords growing out of one another, a mixture of differences, miscegenation of everything living.

The drawings were alive, breathing like fish roe in the warm water of shallows; it seemed they even had a fragrance, spicy, voluptuous; the figures and ornaments met, combined, flew apart, and it was a single act of creating life; the power of the drawings made the earthy black of the fox den vanish from within me; the drawings were not art, not depictions—they were elemental, as if the existence of the people who had made them was transferred completely, without remnant, into them.

They were petroglyphs; I knew they were occasionally found in the tundra here; they were left by tribes that had lived seven or eight thousand years before our era. But at the moment I wasn't thinking about that.

There is a special sense of day in the tundra; a day is an enclosed space, something three-dimensional; in the tundra, where you need not glasses but binoculars, where the summer sun almost never sets, this room of the day is particularly spacious; here in the high latitudes where the meridians almost meet and the parallels are small circles, day reigns, an enormous vault, a single day for the entire world; astronomically that is not correct but that is the true impression.

The stranger gave me a mug; the overbrewed tea was bitter, but the bitterness gently and willfully prompted my heart, making it beat harder and faster, invigorating me and giving me strength.

"You're not following me?" the man asked.

Despite his gun, he was afraid; he would not have hurt me and he knew it.

"People follow me," the man said. "Think I'll lead them to the petroglyphs." He pointed to the drawings. "You can get money for them, if you can break them from the stone and get them out."

The light and the shadows lessened at last; the stone suns dimmed and the earth's darkness melted away. The tension of feeling eased and I saw the man clearly, in full detail.

He had cancer: his face seemed to be inflated from inside, like the caricatures made by street artists, exaggerating lips, cheeks, all the flesh of the face; the overgrown flesh of his lips sagged, the cheeks covered his eyes, the mouth was double in length, and not a single hair grew on his smooth sausage skin.

"This is from radiation," he said. "What's inside my body is worse. The gun—it was given to me as an award—is for shooting myself when I can't stand it anymore."

My unexpected comrade was a military man; long ago he had looked for places in this tundra for underground nuclear tests; he had come from a region with forests and did not know that the tundra could make you lost as well, like a forest, but in a different way: the forest changes where the light is coming from, confuses tracks, while the tundra is open, you can see everything, but suddenly you look around, nothing but hillocks, and your mind, busy with thoughts, has not retained any orientation markers.

And so, lost in the tundra, he found his first petroglyphs, signs of the sun, rolling sun wheels; later, when he was sick, after the surgery, after the chemotherapy, the former soldier returned to these parts, because the drawings chiseled in stone seemed to be the most essential things he had ever encountered; he did not collect petroglyphs, he did not make copies, he simply looked for them, following the path of the ancient artists, and gave the drawings a reason for existing— he looked at them.

We drank *chifir*, the extra-strong tea brew; I asked if it was possible to find someone who remembered this area from decades ago. He said that there were a few nomadic families left in the tundra, who had escaped being forced into a reindeer-breeding kolkhoz; now others tried to show the reindeer to tourists for money, so they moved deeper into the tundra and shot at helicopters that tried to land by their tents. They had no radios, nothing connected them to other people; they accepted only him—sick and looking for ancient drawings for their own sake; at this time of year I could probably run into them in the middle reaches of the river. There was also a village with descendants of the exiled prisoners, it was even farther; he had not been there in close to ten years, and when he was there, people were leaving, abandoning their houses.

The chifir was gone, the fire went out; we embraced, he did not ask me about anything and moved on along the slope, and I went back to the embankment and for a long time as I walked I could see his figure moving along the hills.

Three days later I came out at the former port, where the ruined railroad led; I came out by the river. The water flowed amid low banks in shallows, unattractive, reflecting the gray sky, with a paucity of reflections, sparkle, or light, and the river's width was somehow lost in the rounded banks and unhurried current.

Hundreds of buoys lay in the shallows; they were made of plastic, like fishing floats, metal, and wood, like the top of a lighthouse—the entire history of river boating in one place. The river changed its course, washed up new shallows where never-flowering water lilies, trembling like a bird's webbed foot, started to grow, banks collapsed, revealing the corpses of prehistoric animals, ancient deer, and time was broken open like a hunk of bread in those cliffs—pick it up, run your fingers through the stone age; the river changed its course, but the buoys no longer followed the changes, did not mark its depth, did not stretch out its thread, did not huddle in the dark; when navigation ceased here, the river returned to the complete control of the fish, the fin—forerunner of the oar—replaced the propeller, and the river waters were no longer troubled by the rotation of twisted blades.

Near the shore, only pilings were left of docks; they held trees brought by the river, the rubbish of high waters, and water was sucked beneath them with a slurp and whistle; farther along, in a broad cove formed in an old river bed, barges and tugs sat on the bottom.

Usually an abandoned ship is like an abandoned house; but the barges did not elicit that feeling; they were enormous rusty hulks, grim and clumsy arks; they sank slowly, pushing up a boggy ooze with their weight; the paint came off them unevenly, in layers—you could see that some painters did their work honestly, undercoating first, and others did not—and below the crumbling paint you could see a second layer, a third, fourth, fifth, sixth, seventh; the aging metal was crumbling, rusted chunks of the sides fell into the boat, but the paint layers held on to one another; the barges were half-drawn, they had been used along the river three or four times beyond the limit of the metal's exhaustion, repainting but not repairing, and the metal gave up first, while the baked paint survived.

The tugs were to the side of the barges, six boats: *"… omsom … lets,"* *"Sha …. ter,"* *"Gornya … "* *"Pogranichn … Zapol … ,"* *"Kap … tan P … asolov,"* and *"Boe … "* is what could be read on their sides, as if the names were being transmitted by Morse code with a bad connection.

I walked from one to another and found the only dinghy that looked seaworthy; on the second tug I found oars, on the third a half-barrel of pitch to caulk the sides. I also discovered a rock-hard bag of salt, and I took it—I was sorry to see salt wasted; salt was the missing ingredient in local fresh water and skies, and I tossed it into the box on the dinghy.

I set off, the dinghy was too big for one person to steer normally, so I paddled to the middle of the river and let myself go with the flow; the boat settled, sucked up water once again, and the river carried me away from the old tugs, the buoys on the shore, and opened up a view of the hills beyond the bend; the tilt of the land bore its waters to the Arctic Ocean, and I followed gravity; there was no wind, and there was no time, either—the river had become time, and time inexorably headed for the river's mouth.

Days passed; bare hills, no people, quiet, the measured flow of water, lulling me, telling me that everything in the world was peaceful, calm, and smooth. I made notches in the oar to mark the days, but then I dropped it in the water and it floated away; I ate very little, I wasn't moving, using energy, and I lost my appetite; sometimes it seemed that I would soon become ethereal, transparent, or turn into a young water spirit; fish looked at me from the water, settling into the wake, as if awaiting my transformation. A two-meter pike accompanied me for a while—pikes live for hundreds of years and this one probably remembered people, fishermen, sailors; then it swam off to the side, and once again I saw only water and hills.

That is why I noticed the remains of a bridge—the river had once been crossed by a second branch of the railroad meant to extend to a future settlement in the tundra which had never been built—I first did not recognize it, that is, my eye did not accept it. I saw something odd, unnecessary, out of harmony, a mistake; that must be how animals see what humans build.

In the shallows, where the current is not strong even at high water, stood crates filled with earth and stones, looking like crosssections of log cabins; on the left bank rose the cones of *chums*, or tepees, essentially the enlarged hats of nomads, negating the idea of a house; wherever you toss your hat, there is your hearth. The area was hilly and the chums followed the lines of the bare hills as a wave follows another.

I landed close to the settlement. Below the railroad embankment, steam engines and trains were parked. They must have been abandoned when the bridges were washed away on the line, and now they were rusting and sinking into the tundra; strange only at first glance, it was the trains and not the chums that seemed a chronological inaccuracy.

The steam engines stood there like broken time machines, which they were in other places, where the railroad truly did accelerate time, opening a way through it, where the steam engine truly was seen as a symbol of the future happening now, where tracks, semaphores, and stations connected the scattered times of a big country into a shared ensemble. But here, in the middle of the tundra, those mechanisms did not work; here it was still the time before steam engines, time before whatever would be; I remembered the steam engine from my dream—this was its dead end, the end of its trip, and the tundra, indifferent to the cumbersome machine, extended itself tranquilly and in its entirety, not knowing about divisions into different sides of the world.

Near the chums, hunks of meat hung from sanded poles; the smoke from the campfire fed on wet willow was everywhere, more than was needed to smoke the meat and chase away midges and flies; it seemed it was intended to permeate people, to teach them to stop the flow of tears by willpower or to lose the ability to cry completely; the wind blew in steady gusts, and in rhythm with the gusts the coals flared red under the damp branches dripping boiling juice.

Reindeer grazed nearby; they walked around the pole, two or three hundred head—they had to be counted by the head because below their bodies melded into a single multilegged body, and each back was a bulging muscle; their gait resembled water flowing in a whirlpool. The deer walked by the pole to be free of the midges; the shepherd set the leader in motion and the herd followed. I imaged how it must look from the air and realized that I was looking at a clock, a clock without divisions; the pole was the only vertical point for dozens of kilometers, casting no shadow on the cloudy day, and around it flowed the seasons, measured by the height of the deer antlers.

People appeared suddenly, stepping out from behind the chums; the nomads did not mix blood with outsiders, and they were very similar, a single person in different ages, a bisexual creature as infant, girl, man, old man, old woman; one person, or they were all as one; their faces the color of tea, dressed in clothing that combined fabric with deerskins, they seemed to be living in order to perform the ritual of becoming one with animals, and I probably looked defective to them, lacking an animal half.

Seeing that I was alone, they invited me to the fire and fed me boiled deer meat; there was no rejection and no interest. They asked if I had any salt; I brought the bag from my dinghy and they changed, surrounded me; in this world devoid of material objects I realized salt was the power of bones, the power of what is solid in man, and the nomads felt it, too; now I could ask questions—we had become close, united by the salt, and I asked if they remembered anything about when the barges and people first appeared on the river, many, many years ago.

I was told the story of the barge caravan, not as a myth, not as a legend about floating river houses, yet still I felt that the man was talking from a distant shore, not because he was essentially indifferent but because the subject of the story was like a natural phenomenon or as a phenomenon of a world so alien that the world of nature was much closer to him.

The voice of the grandfather, who saw the barges full of people on the April river after the ice broke but did not understand what was happening, directed the grandson's vocal cords; the nomad standing on the shore must have thought these were arks, entire worlds containing the absolute in life's laws, and if some people threw other, weaker ones into the water, then these were the real laws of those worlds, this was their truth; thus, if all of Christopher Columbus's men had limped, the natives would have probably imagined a land beyond the sea of limping men. And how could a man born where old people were sometimes left to die if the family was moving to new site, how could he disagree with throwing the weak overboard? I entered inside the viewpoint of the storyteller, like entering a room with a wide window, and looked out from there—but with my own vision, recognizing what my unwitting guide could not.

The barges docked at a big island in the middle of the river—that was more convenient for the tugboat captains; the people were left on the island, on the long beach where there was nothing but driftwood; it was a warm sunny day and the prisoners, even though the guards fired on them, jumped into the river to bathe. The water darkened from the filth of several thousand men, remnants of clothing that had been worn in the cramped holds where men stood shoulder to shoulder floated in the water; the icy water chilled them, and the men quickly ran back on shore, running along the sand, embracing, huddling for warmth.

The water, melt water of yesterday's snows, water of new life, washed away the long journey, the rust and filth, and the sun played on the waves so that it seemed fish would appear to lay eggs at any moment; but the sunlight was brief, the nascent day was short, and the few who still had the strength to risk their lives jumped into the water, clutching trees floating by or floes of bottom ice, covered in silt and water grasses, that had bobbed to the surface and were carried by the current; the guards fired, the tight chilling air whipped eardrums, nostrils flared at the gun smoke, acrid and sharp.

Then the tugboats and barges left, and the men remained on the island. Night came, and in the morning it started to snow—storm clouds rolled in from the north; the snow was thick, it put out the feeble fires of wet logs; the exiles sought shelter in gullies, tried to dig burrows in the sand and add some protection from the snow, but the snow penetrated everywhere, even inside the hollow tree trunks where people squeezed in; the nomads could not cross the river in their light, flat-bottomed boats wrapped in skins, and so they could only watch the smoke and ashes thicken over the island, how flames flared and died out; for a few days while it snowed they heard screams, and then, on the coldest night, they could hear only moans; the snow stopped, the fog dispersed, but there was no one left alive on the island; you couldn't see the bodies, people had hidden as best they could and died in earthen dugouts, digging with their hands, with branches, the few tools they had been given.

When the river calmed down, someone went over to the island; there was a stench, birds had gathered; they brought back sacks of flour (the exiles were given food, but no dishes), but they did not eat it; in subsequent years the island was flooded several times, the bones were washed away; only rarely did holes open up, with dead men lying deep in the permafrost.

The next settlers—and many traveled along the river—did not ask about their predecessors; they traveled past the island without noticing it; the island remained as it had been—a flat earthen pancake in the channel, and only the nomad family I met passed on the memory of what had happened there.

The ones I talked to could not say where the island was; I had passed sand spits, shallows, other islands—and they were all the same, all inconstant, all vanished and then were reborn with high waters; islands without features, islands of empty expanses; just islands.

I pushed off from the rocks in my dinghy; the current picked me up, and the people by the chums watched me go the way they had once watched those who were deposited on the island; the river, perturbed by the piers of the former bridge, calmed down, the rapids sank to the bottom, and the dinghy sailed steadily, as if propelled by flying clouds, the movements of the stars, the air currents high in the sky, reflected in the water.

A few days later I saw houses on a knoll; that was the village of exiles. The houses seemed transported by a mirage, an optical illusion; as if actually they were somewhere thousands of kilometers from here, near a small river and woods, and it was the play of light in the atmosphere this far north that placed them on a knoll where they could not be.

I left the dinghy and took a path that zigzagged up the hill. The village, a dozen houses, did not seem completely abandoned: clearly someone had walked down the road, splotches of spilled water dried in the sand. But the weeds were too thick in the gardens, the windows had been shut up too long ago, the nails were falling out of the wood; and most important, there was every indication that people had stopped caring about the place where they lived. Besides which, I couldn't understand how there was dirt, how there were weeds here in the tundra; where did the soil come from?

At the well, which is always kept clean in villages, dogs had dug themselves a hollow, a dusty hole full of fur and scraps of bone; a torn wire hung down, easy to brush against, the pole was so crooked I longed to straighten it; every object in the village asked for human help: supporting, straightening, sawing, lifting. People here seemed to have forgotten all the verbs for creative activity, the sound of a hammer or the song of a saw, and had forgotten about themselves, too: being there was intolerable. There is a special color, the color of old fence boards that have been splashed all winter with the snowy mush underfoot, and in the spring the mud dries, turning earthy gray; the color of carelessness and indifference. The whole village was speckled with it, as if it had been sown over many years of drizzle; someone had hung a lantern by the gate and now its glass cover was filled with rainwater and the canvas wick bore filigree rust crystals. What was intolerable was not the neglect itself but that life could accommodate itself to neglect, take on its image, become identical to it.

One garden was tended: strangely, it was entirely planted with potatoes, leaving only a narrow walk to the house, every bed filled with potatoes, as if nothing else grew anywhere in the village. Someone was inside the house, smoke came out of the crumbling chimney that dropped pieces of brick onto the mossy roof, but the windows were shuttered tight.

Behind the house there was a creaking, grinding noise, metal on stone, ringing and then grinding again; the blue twilight that made the air thicken as it grew colder without losing its transparency settled on the village, and each screech caused goose bumps, warning me not to come closer—only forged steel could sound like that. Three apple trees by the house—how much effort had it taken to grow them here!—had gone wild, all their force going into offshoots and foliage, and the branches untouched by buds dropped brown leaves onto the ground; the color of dead leaves, the color of rotting apples was everywhere, giving the house and ground an aging, debilitated air. Old pruning cuts painted with pitch remained on the trees, but the pitch had cracked and fallen off, and even though the tree had grown a tight leathery circle around the cuts, the trunks were already crumbling and the roots were probably dying off. The wires holding branches that threatened to fall off dug too hard into the wood, cutting the bark.

I went into that small fallow garden, engulfed in the bitter-ash smoke that comes from a badly built or deteriorating stove; it was getting colder and the leaves fell less frequently, as if their twigs were growing torpid.

Behind the house, at a grinding machine made from a converted foot-operated sewing machine, sat a shaggy old man; I saw him from the back, broad and hunched, half covered by long, tangled, gray hair, with apple leaves nestled in them; I thought at first that he was a werewolf with claws, but then I realized they were fingernails, yellow, curved, broken or crookedly cut. The old man was sharpening an axe on a long handle, a lumberjack's axe; it was badly chipped, someone had used it to chop up boards of an old structure and kept hitting nails; long streams of reddish sparks caused by the uneven blade edge on the whetstone flew in the air, illuminating nothing but merely sewing through the dark; the wheels turned and the dry belts creaked.

The old man, the sharpening wheel—rougher than needed for fine sharpening—and the axe; I went farther along, not ready to call out to the man, when I saw a second one. He was on the porch steps, bent over a fishing net on his knees, and the same kind of thick, unkempt hair covered his face. The old man was mending the net, unwinding rough thread from a spool the size of his hand, making loops with a curved faceted needle and muttering to himself—his beard stirred as if a mouse had moved into it. A third old man, also on the porch, just as gray and shaggy, was carving a boat frame; the wooden piece had a bend with an inconvenient elbow, and the old man clumsily moved his long knife along it.

I greeted them. The three old men turned to me, dropping their work. I still couldn't make out their faces: their hair fell over their eyes. Their fingernails belonged to animals or birds, and their hair grew so thickly it could have been moss or weeds.

The old men were silent and uncomprehending. Telling them apart by their clothing was difficult: their padded jackets and trousers had not been washed in so long they had taken on the same indefinite color of grime, and new spots vanished among the old; the one with the axe had a scar across his palm, the one mending the net had a thimble that had become ingrown on a finger of his left hand and in the finger of the right, a fishhook that had jabbed his calloused skin, yellow as candle stearin, was hanging as if from the lip of an old fish; and the one who had been whittling wore a darkened ring.

"The dogs got themselves lost," said the fisherman.

The man spoke as if they were still just three; as if they had always lived the three of them and a fourth never was and never could be, and thus I did not fit into his field of comprehension and he might not figure out for several days that there was a stranger among them. Their solitude together was older than they were, time had vanished within it, and the old men had aged not only with the years but because the days of their lives resembled one another, and the days did not bring new impressions but merely subtracted old ones from their memory.

"The dogs got themselves lost," the fisherman repeated, and the other two replied, "Lost."

Their voices were like old things being used after a long hiatus; the sounds did not fit together properly, hanging on by hook or crook, dangling like a loose button. They sounded like dead men who had acquired new flesh but could not adjust the new voice to the old words.

The man with the axe leaned against his sharpener, the fishermen stuck the needle in his jacket, and the whittler put the knife away inside his boot. Wind came from the higher reaches of the river, the wind moved the old men's hair, pushing it from their eyes.

The men were blind; their minds were damaged and their gazes were stopped like a run-down clock. The lens, cornea, iris, the entire eye was whole, the visual core of the brain was whole, but the mind refused to allow the visible world in, refused to see. The eyes were those of a sleeping man whose lids were lifted without rousing him, and the pupils were like binoculars turned inward, into the head, the dark cosmos of dreams that is not accessible to the waking.

I waited, not knowing what time of day was in their heads, if they had any time at all, at what point they lost their sight, if they remembered the house, the apple trees, the village, the river, the land on both sides, if they understood where I was and who they were.

They were brothers, and no longer able to see, they came to resemble one another even more. Their faces fell into neglect;

the unconsciousness that annihilated their lives also annihilated their distinguishing features. All that was left in their faces was what had been placed there by their parents' blood: their faces had been taken over by their fathers, grandfathers, and great-grandfathers, and it seemed those figures would start coming out, opening the flesh like a door, and exiting one at a time, and once the last one was out, gaping emptiness would replace the face.

The old men finally understood that a stranger had come to the village; they surrounded me and ran their hands over my face and body; I stood and thought that I had truly reached the limit of memory; the blindness of the exiled old men, the blindness of Grandfather II all combined; this place did not exist in geography, an accidental traveler would not find this village, he would miss it; this was a country inhabited by people from the days of Grandfather II, an entire country that had protected itself from the present through blindness and then became trapped in it. While the old men molded my appearance for themselves with their hands, I thought about how not to linger here and destroy the insularity of this world.

Essentially, the old men had one memory for the three of them; separate them, and each one's memory would not be enough for a complete description of the events, so they often spoke simultaneously, creating a collected field of memory that lived only in words. I asked about the apple trees, impossible to imagine here near the Arctic Circle, planted in permafrost that would not allow roots to penetrate, and they told me that the whole village stood on soil that was brought in, stolen— the exiles were not allowed to leave their place of exile.

For a dozen years the people secretly took boats to the upper reaches, where there were forests and soil, they chopped down trees, made rafts to float them down to build huts and sent soil on the rafts as well; it took ten years before the first garden bed appeared in the village—before that, the exiles had lived on imported food products and by hunting. The authorities had set up a cordon on the river to overturn the rafts—they allowed them to cut down trees but not to take away soil; the reindeer herders even wondered if the exiles ate the soil, they were bringing so much, and they couldn't understand what for, since for nomads soil could not give birth to anything but reindeer moss. The villagers might have given up on the idea but most of them were kulak peasants and they put their entire organizing force, their passion for life into a calculated gathering of soil, real soil, without pity for themselves or others; they called the local soil mud, which it was, a runny liquid of mud on ice.

Later, when the village stood on fertile soil, some of the exiles were taken to town, that is, to the camp where Grandfather II had once been warden, where they started a botanical garden, planting flowers in heated greenhouses to show how new life was burgeoning in the Far North, and in the polar night prisoners in the barracks could see the glowing glass cubes behind three layers of barbed wire. The garden was part of the camp economy, and the locals hated it for devouring heat and light, a garden for baskets of red flowers to greet official airplanes that instantly turned to glass in the frost; high-ranking guards brought the flowers home later, and anything left over was taken to the statue of Lenin.

A war ensued over the right to work in the garden, in the steamy heat of the greenhouse, and the criminals won; the guards couldn't do anything about it; the only gardener who knew the job, a former custodian of an arboretum, was soon killed by a live wire, and the garden began to fail; prisoners started eating the flowers, chopping them up with a knife like greens and boiling them in tin cans. The camp administrators, who could not retreat—the botanical garden was now celebrated in the ministry, they promised to send specialists, expand the garden, and turn it into a museum of polar agronomy and gardening—the administrators decided to gather the peasant exiles and staff the garden with them. They simply sent a convoy of guards to the exile village and, without arresting them, the leader picked out ten people to bring back to the camp.

The garden had trees—apple, cherry, plum; in winter they were wrapped in burlap, with straw piled around the trunks, but the burlap and straw were stolen to make clothing warmer; they had to keep a watchman by the trees. They were still too small to bear fruit, so when high-ranking visitors came, fruits were hung on the branches in any season; the fruits were counted, so that the staff would not appropriate any before returning them in compliance with an inventory list.

One time a guest decided to eat an apple and discovered the thin thread that tied its stem to the branch, and angrily threw the small Golden Chinese apple, glowing like a paper lantern, somewhere into the grass; the official was insulted, he had believed with childlike sincerity that he was in a polar paradise where trees bear fruit twelve months a year, and while he was used to human trickery, and an expert on faking reports himself, he was unpleasantly surprised to see that even nature can be involved in deceit. He walked around a few more trees, muttering "I didn't expect this, I didn't expect this," as if the trees had pinned the fruit on themselves like false medals in order to greet him; one of the exiles assigned to the garden later picked up the apple the guest had tossed.

They wanted to eat the apple, it was the first fruit the exiles had held in their hands in many years; they were not trusted to hang the fruits on the trees. The very shape of it—the rounded ripeness—sated their hungry palms that had forgotten everything but tools; the exiles passed around the apple, as if it had just been born in the straw, passed it around and consumed it with their eyes—a case when a metaphor becomes the literal description of what happens: the apple was spiritual nourishment, food for the eyes, and there was enough for all of them.

One of the peasants, who was considered a sage, though this word is imprecise, was a reader and interpreter of the Scriptures, the kind of man who becomes a leader of a small peasant sect of somewhat twisted fanatics. If any of the educated prisoners talked to him about paleontological finds, about animals from other eras whose remains allow us to re-create the history of the earth and disprove the Bible, he would reply: "The Lord thought about you learned men as well when He created the world, he threw in some toys to keep you busy." Among his fellow villagers who were exiled with him, his intellect was revered, for he had a unique way of understanding appearances and reality. This reader, this sect member-to-be, understood what had occurred: just as Christ had fed thousands with five loaves, he said, so are we, many, eating from one fruit and it is not diminished. For it not to be diminished ever, let us save it and send it back to the village—they stubbornly called the settlement in the tundra the village—and let them plant it in the soil so the fruit shall beget more fruit.

I could understand the peasant, even though I did not know peasant labor; I grew up together with the dacha apple trees and lived half the year by the apple calendar; I remember my childhood when the spring frosts occurred, and bonfires were lit in all the orchards, the light frosty fog mixing with smoke hugging the windless ground, and the trembling, flowing, warmed air enveloped the trees, protecting the buds. On a cold night smells unleash their invisible fans, but on a night like that the apple blossoms smelled of the bonfires, and it seemed that it was the fragrance of the stars, the fragrance of promise.

In August came the unremitting thudding—straw was placed under the trees, but the apples were too heavy, too ripe, and the straw did not soften the blow completely; apples fell, during the day the sound was muffled, but at night it seemed that a chronometer was beating in the garden, that a different time was beginning, the time of ripeness. And when I later read about the Transfiguration of the Lord, this incident helped me to understand it as much as I could: that old image of the apple orchard in August on the threshold between summer and autumn; the Transfiguration occurred when His time had come.

The apple is the fruit of time; and even though it is not said that Adam and Eve had eaten of the apple, what other fruit could have embodied the unknown fruit of the tree of knowledge in a painting? Human time began with the apple—Seth begat Enos, Enos begat Cainan.

So the old peasant ordered them to send the apple to the exile village in order that apples would grow there, he was trying to spark the time of the new village, the way you start a motor, the village that arose on carted-in soil, to put down roots in the place where it appeared by accident, by the will of those who sent the exiles; some settlements, even though a hundred years old, stand on bare earth, as if the huts had just been knocked together, while others accumulate time, grow into it.

And now the three old men told me: we had a reason for sharpening the axe today. We've decided to chop down three old apple trees: they no longer give fruit, we have no firewood, and we don't have the strength to take apart the houses. Chop down the trees for us—you are a stranger, they don't mean anything to you; you will leave, and we will have fire and warmth.

The old man handed me the axe with its long handle; an old tub with iron hoops was placed under the roof gutter, and since I didn't know what to do, I moved toward it and leaned on it.

I told the old men that I would not chop down the trees and promised to gather driftwood by the river; then they said, cut our hair, and the fisherman handed me scissors, just like the ones on the wall at the dacha when Grandfather II suggested cutting off all my hair; darkened, charcoal colored, and ancient—you could tell from the shape of the scissors, which made me think people in the past cut fabric differently, touched objects differently, saw differently.

I froze; I thought that cutting their hair would be preparing them for death; they also asked for soap, and imagining its fragrance of artificial freshness, chemical cleanliness—the last cleanliness for them—I felt fear; but then I washed each of them in the barrel with rainwater, cut off their long matted hair, and the old men, changed into white cotton underwear, started touching one another, using one another as mirrors.

I brought them driftwood, sawed and chopped it into logs; the old men sat, getting used to their new selves, and they couldn't, the power of adjusting had waned in them, so they just listened to the whine of the saw, the ringing sound of the axe on the tarry wood, and those sounds—the sounds of beginnings, work, construction—seemed to reach them less and less.

I did not ask them about the island; the past seemed very fragile and unstable to me; touch something in the past and there would be a collapse of honed memory and the heart that had lived with pain would grieve again.

The old men were silent, and I left; words of farewell would not have reached them. The dinghy picked up the bank current and sailed past quickly, the houses on the shore vanished in the twilight, the big apple moon cast shimmering light on the water, and I pointed the dinghy's nose along the moonlight path.

I sailed all night; the river carried the boat over shallows and whirlpools, over the backs of fish; in the morning when a cold fog rose from the river bays, I saw the island.

I recognized it—rounded, unsightly, dividing the river in two; surrounded by fog, it seemed to have been born in the thickening of river evaporation and would vanish when the sun rose; the green shaggy locks of bottom grasses, the streams of the current, all moved toward it, everything pointed at it; it rose from the waters like the back of a whale. The dinghy poked into sand and I stepped on shore; the footprint etched in the sand immediately filled with water.

The island was just a surface, an oval; it felt as if the land had been cut out of the middle of Asian steppes where nomads traveled, bringing along their history, which existed only in the memory of the storytellers, a history that could be rolled and unrolled like a yurt; the land there was virgin soil not only because it was never touched by a plow—only human settlement gives a place existence in time, and where people never stopped time never began, and those places, like the island on which I stood, were not part of shared human memory.

Grass and occasional shrubs of dwarf birch grew on the island; you could see it all, there were no hills, no valleys. If I had hoped to find something, now I saw it was pointless: what had first been a dot on the map now had its real scale but remained just as virtual.

I walked around the island; the fog had lifted and a black kite scavenger appeared in the sky; it circled the island, then came lower, and dove down.

There was a black hole ahead.

A hundred steps more and I could see that it was an actual hole: the water must have seeped in, washing away the soil, creating a funnel with uneven edges, and moss fell into it in raggedy drapes. This pit in the middle of the flatness of the island was the whole point of my trip; it was the only mark, the only opening in the floating ground that the ground could not smooth over, and it beckoned dangerously and terribly. Something had happened inside the island, the ground had opened, from the bottom up.

The closer I came the stronger was the cold that blew from the hole—not imaginary cold arising from anxiety or fear, but real cold. It chased away the weak warmth of the northern summer, it chilled the blood, but also weakened, so that in it ghost smells, corpse smells slowly thawed; they floated, moved by waves of cold, and it seemed that I was approaching ancient, snow-covered ashes.

Hearing me, the kite flew out of the funnel; it had something in its beak, I couldn't tell what; it rose higher, heavily gaining height, and flew in wide circles, seeing from above what I could not see: the bottom of the hole. The black bird drew the same funnel in the air, as if putting a spell on the wind spout or, on the contrary, as if it could not overcome the hole's pull; the black bird, the diving scavenger, a creature that rots from inside and for which therefore corpses present no danger—I was afraid to think what it had it its beak, what it had found in the hole, but I continued.

I stopped a few steps away from the edge; I could see the walls of the hole, layers of ice mixed with soil, the walls were carved by water, but the permafrost did not melt, it simply floated, icing over, smooth and slippery; going to the edge was a mistake—the soil spread, revealing ice, the slope was steep, but it was impossible to remain within three steps and not look at the bottom: I had the feeling that if I went back for poles and ropes the hole would close and vanish, that you could look into it only the way you came, without any hope of survival.

Carefully, millimeters at a time, I moved closer to the lip of the hole; the funnel, like extended throat spasms, drew me in; the world was large, the pit was small, but close up it did not seem that way: its smallness was the dangerous smallness of jaws that would increase with every swallowed piece until it was the size of half the world and devoured the other half. For now, it waited, hiding on a remote deserted island, gathering strength, but the carrion-eating kite already knew where to go.

I do not remember looking over the edge; I was falling into the hole and falling into the dark hole inside me; the very ground of consciousness, so familiar, so reliable that you don't feel it, suddenly faded, and darkness breathed beneath it; when you close your eyes, your inner gaze always finds some light, perhaps weak and distant, but there was no light here at all: it was as if my inner vision had been taken, my consciousness blinded, and I did not feel my fall to the bottom.

What happened next did not take place on the border between reality and delirium, nor alternating between reality and delirium; I was in both states simultaneously; blood from the gash in my hand made by an ice shard flowed onto the ice. The blood was warm but the ice did not melt; the funnel deepened, resembling a well, the circle of bright sky moved off, narrowed, and a black spot circled inside it—the kite. Around me were the pecked-over bodies of animals—foxes, wolves—all those that had crossed the frozen river to find fortune in this gully and then fell inside; the birds fed on the bodies, they were the only ones who could go down into the hole and come out again; the permafrost kept the bodies from rotting, the animals were curled up, their bodies diminishing in size, and it seemed that these children, kits and cubs, had been killed here in the hole-trap.

The dead animals—bird claws had ripped open the belly of one fox and undigested tundra mice fell out of the intestines, as if the fox had not eaten them but was pregnant with them—distracted me, did not let me see the funnel in its entirety, to see what had attracted the animals. The walls were uneven, there were charred logs poking out, and there were logs on the bottom, old logs brought by the water; there was order in how they lay, and I realized that someone had tried to create a dugout here, build a cover, and then light a fire; probably the heat of the flames melted the wall and the logs fell down, onto the people.

With that thought, my vision changed and in the black peaty protuberances, in the icy smears I saw the outlines of human bodies.

The funnel was filled with corpses; the permafrost had preserved them. The opening in the wall filled with grass turned out to be a mouth; a rounded bump was a head; mixed with dirt, dissolved in it, the dead seemed to be trying to step out, to break the ice crust; what I had taken for tree roots were arms; the dead flesh had taken on the color of the earth and you could recognize it only by its shape.

Black, gray, shades of brown—the spot of my blood was the only bright color in here; when I looked at the blood, I stopped seeing the corpses—the color blocked my vision, blinded me with its brightness; the dead had no color, and a long road of my gaze led to each one, gathering particle by particle the features of the body that separated the corpse from the twisted peat snags, boulders, and lumps of peat.

I was in the belly of the earth; my brothers lay here, and their imperishability was not the incorruptibility of sainthood, but the absence of death. They did not follow the path of corruption, they merged with the earth without becoming it; for all the world they had vanished without a trace, and even death was not the last message they could send; and that meant that death had not reached its conclusion; the dead remained only with the dead and the living only with the living. Death is not disappearance, it is not an instantaneous transition from presence to absence; a man dies but not the ones around him, they must complete the deceased's terminal work with grief and bereavement: the services held on the ninth day, the fortieth day are part of the event of death performed by the living. If the living and the dead are separated, this incompletion, this endlessly lasting moment turned to ice stops the flow of time.

I could not climb out of the funnel; the smooth icy walls, licked flat by water, gave me no purchase; I had nothing with which to chop out steps. In my delirium I thought I could make a staircase out of corpses if I could get them out of the embrace of the ice; but then calmness descended—the way out was to dig deeper, not seeking salvation but deepening the hole. I found a broken branch and starting digging in the frozen peat; digging a grave in a grave.

I don't remember how long this went on; I dug an opening, a well, I dug through coal, wood, rubble, I dug between frozen bodies, going around arms, shoulders, feet; and when my strength was gone, I fell into my well, fell on top of a corpse, and in the cold mist I saw my very distant childhood.

It was night, the middle of the night in autumn. I was on the prow of a boat, all its light was behind me, the passenger cabins and the deckhouse, but here where the boat was just beginning, where the oncoming wind blocked the sound of its machinery, where the only smell was that of the ship's metal— here was the place that barely belonged to the ship; I moved together with the boat, but just a second ahead of it.

The river air and the darkness I sensed on that spot were different than what you saw from the cabin or the middle of the deck. Back there the light made out of the darkness a mere indicator of time; voices and music gave to the air the role of a waiter who serves up desired sounds; here, where the ship's prow dug into the night's flesh, and the night did not reel away but left open shell-like shutters revealing its moist, chilly interior, I looked at the night as if from inside it, while the other people on the boat looked at night from without.

Turning around, I perceived the boat the way the darkness ahead of us perceived it; it was gaining ground, I was retreating; I stood on the deck but all the passengers, all the tables in the restaurant, all the potted palm trees, all the beds in the cabins, all the pieces of hotel soap in the showers were attributes of a world to which I did not belong; imitating one another, losing distinguishing features, people seemed like insects crawling and flying toward the light, but there was no humiliation in that comparison: I also was not human, and blackness streamed between my ribs as if I had drowned in it, and my lungs were filled by the wild, wind-tossed air of the river channel.

I stood on the bow of the boat for so long that had I glanced at a watch I would not have understood the object's meaning. I no longer noticed whether the boat was still moving or whether there was anything at all behind me; the rare flashes of buoys and house lights on shore seemed to be eons away from the boat. I no longer understood that had I been in my cabin, I would simply be seeing darkness, that is, I would see nothing and not know how close nonexistence comes to people, I would not feel the announcement of death in the dying of color and loss of features; I was completely in the night, wholly open to it.

I thought that the emptiness was crying out; when the wind died down a bit, I heard singing in lullaby tones resembling the sounds of stone Aeolian harps that never reached musicality but expressed the one-dimensional dreariness of being cast in crystal; the singing came from afar, as if through a series of windows that opened and closed; with that singing, sometimes close to a howl and sometimes thinning to the sound of a flute, I felt a primordial horror, the fear of nonbeing, so ancient that the feeling did not know itself, just as an animal does not know it is an animal. Probably this was what the first human who managed to separate himself from the fact of his existence felt, thus dooming himself to know death; a knowledge still unverbalized, piercing the vertebrae that united bones, muscles, and flesh into the body.

Suddenly out of the dancing darkness came something white and motionless in the river channel, resembling a gigantic bone with four joints. Its whiteness was the noble white of marble, which gives statues their aloofness from the world; the darkness tried to blacken it but could not: the white color did not glow but it did not allow other colors to mix with it.

The white pillar rose above the waters, it came closer, and the majestic calm of its lines became clearer. Five tiers rising one above the other, like sails, and now it seemed it was a ship, a tall ship coming toward us. Amid the chaos and discord of the night, amid the darkness that blurred all borders, all lines that destroyed the horizon and mixed up heaven and earth, the white pillar redefined the separation; its hanging levels, the bottom steps of a great staircase, built the tiers of the heavens, and its soaring line set the vertical axis. The three central levels had openings like keyholes; empty niches, the promise of invisible gates ready to open above the spire, at dizzying heights.

The roar of a foggy siren from the oncoming vessel deafened me, submerged my mental dread in the immediacy of physical fright, and I learned where I was. We were sailing over an old flooded town, of which only the bell tower remained, they had forgotten to blow it up and then left it as a marker for vessels; the Aeolian harps were clots of wind that formed under the vaults of the belfry, and the black ear on shore was a communications antenna.

Deep under the ship's keel, foundations were covered by drifting sands, and drowned leaves floated over former streets; the river was enjoying its own underwater autumn, fish hid in the silt that had settled over the summer, crawfish dug habitats in the dirt of former gardens and during the day cleaned the hulls of boats onshore.

But there were also the white pillar, the white stairs to the invisible gates on high; they existed just as objectively as the bell tower—but the white staircase appeared to me at the bottom of the hole, and when I came to I sensed that the corpse on which I had fallen had been warmed by my body; he had an axe in his hands, the axes had been given to the exiles so they could build, and I could take it out of his dead fingers.

I chopped steps in the ice; I was the first one to get out of that hole, and I sensed that the pit would close and vanish, washed away by high tides; the living and the dead had met and my warmth became their warmth.

The dinghy carried me toward the Artic Ocean. I realized I was mad, I bore the virus of knowledge that should not be passed to the living; something was still not completely understood and without that understanding the knowledge was deadly.

The river grew broader, my wound ached, my temperature rose; madness throbbed in my temples, and I remembered a long-ago meeting with madmen and Grandfather II, when I felt the same fever, the same virus, the same fear.

When I was little we went for walks in the local park; it smelled of sour pea soup; the odor of that soup, wherever you smelled it, meant that a solid fence would soon materialize, sometimes covered with barbed wire; behind it would be a cement block or brick building. That was the situation here: beyond the concrete fence stood the psychiatric hospital.

I led Grandfather II along the paths and told him what I saw; suddenly I heard the bird-like screeches of the patients—they seemed to converse in their own language, inaccessible to the doctors, a language they spoke fluently, or else they had become somehow like gulls, and I thought they might fly up, settle on branches, and grow feathers. Grandfather II shuddered; that was so unusual that it scared me. He never shuddered, as if his body were frozen, and here some memory pushed him and bent him; he tried to pretend he was stretching out of weariness, but the pretense did not help: the squawks of the mental patients—a rare sound for the human voice—had reminded him of something in the past which had remained distinct, and Grandfather II whispered, thinking that I had moved away and could not hear him, "I won't move, I won't!" He whispered and stood stock-still, bringing his feet together as if he were standing in a narrow radiant place of his mind.

Later, when the screaming died down, Grandfather II asked me detailed questions about how the hospital looked and even, to my surprise, whether there was a crack in the wall to see what the patients looked like. I found a crack, but the patients had been taken away; all I saw were slate awnings—we had the same kind at our kindergarten—and two orderlies taking turns pushing each other in a wheelchair: they raced along the asphalt path, avoiding piles of bricks, laughing excitedly but joylessly.

I returned to the park as an adult: I came back gathering up all my memories of Grandfather II—and I met a patient escaping from the hospital.

The man was running through the woods, running like mad, as if it were not he, but somebody else twisted and cramped in the prison of his body; a man inside a man. This prisoner was running and trying to free something within himself; the fugitive fell on the ground, rolled in the leaves, banged against trees; his screams were muffled, as if he was screaming through his stomach. But his running and his fits were devoid of intensity, the body hindered him and sometimes, victorious, the man stopped, took a few disconnected steps, then hurtled himself into clumsy flight again; a person sewn into an animal skin or sack would run that way.

The fugitive came closer and I could see his face—empty of all emotion; his face, which had slipped lower under the weight of his own skull.

The madman ran toward the river; muddy, full of tires and rusty metal, but deep in places; deep enough to drown. You could surely see the river from the hospital windows; full of rubbish, filthy, with a stench of effluvia, steaming, it did not freeze in winter, and on frosty days a toxic fog the color of dog urine hovered over it; it emanated evil, like the filthy passage between garages, there was an affirmation of self-destruction about it, like alcoholics in the final stage of the disease; no wonder the local tramps drank along its shores, the men as murky as the water. The fugitive had not completely taken leave of reason, he could tell that here was the river and he ran toward it to die.

The orderlies cut him off; the fugitive grabbed a bottle, smashed it against a tree and stabbed himself, but the shards were too short, the pieces of glass merely pricked his tightened muscles.

I remembered that I had once seen a man running that way.

For several years I used to come out to work at a remote mountain mine; in those regions, roads exist only in the winter, when the swamps freeze and packed snow gives a better grip than asphalt; in summer you can get there only by helicopter. The remoteness turns these places into storehouses of time, cut off from the country's overall life; the clubhouses still had red banners with white-lettered slogans hanging on the walls, ballot boxes were helicoptered in and police along with them, to deal with fights, thefts, and other minor crimes of the previous six months; essentially, there is no government except for the mine administration, there are no signs of the renewal of time, and people are drawn here from all over the country who could not fit in elsewhere, who are incapable of entering life, as if it were a revolving door that moved too quickly. There, in isolation, there is unity among people who have no one waiting for them, no one to write to.

These are strong men, but they are missing something; they are of necessity harsh but firmness and harshness do not let them feel or understand. These are strong men who secretly fear life; they gradually lose themselves, dissolving in particles; they could have mourned and suffered, but they didn't have the ability to mourn or feel on a major scale, and so all they could do was drink and behave with reckless bravado.

In summer it is tolerable, there is the sense of space, changes in weather, and commensurate feelings. But in winter, when there is nothing but darkness, everything is snowed in and you are alone in the barracks, unspoken thoughts about the futility of life begin to eat at you. You don't know what to do with these thoughts, you don't have the habit of interacting with them, of safely releasing them into their orbits. You become superfluous; the protective carcass of strength and harshness comes off and you have no other defenses.

At the mine, the men lived in big railroad fuel cisterns which had been brought there suspended from helicopters; they cut out doors, laid a floor, insulated the metal walls, and added round windows; but still it was like living in a submarine in the middle of the mountains.

There were two inseparable friends there: Misha and Kolya, the local radio operator and one of the shaft diggers. People viewed them as one person; they jointly owned the only washing machine at the mine, which they used to brew their own beer, they hunted together—they joked that the double-barrel was invented for them. They were the only ones who never argued with each other, and in a fight they stood shoulder to shoulder; there was something strange and unnatural in their mutual sensitivity, as if there were no friction between them. I went there year after year, some things changed, people grew closer and drifted apart, but those two were always together, and at some point I started to think that it would not end well; that once—over some trifle—there would be an explosion, and the two would clash fiercely, making up for years of meekly putting up with each other's weaknesses; I thought they already hated each other but did not know it yet, and every friendly gesture, every service, every word just added fuel to the future fire.

I don't know why I thought that way; whether shadows of the future fell on their faces or if something in their lives gave off a hint; the radio operator had a doormat in front of his house that was actually a druse of centimeter-sized transparent crystals, for people to clean their shoes before entering; when it got dirty, he threw out the druse and put down a new one. The miner once saved and nurtured a dog that had its leg squashed by a truck. The lame dog repaid him once when the miner fell down drunk in the snow by running up to him and keeping him awake so he would not freeze to death; the next winter when the miner's hat was worn out, he shot the dog for its fur. That crystal druse used for wiping feet, the lame dog shot for its fur—those were not random things, they revealed the inner bluster of decay; it passed for braggadocio, for tough manliness, and the poisonous rot infected them deeper and deeper.

It resolved itself one winter night; the radio operator and the miner were coming home drunk from the base; as the miner later told it, the radio man fell down and asked for matches to light a fire, it was very cold, but the miner refused, he had only one match left and he was planning to have a smoke halfway there; he was so looking forward to that cigarette that he wouldn't give up the match, and he thought his friend was fooling and would get up; the radio operator cursed the miner—You won't give up your match!—which made the miner angry. He burned the match and went on alone to the settlement, certain that the radio operator would follow. But the man was too drunk, he couldn't get up, his cries were dispersed by the wind, and he froze, fell asleep turning stiff; they found the burned match in his fingers.

They called for a police helicopter; the miner locked himself in his metal cistern and shot at anyone who got close; they hauled the corpse with a tractor plow and placed it on the billiard table taken from the antechamber of the miners' bathhouse. The diesel generator stopped at eight, and the men played billiards at night wearing miner's caps; the nets in the pockets were torn, so the balls always rolled off into the gloom.

Now the table was outside the bathhouse, its legs deep in snow, and the corpse lay on it; the wind blew snow into his hair, and his head looked like a frozen cabbage—there is a variety of white crinkly cabbage, the leaves almost curly; the mouth and nostrils, everything, was filled with snow, and the head without orifices was sculptural, as if the artist had been called away and would be back any minute to make the eyes, mouth, and nostrils. The snow fell harder, there was a blizzard, and the police helicopter turned back, the mountains danced in waves, the metal cisterns rang when the wind hit them hard; for three days people stayed indoors, drinking to the dead man's soul, and that's when I remembered the radio operator's story of his childhood.

He was born in the settlement where the police helicopter was kept, awaiting summer weather; his father was a radio operator in a polar station on one of the islands in the icy latitudes that were used to cartographically celebrate individuals; they were named in honor of princes and generals, forgotten politicians; captains of polar ships named them for their beloveds, scholars in honor of their teachers; the Soviet regime named them for newspapers, institutes, and anyone deemed worthy of award; the reality of the new era thus appeared on the map—there were islands called Bolshevik, Pioneer, Komsomol, and October Revolution.

One of these islands had a meteorological station; three men worked there—the station chief, the meteorologist, and the radio operator. Every six months, a plane flew in; a solid ice patch was the landing field, they flew in food, newspapers, smokes, and batteries for the radio transmitter. Twice a day the station broadcast the weather information; it was used with many others as a forecast for ships and airports. The radio operator and the station chief were Party members and held meetings, making the meteorologist wait outside; but one summer, when a plane could not land at the station since the ice was melting, the operator received a message: he, as a Party member, was told to arrest the station chief, now the former station chief, and an enemy of the people, and in the same message he was appointed acting chief; the man was to be arrested, isolated and sent to the mainland by plane, which would arrive two months hence.

To arrest and isolate on an island that had only one hut with one large room; arrest and isolate a man he had worked with for four years, four winters; arrest and isolate; the radio operator suspected that if he did not follow through, the meteorologist would later give him away; he had received the message and had confirmed receipt.

The radio operator arrested his chief and informed him of the contents of the message; together with the meteorologist, they made a dugout in the cold ground, built a stone stove and a bunk, and the former chief moved in there; they could have left him free on the island, for it was impossible to escape, they could have lived with him in the hut for two months, but the radio operator did not know what the meteorologist thought, the meteorologist did not know what the radio operator thought, and any question, any word could later mean their own arrest.

The radio operator thought that the chief would try to kill him; but he sat in the dugout, insulated by many layers of rubberized canvas, ate his portion of food—now referred to as rations—and asked only for the atlas. Once he got this, the chief rejected his comrades; he talked to himself, as if they were not there.

The night before the plane was due, in the white night of summer, the former chief tied them up; they had set up a watch to guard him, but the meteorologist fell asleep; he tied them up, took the carbine, clothing, and food, and went off into the ice, toward the Pole, taking along the atlas he had pored over for two months.

As the radio operator later told them, the chief took pity on them, kept them from having to turn him over to the police; the plane spent a long time circling over the ice but never did find the fugitive, the ice was breaking apart, long sheets of water, kilometers long, showed black everywhere. Perhaps some expedition would come across the man, his frozen body; did he shoot himself, drown, starve to death? The radio operator said the chief appeared like a raving lunatic when he left; they had placed him at the very edge of the inhabited world, locked him in a cage of words in the middle of the icy desert where he kept repeating lines from the radio message.

The radio operator was put on trial, and afterward he attempted to disappear in the most remote settlement, surrounded by taiga and mountains; he'd become frightened of open spaces, he imaged he was too visible, too noticeable; he lost his mind, he maintained that a circle was more than 360 degrees, that there were crevices between the degrees where one could squeeze in, and which only looked small and insignificant but were actually very wide; he was removed from work when he could only see one message in every radiogram, one message with an order to arrest himself, and he trembled, and he tore the transcription journal and tried sending a message to nowhere, claiming to know where to find his former chief, that the chief had escaped on the island through that very crevice between degrees, and if we studied this phenomenon it would be very useful because spies are surely using these crevices to get in; he died of a heart attack when crossing a summer field.

The son, also a radio operator, spoke about his father with detachment; he retold the father's torment through his own, what it was like to have a father like him; his father told him everything, and the son was burdened by the trust, he didn't know what to do with his father's honesty, it oppressed him, he was ashamed of his father's breakdown, he hurried to tell it all, to be free of it at least in part; and he died in just as disturbing a manner, incongruously, as if expiating his father's sin; his life turned on a trifle, a burned match.

The blizzard lasted three days; then the snow quieted down, people dug out the entrances to their houses, the clouds passed quickly; the sun was threatening, primordial, as if it had been reborn over the three days of blizzard. The snow still fell, attacking in short raids, and in each raid I imagined the cavalry or flying figures.

The snowbanks in front of the miner's house developed an icy crust, and suddenly everyone saw him running, running from the house, breaking through the crust and sinking, then pulling out his feet as if the earth were trapping him; he ran and shot at the sky, as if fending someone off, someone up there, elusive and light-winged. Shells fell from his pockets, he kept stumbling, his face was bloodied, his hands red, but he would reload the shotgun, take aim, and shoot, one barrel at a time, switching targets between shots as he ran; he shot and ran along a high cliff, its steep slopes overhanging a stream.

Thin beams of light caught the snow clouds, and deep flickering spots moved in the sky. The fugitive shot at anything he thought was approaching from above, catching up to him; every approach of shadow or sunbeam was a threat and he shot at it.

Someone said, with understanding, "He's shooting at angels."

The madman in the park also ran that way, as if it was not

the orderlies chasing after him; and now, lying in the dinghy sailing to the ocean, feeling my own madness, I could see through that madness the wandering souls bearing the weight of sins and the unconsciousness of birth; how bound by the body they ran from angels—who alone could save them—thinking they were angels of vengeance come upon them; they hurried to tear the chains of life, but imprisoned in the fortress of their bodies, they were doomed to bear on their shoulders everything that had not happened, was not understood, was not discovered, without ever knowing what was tormenting them; and I felt my madness recede, its fever leave, and the blood of Grandfather II, who had imagined in the madman's cry the scream of the carver crushed by a falling tree—there was no more of that blood in me.

I was picked up by a fishing trawler; the force of the pendulum dragged me from north to south, through trains, stations, airports, buses—to the shore of the Atlantic, near the edge of Africa; within me the march of time was reversed, unspooled, unwound, I was crumpled and tossed; and now I stand at the boundary of Europe and begin the return trip—in words.